# THE HUNT OF THE UNICORN

OTHER BOOKS YOU'LL ENJOY

—⁓—

*Bones of Faerie* by Janni Lee Simner
*The Game of Triumphs* by Laura Powell
*Guinevere's Gift* by Nancy McKenzie
*Nobody's Princess* by Esther Friesner
*Runemarks* by Joanne Harris
*Throat* by R. A. Nelson
*Warped* by Maurissa Guibord
*Wildwood Dancing* by Juliet Marillier


MORE FROM C. C. HUMPHREYS!

—⁓—

*The Fetch*
*Vendetta*
*Possession*

# THE HUNT OF THE UNICORN

## C. C. HUMPHREYS

BLUEFIRE

Visit us on the Web! www.randomhouse.com/teens/strangelands

Educators and librarians, for a variety of teaching tools, visit us at www.randomhouse.com/teachers

The Library of Congress has cataloged the hardcover edition of this work as follows:
Humphreys, Chris.
The hunt of the unicorn / Chris Humphreys. — 1st ed.
p. cm.
Summary: Despite strange dreams and her ailing father's firm belief in the family lore of a long-ago ancestor's connection to the mythical unicorn, fifteen-year-old New Yorker Elayne remains skeptical until, during a school visit to the unicorn tapestries in the Cloisters, she finds herself entering a tumultuous world where she must fulfill the legacy of her ancestors by taming the unicorn and bringing a tyrant to justice.
ISBN 978-0-375-85872-7 (trade) — ISBN 978-0-375-95872-4 (lib. bdg.) —
ISBN 978-0-375-89624-8 (ebook)
[1. Unicorns—Fiction. 2. Tapestries—Fiction. 3. Fantasy.] I. Title.
PZ7.H89737Hun 2011
[Fic]—dc22
2010030852

ISBN 978-0-375-85350-0 (tr. pbk.)

RL: 6.0

Printed in the United States of America

10 9 8 7 6 5 4 3 2 1

First Bluefire Edition 2012

*To Aletha,*
*Tamer of Unicorns*

# ONE

# THE BOOK

*Thunderstorms rumble nearer, the air charged with static, as sticky-hot as only a New Orleans night can be. Arcana knows that the werewolf is going to come. She prays that all the precautions she's taken are not in vain. Prays that he's brought the goal of her quest—*

"Elayne?"

She jumped. She was not in an old mansion in Louisiana, but in her bedroom in New York. And no muscle-bound werewolf stood in her doorway. Her dad did, skinny as a stick.

"Sorry," said her father. "Did I interrupt something?"

"Uh, reading, homework, you know."

"Well, if you're busy . . ." With a sigh, he pushed himself off the doorframe. She could see the effort it took.

"You OK?"

He reached out a hand to steady himself. "Fine. I was

1

reading . . . this." He held up a book. "Fell asleep. Began to have the strangest dream."

"What about?"

He smiled. "You."

He'd stepped back into the hall. The light glinted on his gone-bald head. Elayne didn't know when she'd grow used to that. All his thick black hair gone.

She leapt up. He didn't look any better the closer she got. In fact . . . She gripped his arm. "Do you need something?"

"No, I . . ." He smiled again. "Yes. I wanted to read you this." He raised the book. "But I'm kind of tired. So I thought you might read it to me?"

It was late, close to eleven. Her dad was usually long asleep by now, zonked on his meds. But he was going into the hospital in the morning. A few days, they'd said. But they'd said that before.

"Sure," she said. "Love to."

He led her back to the living room and sank onto the sofa while she made cocoa. After plopping baby marshmallows into the two mugs, she joined him, snuggling deep into the old leather. He pulled a blanket over the two of them. It was warm in the loft, but beyond the double-glazed windows, snowflakes fell. *A long way from Louisiana,* she thought, and shivered. An ambulance's siren, heading away from St. Vincent's, made her shiver again.

"So, what's the book?" she asked.

"Ah!" He handed her an old hardback, small, a little bigger than her hand, the cover emerald green, fading, the edges frayed. *"The Maid and the Unicorn,"* she read out loud.

"Remember it?"

"Should I?"

"I read it to you when you were about, uh, eight, I think."

"Really?" She shook her head. "It's not a fantasy story, is it? You know I'm not into fantasy."

"The shelves in your bedroom tell a different story."

"Dad," she said patiently, "I'm fifteen now—"

"So what about all these vampires and werewolves, eh?"

"That's not fantasy, that's . . ." She was about to say "romance," but romance was something she really didn't want to discuss with her father. So she settled for ". . . different."

He smiled. "I see. Well, this is different too. Give it a chance."

She gulped some cocoa, put the mug down, opened the book, and read: "'The Incredible yet Nonetheless True Tale of Alice-Elayne Robochon; Her Adventures in Goloth, Land of the Fabulous Beast; and What Happened Next.'" She looked up. "Alice-Elayne?"

"That's your name. Your full name."

"Duh, I do know. I try to forget the 'Alice' part. It's just so 'Wonderlandy.'" She read again. "'Robochon'?"

"An old family name."

"So this 'Alice-Elayne' was, like, an ancestor?"

"Not 'like.' 'Was.' *Was* an ancestor." He pointed. "There's a family tree in the back. But finish reading the introduction first."

She read, "'And What Happened Next . . . ,' uh, 'Her story, passed down through Generations of the Family by Mouth and translated here, in the year of Our Lord 1863, for the first time in Print, by Alice-Elayne Corbeau, her descendant.'" She looked up. "Another Alice-Elayne?"

He nodded. "Now look at the family tree. It's attached at the back. Careful, it's fragile."

Gently she unfolded a sheet of waxy old paper. At the top were two letters, A and E, except the E was reversed. They were done in gold ink and linked by a tasseled cord. The paper's folds had made black lines down its middle. Between them, in beautiful old-style handwriting, was penned a list of names, descending from . . .

"'Alice-Elayne Robochon,'" Elayne read. "So she's the one who gets to go to Beast World, right?" Her father nodded. She followed the names down and whistled. "All the women are named Alice-Elayne." She tapped the gold letters at the top. "Their last names change with the men they married, but . . ." She scanned. "Yep. Everyone down to— Hey! That's me!"

"Yes. I added that."

"Nice lettering."

"Thanks." He leaned over and pointed. "There's Gramma Elly who was Alice-Elayne too. Her mother, and her mother, the same. And there is Alice-Elayne Corbeau. The woman who did the translating and writing down."

"Translating?"

"Yes. The original Alice-Elayne Robochon was French. I think this Corbeau ancestor, the writer and translator, was the first one in America."

"So the daughters always get saddled with the name, huh?"

"Yes." Her father suddenly looked serious. "It is one of the

4

reasons I wanted you to read this book tonight. To learn the tradition. Who knows what will happen in the hospital? I might not be able to—" He broke off.

She seized his hand. "It's just more tests, Dad. A new drug therapy, maybe? A few days, then home for the holidays. You're going to be fine."

He smiled. "Of course I will. But anyway, you need to know this." He cleared his throat. "Before you get married, you have to tell your fiancé, 'If we have a daughter, she is to be called Alice-Elayne. Or the wedding is off.'"

"What?" She snorted. "You think I'll stick my daughter with 'Alice-Elayne' because of a fairy story?"

"Doesn't it say on the front 'true tale'?"

"Yeah, but . . . every book and film claims it's 'based on a true story' and then goes on to be about . . . Nazi killer zombies or something." She held up the book. "Plus, the title says this is about a unicorn."

"So?"

"So unicorns aren't real."

"Aren't they?"

"Dad! Of course they're not. Have you ever seen one?"

"I've never seen a giant sea squid, yet I believe they exist."

"But you've seen photos of them."

"Ah, I see. So something only exists if it has been photographed?"

"No, but—"

"They discovered thirty new species of tree frog last year in the jungles of Madagascar. *They* had never been photographed. Did they not exist before?"

She laughed. "Are you saying that unicorns are alive in the jungles of Madagascar?"

"No. I am saying, Don't always trust that what other people tell you is true." He settled back. "Now . . . read!"

"Yes, boss." She took a swallow of cocoa. It had cooled, and what remained of the marshmallows felt like snails slipping slimily down her throat. "'The Incredible yet—'"

"You can skip that part."

"Oh. Right." She turned the page. "'One,'" she declaimed. "'The Weaver's Daughter.'"

I

## THE WEAVER'S DAUGHTER
### Wherein Alice-Elayne learns of the secret tapestry . . . and receives a shock

It was in the summer of her fourteenth year that the life of Alice-Elayne Robochon changed entirely, in a single day, almost in a single moment. Yet a day that would end in such sadness began so happily. For she was doing the thing she most loved in this world. She was watching her father weave.

François Robochon was the foremost weaver in the land. Indeed, before his coming into Goloth some twenty-five years before (from whence no one knew, but his daughter was, to her sorrow, soon to discover), there was scarce a loom worthy of the name. Before him, weavers were merely poor journeymen who made rough garments to conceal their own and their neighbors' nakedness, and no more. But her father, coming from both a town and an eminent family of the trade, brought his skills and knowledge with him. Once better looms were made, and the poor people of Goloth were better clothed, and once they had been delivered from the terror of certain beasts by the other man who came, Adam, called "the Hunter" (another sad part of the tale, soon to be related), there was time to weave for beauty, for art. François gathered such men as had some aptitude and taught them, though none came close to his skills. Extraordinary were the tapestries that sprang from her father's loom, bewitching a primitive people who thought they were magic and their creator a magician.

Watching him work that fateful day, Alice-Elayne understood the awe in which he was held. The way his fingers danced between warp and weft. Bobbins of thread—indigo and cobalt, argent and lavender—sprang to him as if by thought, not touch. Through they went, used, discarded, replaced, passing between the vertical rows, filling white warp with colorful weft, stitches melding suddenly into shapes, into curves, slashes, shadows, slits.

It was a rare chance, to sit with him thus. Her father's time had lately been taken more with matters of state than of art. For he was, along with Adam, joint ruler of the land. Only recently had he returned to the world of the weave, creating a grand tapestry that Adam had demanded, whose twin, her father said, existed in the land whence they'd come to Goloth. That one was already dispatched to the Great Hall Adam had lately caused to be built. It would be hung the morning of his coronation. For, in three days' time, Adam was to be crowned king, the first that Goloth had ever seen.

Though her father was to be made first duke that same day, Alice-Elayne knew the idea of the crowning made him uneasy. He'd brooded for weeks, scarcely speaking beyond orders, scarcely eating despite her attentions. And then, while the magnificent tapestry was worked on by shifts of apprentices during the day, her father began to return to his workshop each night with only her as company. There, in secret, he began another tapestry on a smaller, older loom, doing the work that six would do, letting her sit beside him on the bench and help only when his fingers and eyes near failed with exhaustion.

This night–this last night, she was sadly to learn–he had worked alone, unceasing, unspeaking, sliding the length of the bench, back and forth. Finally, he slowed, stopped, and hung over the loom as if asleep. His lips moved, muttering words.

"Is it finished, Father?" Alice-Elayne asked.

"Aye," he grunted, drawing his hands over his eyes.

"Then may I see it?"

"You may. You must. And after you, if fortune favors us, then everyone. Everyone in Goloth."

She was startled by his grim voice. But her excitement surpassed her surprise. For a tapestry is worked on in such small sections, thin lines of colored thread building up so gradually, that it is impossible to see the whole. The tapestry is fully revealed only when it is finished, when it can be lifted from the loom and hung. Only then can the weaver see how the visions of his mind have been translated into art.

"Then shall I help you lift it, Father?"

"In a moment," he replied. He turned to face her. "But first, Daughter, I must ask you a question."

They way he said it filled her with dread. Yet she was her father's only child and bold with it. "Ask," she said.

"Do you love me?"

It was a strange question. In Goloth, there was duty. Obedience. And yet she did, even if she never told him so. "Yes, Father. I love you."

"And do you trust me?"

"Of course."

He reached out then and laid a hand upon her shoulder. They rarely touched. It was not the way of their land. He stared at her a moment, then squeezed before withdrawing his hand. "Then come," he said, "help me with the tapestry. And I will tell you everything."

Before one can remove the cloth from a loom, scores of colored threads need to be cut close to the weave, wound tight, the bobbins placed in boxes. So that is what they did, happy in the work, happy in the delay it gave. Until he spoke again.

"I need you to trust me, child. Not obey, as a daughter must. For what I am going to ask of you, duty is not enough. Love may be."

She continued spooling thread, kept her voice calm. "Ask me what, Father?"

"Ask you to leave."

"The town?" she asked. She was puzzled. There was little beyond the wooden walls of the small town. A few outlying villages and farms. The ocean to the east, which no one had crossed. The northern mountains, which no man could climb.

"No," he replied. "Leave this world. Leave Goloth."

No breath could calm her now or still her whirl of thoughts. "But . . . where would we go?"

"To France," he replied, reaching out an arm to catch her if she sagged. But she did not.

"France," she echoed in wonder. "France is . . . a tale. It is not real."

"So I always told you. Because I did not think we would ever go back. Could ever go back. Yet real it is, and we must return to it. We must!"

"Why?"

The sound of the bell came to them, tolling the hour. When midnight finally echoed its last in the room, he spoke again. "There is so much to tell and not the time to tell it. Not if we are to do all we must before we leave at dawn."

"Dawn?" Strangely, this further shock calmed her. "Then let me hear what there is time to tell."

A little smile came to him. "You are as strong as your mother was, child. Stronger." The smile vanished. "And you will need to be." He turned back to the loom. "Help me here," he grunted.

They began to untie the tapestry from its place between the two rollers. As they did, he talked. "What you think is a tale I invented to send you to sleep when you were a young girl is, in the largest part, true. Twenty-five summers ago, I... stumbled from my land into this one. I will not relate the why or the how of it now. That is a tale for when we are safely gone. But I came from my workplace to Goloth, and I did not cross a sea or traverse a mountain to get here. And, as you know, I did not come alone."

He paused, heavy cloth between his fingers, looking down as if seeking flaws. She prompted him. "You came with Adam, Father."

He resumed his task. "With Adam, aye. Adam was from another land, called England. He was a soldier, a guard in the employ of the man for whom I wove in France. But more than this—Adam was a hunter, and he sought a special quarry. One he thought I could lead him to."

Alice-Elayne knew that Adam was simply "a hunter" as her father was merely "a weaver." The foremost man of Goloth, Adam hunted, trapped, and killed as creatively as François conjured worlds from thread.

Her father sensed her thoughts and spoke to them. "You know

what is said here. How the history of Goloth began only with our arrival. It did not. We found a land, simple in its ways, a people ignorant of most that Adam and I called 'civilization.' But a happy people for all that, who grew crops and raised animals and wove the most basic of clothes on primitive looms." He sighed. "In one thing only were they unhappy. For they did not live in this world alone. They shared it with animals. Not just the animals of forest and field. For Goloth, as you know, also holds fabulous beasts. And one of those beasts hunted man."

"The manticore," she said.

"Aye. And there was one manticore who yearned most for human flesh...."


"Whoa! Time-out!" Elayne lowered the book, looked up. Her father's eyes were closed. She wasn't even sure he was still awake. The cancer, the drugs they gave him for it, made him drop off suddenly. "Dad?" she said softly.

He opened his eyes, blinked. "I'm here."

"So, OK, two things." She tapped the book. "First—what the hell's a manticore?"

"A manticore? Let me see." He stared above her, sucking his lip. "A manticore is what's called a 'fabulous beast.' Like a sphinx or a griffin, it's made up of different animal parts. If I remember correctly, a manticore has a lion's body with poisoned spines at the tip of its tail that it can shoot like darts. It has a mane too, surrounding a face that would be almost human—were it not for its triple set of jaws. Made to consume human flesh." He smiled. "I believe it sings beautifully too."

"How nice for it!" She snorted. "So it doesn't exist. It's a fantasy."

"Well . . ." He shrugged. "It's certainly never been photographed—"

"Oh, right!" She smiled. "It's living in that jungle of yours, in Madagascar. With the tree frogs and the unicorns."

He pointed at the book. "Or in Goloth."

"That's my second question." She picked up the book. "This . . . Alice-Elayne. 'Loving. Dutiful. Obedient.' Puhleeze!" She rolled her eyes. "Doesn't she already know her father's story?"

"Most of it, I think."

"So why is he telling her again?"

"He's telling us. The reader. Or, rather, 'the author' is."

She turned the spine. "'Alice-Elayne Corbeau'?"

"Exactly. That was the way they did it when she wrote the book."

"I see. She tells us all that at"—she mimed a yawn—"considerable length and yet doesn't explain what a manticore is?"

"In 1863, people would have known what a manticore was." He smiled. "They were much better read than your generation."

"Sure—those three percent who weren't starving in slums. Jeez, Dad." She shook the book. "I just wish she'd cut to the chase."

"I think she does. As I wish you would."

"OK. OK." She opened to the page. "Where was I? Oh yeah . . . 'And there was one manticore who yearned most for human flesh. . . .'"

"...and the simple people of Goloth were powerless before him. Yet Adam wasn't. Adam had killed almost every kind of creature in our world. Now he discovered a way to kill the manticore and delivered the people from their terror. For that they made him their leader. 'The Hunter,' they call him." The weaver's voice began to shake. "And in three days, they will call him their king. He demands a crown, he will rule in tyranny, and he will complete the evil we introduced into this world when we entered it."

Alice-Elayne stared. "Evil? You have not brought evil, Father. Consider the clothes the people wear now, because of the looms you created. Consider the art you have given them. Before you, they could only daub upon rock walls. Now..." She reached down and caressed the cloth before her.

"Oh yes," he said, his voice bitter, "I have given them 'art.' I have tried to counter Adam as he creates the world he wants, centered on hunting and killing. There are a few who follow me. My weavers. I would have stayed, tried to exert what influence I could. Were it not for the last thing Adam wants. Which he will take if I do not prevent him."

"What is that, Father?" She was frightened again by the look in his eye. "What could he want beyond a crown?"

There was a long pause. Finally he spoke it, a single word: "You."

"Me?" How could that be? The idea was absurd. Adam was as old as her father, close to fifty, while she had seen just fourteen summers. And yet...? Yet his three wives had not been much older when he'd taken them. Others married as young.

She blushed, looked down. It was still absurd. "Why would he want me?" she murmured.

Her father stepped around the loom, took her hands. "'Why?'" he echoed. "Why, aside from your beauty, your grace–"

"I am not beautiful."

"Your talent, which may one day surpass even mine–"

"No–"

"Yes!" Her father held the hands she tried to pull away, bent till he could also hold her gaze. "You are grown into a wonder, Alice-Elayne, so different from any of the girls of this land. And, king though he will be here, even Adam sometimes misses the world we came from. You remind him of it. So he will have you."

It was true. She knew it to be true. "What must we do?" she said.

"They cry it in the town that the Hunter will return within days." The Hunter was scouring the land, catching animals alive if he could, to be ceremonially killed before his people at his crowning.

"We must leave. At dawn."

In her mind's eye, she saw him then, the Hunter, his hands as ever steeped in the blood of some beast, coming toward her, arms wide, laughing. She shuddered. "Why not tonight, Father? Why not now?"

"There is something I must do first. Something I must leave behind. For the people I love."

"What?"

He stepped back to the loom, touched the tapestry, now wrapped around one beam. "Let me show you."

It was hard for just the two of them to manage it, the cloth heavy with the layers of the weave. They began to unwind it from the beam, leading it toward the trestles that waited to bear it unwound. The top of the tapestry was revealed, and she first saw . . .

. . . the initials. As in the other tapestry he had just completed, so here, the letters *A* and *E*, worked in spun gold. She touched them.

*AE.* "Alice-Elayne." Except her father had told her that the letters were not for her but for someone else. "You should know of her now," he said, as if answering directly the question she'd always had, "for if we succeed in our escape, if we return to the land I came from, then perhaps"—his fingers joined hers upon the weave—"perhaps we shall meet the lady again. Alice-Elayne. You are named for her."

His fingers traced the curve of the *A*, the reversed *E*. She saw that sadness in his eyes, dancing in memories. It was strange to think of her father loving another, once. Not her mother, whom she hoped he loved, though she had died so long ago it was hard to remember.

"Was she . . . this Alice-Elayne . . . your wife there?"

"Nay, child." He swallowed. "She was, in her own way, a fine worker in cloth, as noble ladies of our land are. It was her delight to sit beside me each day at the loom, to talk of color and subject and"—he stared above her—"many things."

"You loved her, Father."

He looked at her straight. "I did."

"Then why . . . why did you not marry her?"

"She married the man for whom I wove the tapestries." He went on, over her little gasp. "They were his wedding gift to her. I tried to capture her face in thread—but such beauty, such a spirit, was beyond even my skills. So I suggested that her initials be placed in each tapestry. I remember how she smiled, the light in her great, dark eyes, when I did. And somehow she still finds her way into all my work." His voice grew in force. "Even this one. Maybe that spirit—for she was strong and bold, like you who are named for her—will affect all who see it."

With that, with her aid, he heaved the rest of the tapestry onto the trestles. And the gasp she gave now was unrestrained.

One week before, the trestles had held a tapestry the like of which had never been seen in Goloth. It was the one Adam had ordered, for he remembered it as a glory from the world they'd come from. And François remembered it because he had woven it before, in that world.

This tapestry was different. Smaller; and simpler, for though the colors were as varied, there was little of spun gold or silver in this weave. A simpler story too. The other had been full of people and hunting dogs, a crowded scene of life—and one death. The death of a fabulous beast. The death of a unicorn.

There was death here also. The death of a man.

On one side of the panel stood a girl, with a face not unlike her own, her left hand on a unicorn's neck. Her right pointed to a different scene, in the center of the panel. The death of a man with a face remarkably like Adam's. The unicorn's horn plunged into his chest.

Alice-Elayne reached to touch the wound, almost expecting it to be wet, so vivid was its gushing crimson. "What does it mean, Father?" she murmured.

"Hope," he replied. "You know the tales. How a maid can tame a unicorn, bend the beast to her will." He nodded. "Before we leave Goloth, I mean to hang this from the gates of Adam's new lodge. I want the people here to see and remember it. They may not be strong enough to overcome him now. But one day, perhaps..."

She frowned. "I do not understand. Will a unicorn be tamed and then kill the king?"

"Nay, child. I am a weaver, not a prophet. Yet the unicorn has ever represented purity, the triumph of light over darkness. As has the maiden. The people may see it... and hope for that light." He gestured to the door. "And the first of those people are those I hold dearest—my weavers. I summoned them for midnight. They should be outside. Go, call them in. Let them be the first to hope."

Alice-Elayne was frightened. She had seen what had happened to those few who dared to oppose the Hunter's will. She did not move. She had to know one thing.

"But how, Father... How are we to leave this land?"

"With another's aid. Because, you see, child"—he smiled, no sadness in it now—"I know a unicorn."

# TWO

# FAMILY HISTORY

"Mmmm."

"What?" Elayne looked up at her father's murmur. His eyes were shut. "Dad?"

"Hmm?"

"You look tired."

"Always."

"Oh. Maybe I should . . ." She closed the book.

"No, no. It's just getting to the good bit. I was recalling when my mother first read me the story. I think I was about eight." He opened his eyes and smiled. "Come on! Read!"

"Reading." She opened the book, found the page. "Chapter Two," she announced. "'The Unicorn: Wherein we meet the unicorn . . . and learn what happened thereafter.'" She cleared her throat. "'On the brow of a hill stood a unicorn. His name was Moonspill.'"

"Moonspill," her dad muttered, closing his eyes. "Of course. How'd I forget that?"

He was yet young in years, scarce fifty, of a race that could live to five hundred or more; and small still, if compared to males of his ilk who could make even the largest of stallions, their closest cousins, seem little.

He was purest white, possessed of a flowing mane, a long and thick tail. But he would never be mistaken for a horse. His hooves were cloven like a goat's, not three-quarter moons; a beard hung, as thick and silken as the tail, from his jaw; and his eyes were an iridescent blue that seemed to have no bottom to their depth.

Yet it was the last difference that defined him the most: a horn, a spiraling shaft of ivory above those eyes, standing straight out from his forehead the length of a tall man's arm.

Moonspill stood, scoring the turf with his hooves, uneasy there, so close to this city of men. It was not the unease of fear. No. His unease was born of fascination.

If man had always been drawn to the unicorn, the opposite was also true. And there were times in the history of both species when the two had come together, to mutual glory. Moonspill knew the legends. And now he pondered that glory and his own line's share of it.

*For am not I the son of Darkheart?* he thought. *He who turned the Khan back from the gates of India and saved it from destruction? Whose own father sprang from Ambrosius, whom Arthur of the Britons rode to triumph and to death in the setting sun of Avalon? While his sire was Bucephalus the Mightiest, who both laid his head at the Buddha's feet and then bore Alexander of Macedon to the conquest of the*

19

*world? And did not my own mother, Salvia, who fed me stories with her milk, bear the Maid Joan to the gates of Orleans and the freeing of all France?*

He tossed his head. All he had sought, ever, was the glory of that union—a human worthy of his respect. Together they would transform the world. That yearning had made him reckless, blinding him to consequence. Leading to his terrible mistake.

Looking down upon the island town, Moonspill gouged the earth with his hooves ... and wondered if he was making another mistake now. The weaver had summoned him. The man was not a hero to be served. But they had a bond. So he had come.

It was that darkest hour nearest to the dawn, yet his eyes could see as clearly as if it were midday. Cloaked figures were creeping toward the largest structure of the town, a building erected since last Moonspill had come close to gaze on man, with disgust, with yearning. Some of the figures carried something between them, the shape of a tree trunk; others bore ladders. When they reached the square before the building, they halted and clustered together for a few minutes; then they broke apart, most heading to the gates of the building, two moving toward the bridge that crossed the lake to the mainland shore. Toward him.

A unicorn's hearing is as acute as his sight. Soon Moonspill could hear their boots upon the bridge's timbers. And he could hear something else—from behind him. Along the track that passed beneath his hill and led to the bridge, he heard hooves. Horses were coming; men were riding them, riding them hard. They were yet a ways away, but their speed would bring them soon enough.

Moonspill looked down. The two figures were halfway up the hill. He could see them now, their faces. One he recognized—it was the weaver, older, grayer than he remembered him. The other was a girl. And something about her, the way she carried herself, made the unicorn hold his breath and stare harder.

"Moonspill," the weaver cried, his breaths coming short with his climb. "You have come."

*Why do you speak aloud when you have but to think?*

Father and daughter halted. The weaver bent, resting his hands upon his knees, thinking. *I had forgotten.* He took a deep breath. *I was not certain that you would come.*

*You left the sign upon the rock to summon me.* Moonspill snorted. *I am here.*

The weaver stood straight, spoke. "I will speak aloud, Moonspill, so that my daughter will know all."

Alice-Elayne had been staring. She had seen fabulous beasts before, the ones Adam had killed, or captured so that he might kill them before the people of the town. But not the most fabulous of all. Now she looked in amazement. "You can...talk with this wonder, Father?"

"Aye. In our thoughts. If he chooses, he will talk to you thus also."

"But how...how do you know him?" she asked.

"He saved my life." Overriding a gasp, he continued. "One night in France, I walked in a forest, mistook some berries, ate them. They were belladonna–the 'beautiful lady' that gives visions of paradise before it gives death. I was dying...until Moonspill came and took the poison from me with a touch of his healing horn. It is his great power. One of his great powers."

"Father–"

He raised his hand. "But this, and how he led me to Goloth, is a story for an easier hour. Now there is little time."

Moonspill felt the vibration of hooves getting closer. *Perhaps less than you imagine. Speak swiftly.*

"Then hear, Moonspill," the weaver said. "I ask a boon." He stared straight into the unicorn's huge eyes. "You brought me to this land. Will you now take us back?"

Moonspill tossed his head. It was not what he'd expected. Yet he was willing. Though each had repaid his debt to the other, still they were bound . . . in colored thread. *Mount, then. And hurry. For there is danger here.*

The weaver had taken a step forward. Now he halted. "Beasts?" he asked.

*Worse. Man.*

It was then that the bugle sounded.

"Adam," François breathed. He ran past to the very crest of the hill, Alice-Elayne following, both peering into the dawn light. "May God protect us! He returns early. But why does he blow his trumpet?" He swiveled, squinting down at the town. "I cannot see so far, Daughter. Is the tapestry unfurled?"

Alice-Elayne peered. "No, Father. It hangs, still rolled upon the gate, but"—she bit her lip—"the weavers have fled."

"Cowards!" François sighed, sagged. The bugle sounded again, closer. "How long, Moonspill?"

*Not long.*

Then François stood straight. "I must go back."

He took a step downhill. His daughter grabbed his arm, cried out. "No, Father! Let us leave now."

He halted. "I cannot leave Goloth without some hope. I owe the people that much, for what I helped bring into this world."

22

He took a step, and Alice-Elayne stepped with him, grasping his arm. "No," he said. He faced the unicorn. "Will you see her safe?"

*I will.*

François turned back. "Whatever happens to me, you must go."

"I cannot."

"You must. Obey me, child!" His voice hardened, and he took her hand from his arm. "Do you hear?"

"Yes, Father." She lowered her eyes.

He bent, his voice soft now. "It does not matter what happens to me. But you must be safe. Safe from the tyrant and his desire for you."

She looked up. "He will kill you, Father."

"Adam? No. Punish me perhaps, but . . ." He shrugged. "He needs me too much." He lifted his hand to her cheek, fingertips touching her there. "And perhaps I will find a way to join you later." His hand dropped, and he turned to the unicorn. "Take her now."

Moonspill nodded. *Go well, weaver.*

Without another word or thought, François turned and began running down the hill.

For the first time, Moonspill reached out his mind to the girl before him. *Come, maid. Mount.*

Alice-Elayne staggered. Words were sounding inside her head! And the voice that spoke them! It was as if language had turned to velvet, words lulling as they stroked, pulling her toward him. She took a step.

*No.* She forced herself to halt, to turn back. *I will stay and see.*

Her voice in his head. He had never heard a maid before. It . . . surprised him, the force of it, of her. *Well,* he thought, and turned, like her, to watch.

They saw François run across the bridge below. As he did, the bugle sounded again, much closer. Now both could feel the vibration of hooves upon the earth.

"'Well!'"

"Huh?" Elayne looked up.

Her father smiled. "A simple word, *well*. The beginning of something. Something huge."

"What?"

He didn't reply, just pointed. She looked down. She had to admit, she was hooked. "It's a new chapter. It's called 'Weaver's Blood.'"

Her father laid his head back. "Cool," he said, closing his eyes again.

III

## WEAVER'S BLOOD
### Wherein the plot is discovered

François ran past the two gate guards. They had not tried to stop him before—him, the second man of the kingdom. They did not try now, just stared toward the road. "He returns," one murmured.

The town of Goloth was not large, and it took little time to run to the square before Adam's new hall. The light had grown. Everything was clear to the weaver's first glance: two ladders, one still standing, the other fallen; the tapestry hung in place, its furling ropes still tied.

The youngest of his apprentices crept from the shadows. "They ran off, master! When they heard the tyrant's trumpet. I could not stop them. And I could not reach the ropes with no one to hold the ladder."

*Youngest and smallest,* François thought. *And most loyal.* "I will reach them, Albert," he said. "Go to the tower and ring the bell. Summon the people as if for fire."

"But ..." The apprentice pointed past, to the hills.

"Sound the alarm. Then join your family before you return."

"Master!" The boy bowed and was gone.

The tapestry was tied to a wooden bar. It sat atop three metal stakes where the heads of beasts, both fabulous and otherwise, were often placed, trophies of the Hunter's prowess. When he climbed up, François could see rust-red stains that rust had not made.

He had cut two of the three ropes before the bell tolled. In a town made of wood, such a summons drew people swiftly from sleep. The first townsfolk were already entering the square when the last toll came. François had just moved the ladder to the middle, had just climbed to the top, when the murmurs of both fear and wonder changed. Shouts of acclaim vied with the snarl of hunting dogs and hoof-falls as many men galloped into the square.

"Hunter! Hunter! Hail the Hunter," came the cries.

A powerful voice cut through them all. The words were in English, the language he had forced the people of Goloth to learn and speak. Being English, he would learn no other. Being leader, he had no need.

"What," he shouted, and all voices ceased save his, "do you do there, weaver?"

François turned. He saw it all in a moment. The tyrant's black-clad guards drawn up behind him, their horses foam-flecked from hard riding, panting hounds at their hooves. In their midst, a face he knew well—for a weaver sat ahorse among the hunters, a dwarf among giants,

25

trying to make himself still smaller as François's gaze found him: Charles, who had been part of the inner circle. His betrayer.

Finally, there was Adam himself.

The Englishman was the largest man there, upon the largest horse. He had grown from the whip-thin hunter who had dragged François into Goloth with him all those years ago. If age had silvered the blond curls and grizzled his beard, power had swelled him, while the blood—of man, of beast—sustained him. This was he whose crueler impulses the weaver had tried, and largely failed, to restrain.

François could see, beyond the hunters, the edge of a sunbeam peeping over the hill. *If I can but wait a few moments longer,* he thought. *It would be better to die with the sun on my face.* So he said, "Have you had good hunting, my lord?"

The Englishman could usually be distracted thus. "The best," he bellowed. "For see..." He gestured back, just as two more horsemen galloped into the square. Their mounts were even more lathered than the others, for they carried a heavy rope net between them. Something whimpered within it. "I have trapped the three-headed dog at last. Two pups in there. Six heads! Their mother led us quite a hunt and killed two of my men before we dispatched her and snared her brood." He frowned. "Didn't the Greeks have a three-headed dog, François?"

The weaver squinted slightly. The first sun was upon his face. "They did, my lord. The Romans too. They called him Cerberus. He guarded the gates of hell."

"'Tis so. I haven't decided whether to breed them or sacrifice them." He smiled. "Always rely on you, weaver, for the answer. Always rely—" The smile was displaced by a frown. "But you have not answered my question. What do you do up that ladder?"

26

There were enough people in the square now. Enough witnesses. The sun was rising fast. François turned away from it, raised his knife, and cut the last restraining rope. The tapestry unfurled.

Aside from on the chase, the Hunter was never the swiftest to comprehend. "Another woven tribute to me?" he said. But then he saw what had caused the gasps around him, and he pushed his horse closer to study. The crowd was silent, scarce breathing, awaiting the fury they knew would come. Some slunk away, recalling that the Hunter's rages could be indiscriminate. Most stayed, too stunned to move.

However, no roars came, no lashing out. "Well," breathed the Hunter, "I think you have not quite captured my nobility, weaver. But I do look like I am dying painfully, so..." He shrugged, looked up at the man on the ladder. "What does it mean? That a unicorn will be tamed and then kill me?"

"No," replied François. "It means hope. The hope that one day tyranny will fall to purity."

"Truly?" Adam's voice was still dangerously soft. "You would give people that hope? These people for whom you care so much? How often have I told you, people need to be ruled, not coddled. We know that, weaver, don't we, you and I? As for me..." He drew the sword that hung at his side, leaned forward, and tapped the weaving with its tip. "*I* hope the unicorn does come. For I will kill it. Like I have killed all the others. Like this!" He drew the sword back, thrust it through the weave, straight into the white breast. "And I will do it before all your hopeful people," he cried, his voice rising. "For this I now vow— I will trap one, tame one perhaps—then kill it in the arena to celebrate my coronation, to prove my right to rule."

His loyal hunters behind him shouted their acclaim. Some of the people did too. Adam beamed. "When I was a filthy peasant in the fields of Kent, we used to chant a rhyme." He rose in his stirrups, withdrew the sword from the tapestry, and waved it.

> "The lion and the unicorn
> Were fighting for the crown.
> The lion beat the unicorn
> All round the town."

His face flushed, his voice lowered. "I will be the Lion. I will beat the unicorn."

More men shouted, many townsfolk joining in now.

François waited for the acclaim to die a little. "You cannot best a unicorn, Adam," he said.

The shouts died in an instant. No one called their lord by his name. No one who wished to live.

But again, no roar came. "Oh yes, I can, *François*." He said the name deliberately, sneeringly. "For are not all the myths of our world real in Goloth? Is that not the wonder that we discovered here? The manticore stalks the forest, the cockatrice hunts in the desert, the griffin soars over the mountains? And have I not found ways to capture them all?" His voice dropped, and he peered again at the tapestry. "You have reminded me here how it is done. For a maiden, chaste and pure, can tame the unicorn. And there is something else too. What? What?" He snapped his fingers. "Mirrors! Is that not so, my scholar?" He smiled. "Well, I will cause great mirrors to be made. And I will choose a maiden..."–he faltered, glancing at the tapestry again, at the girl's face–"a maiden..."

He hefted his sword, placing it against the weaver's chest. "Where *is* the maiden? Your daughter? My bride?"

François looked above the blade, over the walls, up to the hilltop. He did not have long sight. But he saw something glimmer there. Sunlight upon ivory, he thought. "She is safe, Adam. Beyond your grasp."

Adam, seeing the direction of his gaze, turned. His eyesight was perfect. He could see a unicorn and a maiden atop the hill. He recognized both. And for the first time, he began to scream.

"Go!" He waved his sword at his men, pointed with it. "The unicorn and the maid! Capture them."

Hunters turned their tired horses, jabbed cruel spurs into their flanks, rode for the bridge. But on the hill, François saw the two blurs of daughter and unicorn become one. In a moment, the glint on the hill, sunlight on ivory, was gone, and he looked down. "You will not catch them, Adam. They will soon be beyond the reach of swiftest horse and scenting hound. Moonspill's horn will open the door of worlds for her, as he once opened it for us. You will see her no more."

The horse was large and Adam tall. His head was only just below where François stood on the ladder. This close, the weaver could see the other man's green eyes quite clearly. See the red rage sweep into them and take away all thought, except one.

"Neither will you," he yelled. Rising in his stirrups, he swung his sword in a great sideways arc. Some screams came as François's head was struck from his shoulders and tumbled onto the ground. Some more when, a moment later, his body crumpled and followed it.

"Place his head there, in the center of the wall," the Hunter commanded.

Men rushed to obey him. One, a little bolder than the rest, asked, "And the tapestry, my lord?"

Adam was about to shout another command. He halted himself, breathed deep, then leaned in to wipe the weaver's blood onto the cloth before him. "Let it hang there a day and a night, with its creator's dripping skull above it. Let all see the weaver's prophecy. Then let it be brought to me. And know this, all who would hope..." His voice rose to a roar. "I am the Lion. And I will kill the unicorn."

Elayne sat back. "Whoa!"

Her father opened his eyes. "What?"

"Kinda gory."

"Too much?"

"No, no. I like a little blood. But wasn't it a bit much when"—keeping her finger in to mark her place, she looked at the cover—"Alice-Elayne Corbeau was writing? In 1863, wasn't it?"

"Don't think so. Those Victorians liked a bit of blood too. Sir Walter Scott, all those boys? You couldn't move for lopped heads."

They both laughed; his turned into a cough, which went on for a while. She fetched him water, and he drank and coughed till the spasm passed, sinking back into the sofa. "Dad," she said, "we should stop. I've got school tomorrow, and you've—"

"Got the hospital. I know. All the more reason to finish."

"Finish?" She hefted the book. "There's way too much."

"Not all of it. Most of it's about her life later anyway. But the Goloth part—" He coughed again. "Let's finish that. There's not much more, if I recall."

"I don't know...." The doctors had told her father—and he'd told her—that they wanted him well rested. In case the test results showed he needed an operation.

"Oh, come on." He leaned toward her. "Because at the end of the next chapter, I have a present for you."

"A present? What is it? Gimme. Gimme," she said, in her best greedy-girl voice.

He pointed. "Read first."

"Tyrant!" She pouted, sat back, opened the book, read on.

IV

## THE LEAVE-TAKING
### Wherein Alice-Elayne rides a unicorn, sorrows ... and receives a parting gift

She had never ridden before. Yet her terror passed swiftly as she realized that Moonspill was not going to let her fall. He had her safe, despite the roughness of the path they took–soon leaving behind them such track as man had made, fleeting over the open countryside, clearing any obstacles with leaps that felt like flight. Alice-Elayne did not know the land, for she had not ventured far beyond the town's walls. She could not note much now, for streams, forests, steep ascents, swooping plunges, all passed in a blur of speed.

The unicorn was silent. No words caressed her mind, and for this she was thankful. His voice had sounded in her head when he bade her mount. She had replied, obeyed. But in that brief exchange, those few thought-words, a connection had been made as if ... as if she were the warp, he the weft, their thoughts entwining like threads upon the loom.

With his silence, she could be alone in her mind, consider the changes that had come to her life; wonder about the greater change yet to come. She was going to France, her father's land. He had spoken little of it. He had never told her where it was, how far away, how it was reached. Had spoken of it as if it were a dream almost. All she knew was that it would be very different from Goloth.

Yet her future concerned her less than her present. What had happened to her father? Would he be joining her soon? For, truly, how could she leave without him?

Moonspill knew what had happened to the weaver. What linked them had long been dormant. But it had, once upon a time, been strong. And it had vanished. He did not need to see his blood to know the weaver was dead. Killed, he was certain, by the other man Moonspill had allowed to slip into Goloth behind him twenty-five summers before, when he was young and foolish.

Each in their own mind, maid and unicorn flew across the land. Though she knew she would not fall, still she gripped his silken mane. It tired her, she who was already tired from a night of sleepless watching. At last, when the sun was at its zenith, she thought her plea.

*Stop! Please stop!*

The blurred world came into focus, the speeding darkness on either side resolving into trees. They were in a narrow, forested valley, on a path threading through stands of beech, oak, and maple.

He slowed—but he did not stop. *We are close,* he thought to her. *Hold a little longer.*

She sighed, gripped again, and studied the trees she now could see. They began to thin, as the land started to rise, there were gaps in the canopy, glimpses of blue and clouds ... and something else. Something that loomed above the world. When the trees finally ended, she saw what it was—a vast spire of darkest rock, thrusting high into the sky.

*What is that?*

*Black Tusk. And our destination.*

The faint track swung between outcrops of stone, up to the very base of the rock, rounded it, then dropped again through a tree-lined path, finally into a bowl of land. A stream spilled over the lip, carving its way down one slope to disappear into the earth beneath the spread branches of the only tree there—a small oak.

*Drink.*

She slid from his back and walked unsteadily to the stream's banks. The water was cold, clear, and refreshed her instantly. After a moment, Moonspill came, reached down his long neck, and drank too.

*What is this place?*

*A gateway,* came the reply.

"What?" she said aloud. "There is nothing here but—"

*The tree.* He moved to it. *It has grown since last I was here. Since I crossed over. Your father followed. He . . . and another.*

*Adam.*

He tossed his head. And she felt it, along the current of thought that joined them. Anger, yes, but . . . something else too. She stepped up to him, stretched an arm slowly up to his neck. His great eyes widened, but he did not jerk away as she placed her hand on his neck. *You fear him,* she thought.

*I fear what he will do. Not to me. To others. To this world. It is my fault he is here. I left the door ajar. I let him in.*

*What . . . door?*

He raised his horn, pointed it at the tree. *There. In this world, it is an oak, of wood and leaf and branch. In the other, the world your father came from, it is made from cloth. A tapestry. Your father's tapestry.*

Confusion seized her, panic. *What can you mean?*

*I will show you. For you must go. Now.*

"Now?" she cried aloud. "No. I must wait here for my father."

*Your father is dead.*

She fell, as if his horn had struck her. "He is not," she gasped. "How can you know?"

*I know. In my mind, there was you and there was him. Now there is only you.*

He did not know how humans mourned. A unicorn would journey to a mountaintop and roar at the sky for days. But he marveled now, as he saw a single tear move slowly down her cheek.

Their silence lasted the time of the tear's course. Until she stood and spoke again. "Then I will stay. And I will kill the man who killed him."

*Well,* he thought, as he had thought before. He saw her strength, admired it. Desired it. But he had no way to protect a maid in Goloth for long. And he had promised her father to see her safe. *You cannot stay. You must remember him. Obey him. Honor his death with your life.*

She reached up, took the tear upon a finger, staring at it as if it were a jewel. Then she rubbed it away. *So. I will go. How?*

*I will open this door for you. My horn is the key to it. When you step through, you will step through a weaving into your world.*

*Into France?*

*If that is where the weaving now hangs, yes.*

He stepped toward the tree, lifting his horn to it. She did not move. "Wait!" she called. "How can I leave all I know? My father unburied, unmourned?" Another tear came. "And what awaits me there?"

Moonspill stared at her. She was strong . . . but she was just a girl. And she was venturing alone into the unknown.

His horn was already almost touching the oak. With a hard flick, he struck the trunk. Something fell, and he reached her again with his mind.

*Pick it up.*

She obeyed. In her hand, only a little bigger than her thumb, was a length of spiraling ivory. She gasped and looked up, to his horn. Its end was flat, for the very tip was gone.

As she wondered, words came into her mind. *Do not fear. My horn grows still, and I will sharpen its point again. Yet know these two things. First, that it is the touch of the unicorn's horn, on magic tree, on magic weave, that opens the doorway between worlds.*

She looked at what she held, seeing it now not as a mere piece of ivory but as the key it was. She nodded, looked up. "And the second thing I must know?"

He bent his head to her. *If your need is dire, beyond all mortal hope . . . then hold this piece of me and call. I will come.*

She stared into his eyes. "Is it true you saved my father's life?"

*It is true.*

"And now you have saved mine." She hesitated, then continued, except this time in her mind. *So know, if you need me, I will return. And if I die before you call—for you live far longer than we mortals— I will pass on this vow to my child. She to hers. For what you have done for our family, our family will honor our debt . . . for all time.*

For a while, they stood there, unmoving, staring. Until he nodded his great head, stepped away, and the link of eye and mind and ivory was ended. *Come,* he thought. *Cross over.* And turning, he plunged his horn into the tree.

Slipping her fragment of horn into the pocket of her dress, Alice-Elayne stepped closer to the trunk, pressing herself against it, feeling wood, the roughness of bark . . .

. . . the denseness of weave, the softness of wool and silk. . . .

She was gone. Though there was no door to see, Moonspill knew it was ajar, would stay so for some moments more. There was time for him to cross over, should he so choose. And he was tempted, to run once more across the world of men. There were adventures to be had there, heroes to be found.

Perhaps he had just guided one through?

With a great shudder, he backed away from the gap between worlds. He turned again toward his own world—toward Goloth, the Land of the Fabulous Beast. And he began to run.

# THREE

# LEGACY

"Dad?"

He was definitely asleep now. The light snoring kind of gave it away. She studied him. He didn't look good.

Hairy cell leukemia. A name that could have been funny if it wasn't.

Eighteen months since he'd been diagnosed. Eighteen months of tests, hospital stays of increasing length, chemo; and all *that* had seemed to achieve was to take most of his thick black hair and any spare flesh. He hadn't had much before, so . . .

The one place he appeared to have put on weight was at his belly—and that was his spleen, enlarged, pushing out. Elayne knew these next few days of tests were about that, though he hadn't told her so. Hadn't told her about the possible operation to remove it either. She'd read all that online.

He shifted, winced, muttered something. Elayne considered leaving him on the sofa. But he'd sleep much better in his own bed.

She closed the book, placed it on the table. "Dad?" she called again, gently shaking his shoulder.

His eyes opened immediately. "Moonspill," he said.

"Yeah. You missed it, Dad. He sent her through. Come on, let's get you to bed."

She tucked a hand under his arm, tried to lift. He resisted. "There was something else. He gave her something." He blinked. "What was it?"

"The tip of his horn. Come on."

"The horn! That's right!" He slipped his arm from her grasp. "And you must have it too. It's here."

They'd tried some experimental drugs on him. Sometimes they made him . . . a little out there. He'd see things, say things. "Uh-huh. Why don't I just, you know, look for that when you're in bed. Now, work with me here." She reached again.

He laughed. "No, no. It's here." He reached to the side of the sofa, his hand ranging around.

"Dad!" she said gently. "It's a fairy tale."

"Is it?" he replied. "Then how do you explain . . . this?" And with a "ta-da" flourish, he brought his hand up.

There was a small box in it. It had a lock and looked as if it was covered in the same fraying material as the book, the same emerald green. "A present," he said, handing it over, then drew a tiny gold key from his pocket, "for you."

"OK." She sat again, slipped the key into the hole, turned it. There was an audible *click*. The lid rose with a slight screech. One she echoed when she saw what was inside.

"Oh . . . my God!"

She was looking at a nub of ivory, yellowed with age, about the length of her thumb. It spiraled from a wide base to a point.

Her father grinned. "Moonspill's horn," he said.

"Oh, come on!" Someone had bored a hole through the ivory's thicker end and threaded through a silver chain. She picked it up by that, letting it spin as the chain unwound. "Where'd you buy this, Dad?"

He looked offended. "I didn't."

She felt a sudden wave of excitement. "Or is it . . . is it another of Mom's old things?"

Her mom had died in a car accident when she was a baby. They didn't talk about her much anymore. But sometimes her dad would "discover" some old piece of jewelry and give it to her.

"Sorry, lovely, no. My mother gave that and the book to me, since I was her only child. Told me to have a daughter and give it to her. And I always obeyed my mother!" He pointed. "Try it on." As Elayne slipped the chain over her head, her father continued. "You know, one of the myths of the unicorn—and I don't mean 'myth' in the sense of something that's supposedly true but isn't; I mean what people actually believed—anyway, one myth says that a unicorn can cure all illness."

"Where's one in Manhattan when you need one?"

He smiled. "Indeed. But even a touch of his horn is meant to help."

She looked at the still-spinning chain. "How'd that work out for you?"

"As you see." He shrugged. "Still, lovely, isn't it?"

The chain stopped. "Yes." Actually, she wasn't sure about it. It wasn't exactly pretty—but it was interesting. "So you're saying that Gramma Elly passed it on to you and that she got it from her mother, who—"

"Got it from hers, all the way back to the original Alice-Elayne, who as you read, brought it from Goloth." He pointed at the book. "You have to read the rest, by the way. Her return to France through the tapestry, how she finds the family François left behind there, her life after . . . Wild!" He leaned forward. "Maybe we could read a little more now?"

"No. Dad, it's late. I'm exhausted." She wasn't but faked a yawn anyway. "And you've got a big day tomorrow."

"Who's the parent here?" he grumbled, but started to rise. She got a hand under his arm again, helped him up. "I'm good," he said, bending to kiss the top of her head. "Night, sweetie."

"Ni-night."

He began to shuffle toward his bedroom. She looked down, running her finger around the spiral of the horn. *Maybe*, she thought, *the horn just needs to be, like, powered up, to work. Maybe I can get it going and Dad will be fine. Maybe . . .*

The door closed. But through it, she still heard the burst of thick coughing he'd been holding back.

"Yeah, miracles," she muttered. She reached up to undo the clasp, then thought, *What the hell*. It was a present, after all.

# FOUR

# FIELD TRIP

First there was blood. Then more blood.

It flash flooded Elayne's dream. This scarlet gush surging over the whiteness of . . . a side? No! A *flank*. That was the word. As white and sculpted as marble, but moving beneath the surface, muscles, tendons highlighted by sheets of red.

She could see hands—hers?—reaching out, trying to stem the cascade. But there was so much of it, oozing over her flesh now, pooling in the half-moons of her nails. She jerked her hands away . . . and for just a moment, the prints of them remained, white in the red. Were they the ones she'd done in kindergarten, framed now and hung in the bathroom?

Handprints gone in a moment. Swept away.

What had she learned in first aid? If it's an airway, clear it. If it's a wound . . . plug it! Stuff something into it. Reaching, her hands miraculously white again, slipping over the reddened marble flank, searching for the source of the blood rising until . . . An eye! A blue eye so dark it was almost black, so deep it went on forever, and in its depths . . . stars! Not spots, not flashes. Stars! A million memories in that eye, memories Elayne could almost . . . hear, feel, touch.

A voice came from the galaxies.

*Cross over.*

Then red blotted out blue, submerged the eye, drowned the stars. Reaching higher, still seeking the source, still hoping to stanch it, her fingers met a hard, cool . . . column. Maybe this *was* a statue, marble not flesh?

But how could marble bleed?

Thoughts from behind the lashes. Whispers through a blood-steeped veil.

*Cross over.*

"What?" Elayne cried, and sat up. But for a few moments, she still straddled the border between sleeping and waking. Something linking the two, melding them . . .

It was in her hand. "What?" she said again, and reached for her bedside lamp. The brightness dazzled until she blinked it away. Then she saw what she was holding.

The unicorn's horn.

And it all came back. Getting up to see her father into the cab at seven a.m. Him kissing her, saying brightly, "Back in two days." She'd meant to stay up then, get a jump on the day, but she'd lain down for a minute, and . . .

She looked at her clock. Eight-twenty. She still had time. Her class was going on a field trip this morning, an end-of-term treat, and they were meeting wherever it was, later than usual.

She rubbed her eyes. Still didn't explain the horn. She remembered going to bed, putting it under her pillow, sticking to the theory that it just needed to be "powered up" to cure her dad. She must have grabbed it in her dream.

She fell back onto the bed, moaned. Did she have to go? Didn't she have a good excuse not to? But she had missed a lot of school lately, and she hadn't always told them she wasn't coming. She was on warning—one more time and suspension loomed. And even if this was the last day before the holidays, they'd carry punishment over till the next term.

She fell out of bed, into her shower, into her clothes. The Alexander Macpherson Academy for Young Ladies believed that kilts and argyle sweaters built character. Or maybe they just wanted to make their students undatable! They frowned on jewelry but Elayne slipped the unicorn horn necklace over her head anyway, and tucked it under her sweater. *Hell with them*, she thought.

At the kitchen counter, while cramming a Pop-Tart into her mouth with one hand, she reached into her bag with the other. Ms. Melcher had given the students a briefing on the field trip, but Elayne had got to class late—again!—and not heard it. Where was she going?

She pulled out an explanation sheet from her bag. "'The Cloisters,'" she mumbled aloud, through crumbs. It sounded familiar. She thought that maybe she'd been there with her dad when she was a kid.

She read on. "'The Cloisters is the medieval department of the Metropolitan Museum in Fort Tryon Park. We will meet outside the 190th Street subway at 10:00 a.m.'"

*At 190th? Excuse me?* She got nosebleeds anywhere higher than Central Park! And it was nine-ten. She'd have to run for the A train. She really, really couldn't be late again.

• • •

"The tapestries are one of the greatest mysteries in all art. No one knows for whom they were made, nor for what occasion. No one knows who paid for them, designed them, wove them; where they were woven; or even where they were first hung. Only one thing is certain: these pieces of cloth are among the most magnificent works of art of the medieval age . . . of any age. And the mystery of their origins only adds to their magical allure."

The tour guide at the Cloisters museum had a strong voice that vibrated with passion for her subject—a passion unshared and largely ignored by most of Elayne's classmates, who stood around the large stone room in various poses of boredom.

Not Elayne. She had been riveted from the moment she walked into the room and saw . . . the unicorn!

He was in every tapestry, the center point of each one. And though she knew it was only a story, the "unicorn's horn" that dangled at her chest seemed to get hot against her skin as she stared, openmouthed. What had she said to her dad? "Where's a unicorn in Manhattan when you need one?" At 190th Street, it seemed.

But there was a bigger shock even than the unicorn. Because in every tapestry there were woven letters. Two of them. An *A* and a reversed *E*.

*Her initials!* Not only that—the initials of all her female ancestors. The ones the book had said her ancestor had put into the weavings in Goloth. Which were based on tapestries he'd woven before . . . in France. Which could mean . . .

*Wow!* She was tempted to shout, *You're wrong! We do know who wove them. His name was François Robochon. My great-great-great-* . . .

She kept her hand down. There was stuff to learn here, and the guide was continuing. "Why are they so magnificent? A combination, surely, of subject, its expression, and its execution. Consider. These are not paintings. They are made of threads, mainly wool, some silk, woven together. Plain spun wool goes across, as you see—that's the warp. Colored ones are twined through on a loom in what is called the weft. It is a series of straight lines. Yet look at what pictures it makes." She smiled. "Look at the faces of the hunters, the lords and ladies! Each one distinct, each filled with human traits—love, envy, desire, anger, boredom, revulsion. Look at the clothes, how each item has depth, texture, weight. Look at the trees and flowers and fruit, how every plant has bend and grace and seems to move in a breeze. There is action, a story being told; a hunt is in progress that proceeds like the frames of a film." Her voice rose. "Vibrant life is here. All achieved by threads going down, going across."

Her audience was mainly too cool to care. Not Elayne. She thought the tapestries were awesome. The four biggest ones were twice her height, more than that across. And they were hung in a room that could have been in a dream castle—polished wooden floor, huge stone fireplace, medieval furniture all around. Yet it wasn't the grandeur of the setting or the beauty of the art that truly gripped her.

"The unicorn," she murmured under her breath, staring.

"The unicorn," the guide said, as if echoing. "The most fabulous of beasts. A fantasy? Perhaps. Yet the unicorn was believed in for centuries, far longer than it has been considered a fantasy. The people who created this tapestry, those whom it was created for, almost certainly believed in it. As a real animal . . . and also as a symbol of mystical things." She looked around. The small group of the really interested had come closer; the majority had drifted away. She sighed, spoke a little softer. "Remember that for our ancestors, the world was often a black place, full of sickness, danger, and darkness. The unicorn was white, filled with light and blessed with healing powers." She smiled. "And it was the hunter's ultimate dream—for this fabulous beast was almost impossible to capture. It would go mad, and fight to the death rather than be taken by man. Such ferocity led many knights to adopt it as their symbol, to put it on their shields. Yet it had two flaws, two weaknesses that *could* lead to its being tamed. For one myth of the unicorn says that it could be beguiled—lured and lulled—by its own reflection. Another that it could be 'gentled,' as they called it, by 'a maiden.' What we today would call a virgin."

It was the sort of word that roused even half-listening schoolgirls. There were a few giggles, which the guide ignored, continuing, "Yet if you did succeed in the hunt of a unicorn, a fortune awaited—because its horn, ounce for ounce, was more valuable than gold. For it could detect all poisons—they would foam in its presence—so pieces of it were molded into drinking cups and used by kings and rich nobles. Shavings of the horn were powdered and mixed into potions to be drunk—you see, the horn could cure poison as well as detect it. Every pharmacy had to have a large bottle labeled 'Fresh Unicorn's Horn' on its shelf if it wanted to stay in business."

*Is that what I should have done?* thought Elayne, feeling the horn under her sweater. *Powdered it and put it into Dad's cocoa instead of marshmallows? If only it were that simple.*

The guide had moved away, to stand before one of the tapestries. "And if a unicorn dipped its horn into a poisoned stream," she continued, "the foul water would be transformed to sweetness." She pointed. "See here, in *The Unicorn Is Found.* The beast has laid its horn in the stream. This is called 'conning.' Clearing the water of harm, so all these waiting animals can drink." She turned back. "In our polluted world, with rivers choked with garbage and chemicals, with half the world's population unable to obtain clean drinking water, with poisons everywhere, what price would we not pay for a touch of the unicorn's horn?"

*I'd pay anything, if it worked,* Elayne thought, her gaze moving over the various tapestries. In one, *The Unicorn at Bay,* a dog had been knocked on its back, its belly gruesomely pierced by the horn. But the unicorn had been wounded too, a thin red stream running from a wound high up on that pure whiteness. . . .

Blood! Her eyes filmed, and she staggered a little. Looking up to steady herself, she stared into the unicorn's eye.

*Cross over.*

"What?" She jumped, looked around for the person who must have spoken. But no one was close. Besides . . . she was sure the words had sounded in her head. Or . . . echoed? Because she'd heard them before, recently. In a dream. A blood-soaked dream.

Then she heard them again. "*Cross over* to the other side and you will see what I mean about movement in the second tapestry, which is called *The Unicorn Leaps Out of the Stream.*"

Elayne raised a hand to scratch her head. But the guide thought it was for something else. "Do you have a question?" she asked.

"Um, yes. What are those?" Elayne pointed at the two letters, hanging in an oak, dead center in the tapestry. The *A*, linked by a tasseled cord to the reversed *E*.

The guide smiled. "If I could answer that question, I would have solved one of the great mysteries of medieval art. Are they the initials of the man who commissioned the works? Perhaps the Christian names of two people, a couple about to be married? Some scholars speculate that the tapestries were a wedding gift. Or were made to celebrate the birth of a child, some heir to a rich estate? Or perhaps—"

They heard no further speculation because the lights flickered . . . then went out. It was such a dark day outside, with snow clouds looming, that the room, despite its tall windows, was immediately plunged into near darkness. Almost simultaneously, a very loud, harsh ringing began. Everyone jumped as yellow emergency lights began flashing on and off.

"It's the theft alarm," the guide called. "There's no cause for concern; we've been having problems with the electrical circuits lately." She sighed. "The backup generator should come on soon. Meantime, we do have to exit, I'm afraid. Please make your way to the front of the building and reassemble in the Main Hall by the bookstore. We will return as soon as this infernal din has ceased."

She began to herd the class toward the door. But Elayne hung back. It wasn't that she didn't want to move. She just couldn't.

It was the blood that did it. That red trickle down the unicorn's . . . down the unicorn's . . .

"Flank," she muttered. The word from her dream! And as with most dreams, when she remembered one part, the whole thing rushed back. Blood, then, streaming down the sculpted whiteness of the flank—though in her dream, there had been so much more.

She looked around. Everyone had left, even the guard. And yet . . . she didn't feel alone.

*Cross over, Alice-Elayne.*

Her name! Spoken by a voice that seemed to be both in her head . . . and coming from the tapestry. She jumped, staggered a step forward. Maybe it was the yellow flashing lights. But the scene before her was no longer just hanging on a wall. It was something *happening*, an arm's length away. Every plant moving in a breeze. Every hunter breathing in. Every animal crouching to leap.

And the unicorn . . . The unicorn was no longer in profile. She could see both its eyes, which were an extraordinary, fathomless blue. They sparkled with a universe of stars, beneath a column of spiraling ivory. . . .

The unicorn's horn.

*The unicorn's horn!* She clutched its shape beneath her sweater as if it could steady her for the words that came again.

*Cross over.*

She didn't know if she fell or reached out to stop herself from falling. She just knew that when her fingertips touched cloth, they sank into it.

And the room turned upside down. Tapestry dissolving; her, falling. Into a woven tree, through the tree. No fear in the falling. No time for that. Time only for one question, one answer.

*What do you do when a unicorn tells you to cross over?*

*You cross over.*

FIVE

# MANTICORE

The Cloisters were gone.

The museum had been replaced by a chill mist. It enveloped Elayne, so thick that when she lifted her hand, she could only see her fingers at the tip of her nose.

Slowly she straightened her arm, then began to sweep it in a semicircle in front of her. Nothing, nothing, nothing—Ah! She jerked her hand back because, just behind her, she'd touched something hard. It didn't move, no sounds came so, tentatively, she reached again . . . till her fingers met a surface slick with condensation. She turned, explored bumps, grooves. The hard surface curved back. . . . A tree trunk? The last thing she'd seen in the museum had been the woven oak in the tapestry. Her fingers had touched it, the alarm bells were going off, those lights flashing, she'd felt dizzy. . . .

Her mind began to chatter as much as her teeth.

*Elayne, face it—you've fainted. So someone will find you soon, sprawled in front of the tapestry. Just sit and wait.*

She lasted two seconds.

*Wait? I can't wait. What if I've had a stroke? Aren't stroke victims supposed to feel really, really cold? I could be in some sort of coma. For weeks. Years! I can't just sit here. Besides, this coma is fr-fr-eezing! Gotta get help.*

"Hello?" she called softly.

"Hello?"

The reply was soft, as if coming from a little ways off. It still startled her, and she used the tree trunk to brace herself and shakily stand. Pressing her back against the wood, she called, a little louder, "Who's there?"

"Who's there?" This echo came from closer. Except it was not so much spoken as sung, and eerily beautiful. Another time, she might not have minded listening to it . . . if it wasn't coming out of a freezing mist, in the middle of a faint! And if it wasn't just repeating her words like some annoying four-year-old.

"Look, whoever you are . . ."

"Look, whoever you are," came the reply, much closer now. This time it was followed by a kind of laugh. Not a nice one.

Elayne opened her mouth, then shut it fast. She began to edge around the tree, to put it between herself and who-ever . . . whatever was out there. The mist on the other side seemed less thick, a pale sunlight breaking it up. She could even see the ground in front of her.

"Look!"

This word was shouted, cruelly beautiful, triumphant . . . and from right in front of her. Something was rising through the mist, solidifying within it. When it stopped growing—and that took a while—the mists shredded around it, clearing so she could see.

So she could scream.

It was the height of a tall man. It had a man's face, kind of. Except no man she'd ever seen had three rows of teeth. Or a red-gold mane or a lion's body. And no lion ever had a tail like this one—its ball end bristling with sharpened quills.

"A manticore!" she cried. Her father had described one to her only the night before. And there was something else about them too. . . . What was it? Oh yeah. . . .

They were man-eaters.

"Help!" she screamed.

"Help!" the creature sang, laughing with mockery—before it whipped its tail back, shot it forward. Elayne ducked, and something whistled just above her head. She looked up . . . and saw a dart, six inches long, sunk into the tree. Bark sizzled, frothed, dissolved.

She screamed again . . . and the man-lion laughed. Leaping, she put the trunk between her and it. . . . It was in front of her again in a moment, triple rows of teeth spread in what could only have been a grin.

"Please," she whimpered, sinking back against the tree, as the creature dropped onto all four paws, took a pace forward, another.

"Please?" the creature echoed, but in a question, singing

the word, stepping nearer, leaning in, close enough now so Elayne could smell its breath, the stink of rot. Flecks of raw meat were caught between its teeth, which she saw ever more clearly as it leaned closer, closer. . . .

She felt a vibration. Something heavy was moving over the ground. Instantly the manticore reared up onto two paws, spun around, its tail waving back and forth.

The vibration came and went, as if something were landing and taking off, landing and taking off again. Closer and closer it came, the gap between landings narrowing . . . until a huge white shape split the mist. The manticore whipped its tail forward, hurling a barb. There was a sharp *crack* as the dart was knocked away. Then the last of the mist was dissolved by flailing hooves, and the manticore's furious cries were drowned by a single, earsplitting roar.

What stood before Elayne now confirmed she *was* dreaming. Because the creature rearing up on hind legs, a great horn spiraling from its forehead, could only be a fantasy.

A unicorn.

The pain! The manticore's cries were gentle compared to the unicorn's roar. Elayne slapped her hands to her ears but couldn't shut her eyes, couldn't turn away as the man-lion jerked its tail back, shot it forward, and sent six darts flying toward the huge white chest. Nothing could stop them.

And then the horn moved through the air so fast she could barely see it. *Tac, tac, tac tac tac, tac* came the sounds as, like some cinema swordsman, the unicorn parried all the poisoned quills. The manticore shrieked in rage, whipped back its tail to fling again. . . .

And the unicorn charged. The manticore leapt to the side, then sprang, savage claws rending, terrible triple-rowed teeth biting down. Blood gushed. Elayne gasped! Just as in her dream, sheets of crimson streamed down white flanks.

The unicorn reared, then shrugged its massive shoulders, and the beast flew from its back. It landed right beside Elayne, turning at her yelp, its yellow eyes narrowing, its rows of teeth opening, oozing saliva, blood, and the stench of half-digested flesh.

But her next cry was lost in the roar of the unicorn, rising on rear hooves, front ones beating the air. The man-lion turned back and rose too, shrieking defiance. The unicorn charged and knocked the beast backward. It rose but again, the blood-flecked chest smashed into it. And again. . . . And at last, with a high-pitched wail of fury, the manticore fled.

Sunlight was streaking through the last tendrils of mist. Elayne watched the manticore as it ran up a slope. They were in a steep-sided scoop of land, and the beast vanished over the edge. Gulping chill air, she turned to the creature still before her. The unicorn was breathing as hard as she was, red-stained flanks heaving. It was much bigger than the one from the tapestry, far bigger than even the largest horse. Its mane and tail were thick, full, and a little darker than the marble white of its body. Unlike any horse, though, it had a little beard of the same hue.

But what drew her eyes was the horn. She couldn't stop staring at it. It began a handspan above the eyes and had to be five feet long, bone white and spiraling to a gleaming point.

The unicorn had been following the man-lion's retreat.

Now, realizing he was regarded, he turned and looked at her . . . and she breathed even deeper. Because he had eyes she'd seen before, once in a dream, once staring out of a tapestry. Entirely blue but of such an extraordinary shade, so dark they were almost black, so deep they seemed to sink forever to a depth that could never be reckoned.

They stared at each other for long moments of heaved breath. And then, though that silence was not broken, words came . . . inside Elayne's mind.

*Come. The manticore may yet return.*

It was a voice wrapped in silk. . . . *No,* she thought, *in velvet,* because, though it was soft, it had weight as well, and depth.

Her voice came out all shuddery. "Why . . . why . . . why didn't you just kill it? Stab it?"

*It was only doing what it must. It did not deserve to die for that. Come now. Mount.* And as he thought/spoke, he knelt upon the turf.

Elayne stared. "Are . . . you . . . in-insane?" she blurted. "I've . . . I've never ridden a horse in my life. I'll fall off."

The thought was a caress in her head. *I am not a horse. And I will not let you fall.*

Elayne hated riding. Her father said that she'd been traumatized by falling off the carousel in Central Park at age two. But she had smelled the manticore's last supper on his teeth, and she did not want to be his next—even if she was in a coma!

She forced herself to stand, to cross to him. As she did, she thought but did not say, *I wonder who you are.*

He thought but did not speak, *I am Moonspill. And I summoned you here.*

"Moonspill? But you're . . . ?" she cried. "Now wait a min—Whoa!"

She'd slipped a leg over the great white shoulders. As soon as she did, he stood.

*Hold fast,* came the thought.

Elayne grabbed fistfuls of mane. "Um . . . giddy-up?" she ventured.

He went from still to gallop in a blink. She yelped, felt as if she was slipping, grabbed the mane tighter. There was one faint path out of the bowl, and they charged up it, passing under the blackened limbs of a lightning-struck oak. There was a fork, two avenues of trees, and they took the one to the left, heading down, emerging soon into a grassy valley. She was aware of something looming above, shot a nervous glance back, saw a tall spire of black rock. They were soon galloping away from it, toward far hills that got close, incredibly fast.

*Where the hell am I?* she wondered.

*Goloth,* came the reply.

"What?" But she had no time to yell more or think even one of the thousand new questions in her head. Because suddenly their speed quadrupled, and all she could think of was holding on.

Mounted on a unicorn, Elayne flew across the land, toward the gleaming hills.

# SIX

# HORN

It was hard to bear someone on his back. Not difficult. Keeping her centered, when her terror made her likely to fall, was easy enough. It was the bearing itself. Being ridden. As if he were a horse. As if he were . . .

*Tamed.*

Anger flushed Moonspill. He released it over water, clearing a stream as if it were five times as wide, flying high above it, yet landing with hardly a jolt to frighten his burden.

*Burden.* How could he think of her thus? For had he not knelt for her, bidden her mount? More, had he not sought her out? He had not truly believed she existed, nor that she would—could—come, until he heard her scream. He had only a tiny, tiny hope—that one of the weaver's blood still lived, lived and still possessed the treasure he had given . . . to the only other he'd ever borne upon his back.

Alice-Elayne. Weaver's child. She had vowed to return,

should his need be great. In five hundred years, through all the sorrows of Goloth, such need had never arisen.

Now it had.

Moonspill began to run faster, trying to purge anger from his thoughts. There was no place for it. If anger could have won his desire, he would have kicked down the gates of the Castle of Skulls long before. No. He needed something else. Someone. She was there, the burden upon his back, clutching at his mane. Hope was alive, the smallest of flames. A storm had come, yet it burned.

He ate distance. Up ahead, the hills got close, fast. Near the summit of one was the place where he would tell her all. And ask her for his greatest desire, which was also his greatest fear.

• • •

Elayne felt that she'd earned a bit of hysteria.

After all, she had fallen through a tapestry. Nearly become a manticore's dinner. Was now riding a unicorn. Going where, for what, who knew?

She couldn't help it. She laughed. But it came out all jerky, a kind of *huh-huh-huh*.

*Peace.*

"And-that's-another-thing," she said, out loud, her speech as fractured as her laugh. "You. In my head. Hello? I am talking to a unicorn." She laughed helplessly. Then went, "Oh!"

It was as if someone had suddenly laid a warm, wet towel directly over her brain. "Mmm," she managed, then continued, her voice as slow as it had been quick before, "Where am I again?"

*Goloth.*

"Goloth. That's right!" Her heart accelerated, and again she felt that warmth come. He was doing it to her, calming her. She liked it . . . but it disturbed her too. "Stop," she said, shaking her head, as if pushing a caressing hand aside, "and listen! I've heard of Goloth."

*How?*

"It was in a book I read. A fantasy—or . . . or family history." She hesitated. "There . . . there was a girl called Alice-Elayne. . . ."

She felt a ripple go through him. *So you are . . . family?*

"I guess. Alice-Elayne"—she shrugged—"is my name too."

Ripple turned to surge. Whatever had been caressing her mind went choppy. She began shaking again, with cold as well now, and cursed that they'd made her check her parka at the museum. The sun had sunk low in the time they'd ridden toward it. There'd been some leaves below the oak tree. Fall in Goloth? But she'd left New York with its first big snow warning.

They'd quickly reached the hills that had been distant, began climbing steadily. In a blink, they were among trees, surging uphill. It got even cooler; the path got steeper, and Elayne clung harder to stop herself sliding backward—though she still had the sense that he was not going to let her fall. "Where are we going?" she whispered.

*Here.*

It was a clearing. Tall pines pressed thickly, forming three-quarters of an open circle, the rest defined by rock, a cliff face that disappeared into the mist still clinging to the treetops here. Set into it, disappearing in darkness, was a cave.

"Uh, is this where you live?"

A strange sound came, a sort of punctuated humming. It was only when words followed that she realized what the sound was. Amusement.

*I live everywhere. This is . . . shelter for you.*

"Shelter?"

He shrugged, causing her to slip from his shoulders. Wobbling as her feet met earth, she steadied herself against him. When she was set, he moved away, toward the path they'd come up.

She took a step after him. "Wait! You're not just going to leave me here, are you?"

*There are things you need.*

He was gone. She looked around, shivered. Truly, where the hell was she? And then he was back. But he didn't come empty- . . . horned. Wedged onto it were half a dozen small logs.

*Can you make a fire?*

"I know how, but . . . what would I light it with?"

*I will light it.*

He shook his head, and the wood tumbled off before a low, flat-topped rock. Elayne went to the forest's edge, gathered twigs, took them back, arranged the logs in a pyramid just as her dad had taught her on their many camping trips.

62

The activity, its familiarity, calmed her a little. When she'd thrust in the last of the kindling, she looked up. "Um . . ."

Moonspill lifted his head, then brought it down hard, striking the horn against the rock. Sparks cascaded from the impact onto the wood. In a moment, the kindling was ablaze at a dozen points. She bent, poked, blew. The logs caught, and she sat on the rock, her hands held out. The shaking began to ease.

A thought came into her head that she didn't catch. "What . . . ?"

*Go to the cave. In the entrance.*

Just inside the darkness—she couldn't see to the back—something gleamed. She bent—and picked up a silver bowl. It was the size of her cupped hands.

"How did you—?"

He interrupted again. Answers were obviously not his thing, not now. He gestured with his horn. *There is water there. It is good.*

Beside the cliff face, she found a little spring. She dipped the bowl and drank. It was beautiful and cool, clean, fresh, better than anything she'd ever had. She filled and drank again, sipping, relishing. Her mind cleared . . . and she looked up at Moonspill.

His huge chest was scored with gouges from the manticore's teeth and claws, blood congealing around frayed skin. She dipped the bowl, filled it again, looked around. The spring was lined in a bed of thick, spongy moss. Tearing off a chunk, she turned and walked to him.

*What are you doing?*

"This." She dipped the moss and began to wipe away the blood. He flinched at first, then calmed, his head slowly lowering as if it had been held stiffly for too long. Thick lashes drooped to half veil the universe of his eyes. Soon, all that moved were occasional flicks of ears and tail.

It took many bowlfuls, many wads of moss. But eventually the wounds were cleaned. They still gaped, though, raw and ragged.

He must have sensed her concern. *I heal swiftly.*

"Oh. Good." Shivering again, she moved to the fire, bent to restack, to blow, to feed flame.

*There are things that you would know,* he thought to her. *Ask.*

She looked at him. *Where to begin?* she wondered. *Uh, OK. Well, this . . . thinking to each other? Can you, like, understand all my thoughts?*

*No. But think to me and I will hear you.*

*OK.* That was a relief. But there was one other thing she needed to confirm before anything else. "I am not . . . not dreaming this, am I?"

*No. You are in Goloth.*

"So my world, the world I came from, is, what . . . 'Earth'?"

*No. Goloth is "Earth" too. Yours is the world of man.*

She scratched her head. "So are we talking, like, parallel worlds?"

*I do not know what that means. Goloth and the world of man are separate—but there have always been doorways between them. Crossing points. Woven from visions.*

64

"Woven?" A lightbulb went on. "You mean 'woven' as in a tapestry?"

*That is the last door. There were others before it. Not always woven. Created by seers of visions, by the realizers of dreams.*

"By . . . artists?"

*Yes. By men and women who scratched and painted, carved and wove.*

"So you're saying that this world"—she waved at the forest—"is just as real as the one I left behind."

*Yes.*

"So it really wasn't a fantasy," she muttered, thinking of the book she'd read to her father.

*The land of man and the Land of the Fabulous Beast have always existed, side by side. They are both real.*

"Fabulous beast?" she echoed, then shivered, despite the fire. She had met two—one had tried to eat her, one had rescued her. "There's more than you and the . . . the manticore?"

*Many more. As you shall see. Soon.*

"Soon?" She swallowed. To distract herself from the fear, she picked up the bowl. "Did this come . . . from my world?"

*No. That was fashioned here.*

She studied the vessel, turned it over. On the bottom was an engraving. . . . No, a hallmark, she remembered it was called. She ran a finger over it. "A lion," she said.

Moonspill tossed his head. *He marks everything he owns. And he claims he owns everything.*

"'He'?"

*Leo.*

She knew her astrology. "Leo" was "the Lion." And she suddenly remembered— "Adam!" she gasped.

Moonspill lowered his horn toward her sharply. *You know of him?*

"It was in the family story I read! Adam, the English hunter, was going to be crowned king. And when he'd killed the weaver"—she faltered, glancing down, running her finger over the groove of the stamp—"my . . . my ancestor, Adam vowed that he would be 'the Lion.'"

*Yes. He and his descendants have kept that vow. Each tyrant in Goloth rules under the name of Leo.*

There was something in his tone that made her look up. Moonspill was staring away, into the forest. Their communication must have gone two-way because she picked up something. Not fear exactly but . . . dread? And if a unicorn dreaded it . . .

She looked back into the fire. "What am I doing here?" she whispered.

His gaze swiveled back to her. *I summoned you.*

Fear slipped easily into irritation. "Well, thanks for the invitation! But I was kind of busy, you know?" A vision came: her father in his hospital bed, hooked up to monitors, jabbed with needles. "What could I possibly do for you?" He stepped toward her, and her rage faltered in fathomless blue. "Besides," she mumbled, "how was I able to come?"

*How? Because of who you are. And because of what you possess.*

"What do you mean?"

*The horn. Show it to me.*

"The horn?"

*You must have it. You could not have crossed over if you did not possess the key to the doorway.*

"You mean this?" Elayne reached beneath her sweater, pulled out the piece of horn by its silver chain. "*This* opens the door between home and Goloth?"

*That . . . and this.* He dipped his own horn toward her.

"But . . ." Suddenly the questions overwhelmed her again. She couldn't decide which to ask. Why was she here? What did he want from her? Most importantly: when could she go back?

His thought came, as if in answer. *I will tell you all. You will need to know everything. Before you decide.*

"Decide what?"

*Your destiny. Mine.*

It was way too much. "What do you mean?" she cried again.

He jerked his horn into the air, like a hand shot up to silence her. *A question leads to two questions, which lead to four. If you let me, I will tell you what you need to know.*

*What* you *need me to know,* she thought, but said, "I wish you would—"

*Then listen and do not question.* He backed up a step, lifted his head, stared for a long moment into the forest before his thoughts came again. *It begins with your ancestor, François Robochon. When I found him in a forest, he was dying. Poisoned.*

"And you . . . cured him?"

*Yes.*

"How?"

*Understand this. Goloth is the land where man's myths live. Not only the beasts of myth but the beasts' powers too. Thus the myth of the horn has always been, and remains, true: if you are poisoned and are dying, a touch of that horn, bestowed by a unicorn, will cure you.*

It was insane! It made Elayne want to pinch herself to finally wake up. Because she'd said something to her dad only the night before—half prayer, half joke—about finding a unicorn to cure his "poisoned blood" . . . and here one was. She nearly blurted out, "Hey! I'll do anything for you. But there's something you have to do for me first." But she just stopped herself. She had no idea what Moonspill was really like, or what he was really after. She needed to know way more before she started . . . bargaining.

"OK," she said carefully. "But my ancestor's tapestries were woven in the . . . the, what? The"—she tried to remember what the museum guide had said—"the 1490s or something. So that would make you—five hundred years old?"

*We do not reckon our lives in such a way. We are born, we grow stronger, strong, we weaken, we die. But I know how man likes to eat his life in marked stages. So, yes, five hundred years and some more. I am near the end of my time.* His tail swished, as if shooing flies, before he continued. *I was perhaps twenty when I met the weaver. Past my first youth. Old enough to realize how foolish I had been.*

"Foolish?"

*Yes. For I was the last of the unicorns. Had chosen to be last.*

She scratched her head. "Where had all the others gone?"

Moonspill swished his tail. *Here.*

"Chosen? What do you mean? And how...?" She couldn't settle on a question. There were just too many.

*Peace*, he said, as he'd said before. *And hear my story.*

His voice in her head was calming. Besides, she didn't have much choice. Settling back against the rock, she raised her hands to warm them before the fire. Thought of the many campfires where she and her dad had shared stories, as Moonspill began his.

*I was born here, in the Land of the Fabulous Beast. The second of two, a sister born a moment before me. Salvia was our dam, Darkheart our sire, though we saw little of him. Unicorns run alone, once they can run fast enough, once their mother's milk has strengthened them. Five years in your time, perhaps. Less. It was less for me, for I was ever anxious to be gone. To cross over to the world of man.*

He moved to the edge of the clearing, laid his horn against a tree, rubbed it up and down.

*I was drawn there by the tales. Heroes had ridden us—Alexander had conquered the world on a unicorn's back, Arthur of the Britons had held off the darkness astride another. Yet another, my own sire, Darkheart, had appeared to the great Khan as his armies were about to ravage India and warned him away from its destruction, offering himself as reward for the Khan's pity.*

Moonspill's chest rose and fell. *Was it a sigh?* Elayne wondered.

*But the time of heroes was passing. And when the last continent was found by men of Europe, the unicorns decided that even that New World would eventually be no shelter for us, such is man's greed to possess all he can see. Unicorns have always been,* in their way, the shepherds of fabulous beasts. They decided that we should return, every species, finally and forever, to Goloth. To leave only a memory behind—one that man would begin to trust less and less.

He turned back to face her.

The decision was agreed and communicated through the minds of all the fabulous beasts. And on the appointed day, when the sun was closest to the world, we gathered at the crossing places. At the painted caves of Lascaux and the crouched Sphinx of Egypt. By the winged bulls of Assyria and within the Minotaur's labyrinth of Crete. In the forests of the Mohawk, in the mountains of Tibet, on the great plains of Africa—wherever a fabulous beast was depicted by true visionaries, there a gate was, there we met, there we crossed. And when the last passed through, that last destroyed the gate in Goloth, so no man could follow.

He glanced to Elayne, then looked away again.

But not all crossed over. Some chose to remain behind. Others failed to keep the time. The kraken who dwells in a lake in the north of the island of Britain. The man-ape of Tibet. The man-bear of America.

I.

He raised his horn, pointing it straight into the sky.

I was Moonspill, and I was wilder than any of my kin. I sought to be a mount for an Alexander, an Arthur. And I had searched through the world of men such a little, little time. So I hid. And when they all had gone, I laughed and ran free, the last unicorn. And if I never found a hero worthy to straddle my back, I had many adventures seeking one. For a few years, I was happy.

His thoughts fell silent. He stared at the cliff face. And

Elayne felt certain he was not seeing it but his past dancing upon the rock. It took a long moment before his voice came again into her head.

*I was young when the others left—scarce more than a boy in your terms. It took time before I saw what I had cut myself off from.* A shudder ran the length of his great, blood-tinged flanks. *For even though unicorns run alone for much of their lives, there are times of coming together. And there is one unicorn, one alone, who is their destiny. I did not know her. I knew only that somewhere beyond the Ishtar Gate, within the shadow of the Sphinx, she wept for me.*

"So you . . . mate for life?" Elayne murmured.

*Yes.*

"And you abandoned your mate?"

*I did not know her. And I was too wild to know what I would need and desire. Until it was too late.*

"So? What did you do?"

*I visited the gateways, all of them, from the highest mountains to those lost to jungle, hoping that perhaps the last through had been careless in their closing. None had. There was not a trace that fabulous beasts had even passed that way, save for the pictures of them that artists had created. I despaired.*

He turned to look at her.

*And then I came upon a weaver, dying in a forest. And I saw what he dreamed of depicting. Saw that I could help him realize his dreams. And that he could realize mine. So I cured him.*

"François Robochon," Elayne said softly.

*Yes.*

He stared at her for a few seconds before he went on.

*In the months that followed, I came to him sometimes. And I joined him often in his dreams. I helped him weave what you have seen, wondrous tapestries. And some nights, when his assistants had left, he let me into his workshop, and there, within the slits and the shadows of the warp and the weft, he wove for me a doorway. It was a part of the whole, would not be complete until the whole was complete. Until the entire vision was rendered. I did not chafe to go, now I was so close. I thought we were safe.*

Moonspill dragged a hoof across the ground, scoring the turf. *We were not safe. The lord who commissioned the work had appointed a man to command his guards. His name was—*

"Adam?" Elayne blurted.

*Yes, Adam. What do you know of him?*

Elayne thought back. "Uh, that he was . . . English, I think, and a great hunter. . . ." She swallowed. "Not much else."

*Then I will tell you more.* Moonspill had begun to walk as he talked, circling the outer edge of the clearing, no longer looking at Elayne. She stood, so it was easier to turn with him.

*The tapestries were complete. A great event was planned for their viewing, noble lords and ladies invited to a feast. Like the others before me, I chose to leave on the longest day of the year. The door was woven. It needed only the touch of my horn to allow me to pass through it.*

*The guards snored in the barns nearby, lulled by wine the weaver had bought them. Only the Hunter did not sleep. And I, usually the wariest of game, had left my mark before the door. A single hoofprint. And that night, in my eagerness, I did not see or scent him. So this Adam watched man and beast lean together, heads touching in farewell. But when I pushed through the slit with my horn, when I followed horn and vanished . . .*

He paused. "What?" Elayne breathed, her voice barely audible.

Moonspill gave another deep sigh. *I learned what happened later. For the doorway between worlds does not slam shut. The magic of the horn lingers. Time enough for an enraged hunter, deprived of his prey, to burst in, denounce the weaver as a witch, tell him that he and his entire family will burn, having first suffered every torment that cruelty can devise . . . unless he guides the hunter to the ultimate quarry.*

*The weaver wept . . . but there was nothing he could do. He yielded, revealed the hidden doorway between worlds, still closing slowly. At spearpoint, Adam forced François to go with him. They stepped through.*

"You hadn't destroyed the door."

*No. Another beast was nearby, a manticore, the father of Scarax, whom you . . . met. I fought him in the forest there. And when I realized what I had forgotten, it was too late. The Hunter had come to Goloth.*

Moonspill stopped. Only his tail moved. "But," Elayne said, stepping closer, "there must have been hunters already there. Uh, here."

Moonspill turned to face her.

*Not like Adam.*

# SEVEN

# TAMING 101

Moonspill was staring at nothing before him. Perhaps, like her, he couldn't see much beyond the fire glow, it had gotten so dark. She stretched her hands to the flames. She wasn't really cold anymore . . . yet she started shivering when he turned to face her. Something in the way he looked at her. Because he wasn't simply *looking*.

He was expecting something.

"What? What do you want?"

There was a long moment before his thought came.

*You must tame me.*

"I must . . . what?"

*You must tame me. For it is told that a maiden, unknown to man, can tame a unicorn.*

"Unknown to man"? Elayne thought back to the museum, the guide talking about the taming myth of the unicorn. "How do you know I am . . . am a maiden?"

His thought took a while before it came. *I do not . . . know. Yet I cannot think that destiny would cause us to meet if you were not.*

"Destiny?" she yelped. "Look," she continued desperately, "why me? There must be someone here who could help you out!"

*There are no maids in Goloth.*

"Huh?" That didn't make sense. He'd said there were people. That meant that—

But his next thought interrupted hers. *Yet that is not what truly matters. What matters is that you are Alice-Elayne, of weaver's blood. You have the horn. A vow was made upon it. A vow that must be kept.*

Elayne stared. He couldn't really expect her to keep a promise made five hundred years before by an ancestor.

She was about to tell him so. Tell him to forget it all and send her back to Manhattan . . . until another thought hit her, with a force that actually made her gasp.

*Tame? You tame an animal, it obeys you. Obeys your every command.*

She knew what hers would be: Take me back to Manhattan. Cure my dad!

She'd looked down so he couldn't see the sudden excitement in her eyes. *Careful,* she thought to herself. *Don't appear too eager.* "Well," she said softly, "if you think I can do this. . . ."

*I think . . .*

It was the first instance in their time together that she sensed any hesitation in him, any doubt. He'd been so certain. "You don't know?"

*I have never been tamed.* He tossed his head. *I cannot . . . know.*

"But someone must have told you. . . . Your father . . . Your . . ."

His thoughts came at her, choppy still. *No one . . . tells. Each unicorn . . . discovers. Darkheart, my sire, must have been tamed to allow the great Khan to ride him. But he did not tell. It is not our way. But it must be so. For if it is not . . .*

He backed away from her. She could see he was getting more agitated. For whatever reason, he needed this, even if it frightened him. Well, so did she.

"So," she said, trying to be calm, rising slowly, "what do we do?"

He stepped toward her. *You must sit. I must lay my head upon your breast.*

"What?" She couldn't help her cry. But then, taking a breath, she sat back upon the rock.

He dropped to his knees before her. Lowered his head, the horn passing in front of her face, so close she could see its spiral grooves. She blinked, scarcely breathing, bracing for the huge weight that was to come. But when his muzzle touched her, running from her shoulder down to her hip, she was amazed at how gentle he was, how light. She almost laughed when one velvet ear flicked at her neck. Until the veil of eyelashes slowly opened—and she was staring into his eye.

It had dazzled her from afar. She had seen universes there. She'd undersold it.

It was like no blue she'd ever seen. No single shade could sum it up. Layers of blue, from darkest midnight to the most violet of dawns. Swimming with stars, galaxies dancing over the void, spirals of nebulae like the spirals of a horn, twisting through the heavens. Everything spun out from the center, from the globe of the pupil, which seemed black until she looked closer. Until she saw that it too was bottomless. Until she began to fall through its depths.

"Ahhh!" Elayne's sigh was long, and his head rose and fell gently with her breath. She didn't know if she was supposed to do anything. But all she *could* do was stare into infinity.

Time passed, or paused, so suspended did it seem. Until he began to quiver, and she thought, *Is this it?* and readied herself, for what she could not know. And she was staring so hard at the circle of the pupil, sunk so far into it, that when it suddenly contracted, closed almost to a line, it was as if she had been shot violently from it. She gasped, as his head pressed hard against her for the first time. Then he was struggling to his hooves, looming over her, ears, tail, eyelashes, his whole body, twitching.

Something was wrong. She whispered, "Are you . . . tame?"

*Tame?*

The thought came on a roar—like the one when he'd fought the manticore, even louder, rage that deafened, a note in it that pierced, high and low and everything in between, booming off the cliff face, reverberating out of the cave. Bats shot out of it, thousands of them, their shrieks adding to the din. Birds took off from hidden roosts, a mass of blackness rising above the treetops, cawing harshly.

Waves of fury lashed at her. She cowered. But he turned

from her, charged at a tree, driving his horn into its trunk, jerking it out, thrusting in again, as if it weren't solid wood before him but someone's flesh. Then he reared up, front hooves flailing, and in seconds bark had turned to kindling, the exposed flesh beneath slashed, sap spurting like blood.

Elayne covered her ears. It didn't do much good against the storm. And none at all against the words that came.

*Tame? I am Moonspill, son of Darkheart, and I am for the wild moors, not the stables. To bear you upon my back is agony. In five hundred years, I have not ceded even a part of my will to anyone. And you think you are worthy to ride me?*

"I didn't—"

*Crack!* The pine gave, its top half—for the unicorn reached so high—smashed backward. And then he was off, charging between the trees. Gone.

"Moonspill!" Elayne cried. But he was beyond voice, beyond thought. She heard his crashing progress, felt the weight of his landings on the ground, receding fast. Then both were gone as well. Staring at the wrecked tree, at swooping birds and bats, she yelled, "You're not going to just leave me here, are you?"

She waited, not moving, staring the way he'd gone, willing him to return. Slowly, the forest settled again into night, birds returning to their roosts, bats, singly now, darting about their hunt. He did not come.

She sank down onto the stone. What could she do except wait?

And cry. She felt like it, though no actual tears came. It was all too weird—too scary. The forest was filled with the sounds of bird and beast—and she knew what sort of beasts this world contained. So different from her own world. What was happening there? she wondered. Had her disappearance been discovered? Would they tell her . . .

"Dad!" she said it now, out loud, the word a constant shadow on her mind. A tear did come then, a single one, running down her cheek. She saw him there, in the hospital, awaiting his test results. Alone. "Back soon," she whispered.

She wiped the tear away. But when? How? Her only method of transport had just charged off into the night. Was he even coming back? If he didn't, what would she do? Well, find some of these Goloth people, she supposed. If he did . . . would he still want to be tamed? Even though he hated the idea—the tree was witness to that. Even though their first attempt had obviously been a failure.

Elayne shivered. The fire had got low, so she forced herself up and over to the shattered tree. Moonspill had actually shredded it into some manageable chunks, so she dragged them back to the fire, collected more kindling, stacked, dug up embers, blew. Flames rose, a little warmth for hands . . . and spirit.

"Come back, please."

## EIGHT

# RED RAGE

Fool! Fool! Fool!

What had he expected? Five hundred years of running free, of never letting another choose for him, ended in a moment? His great spirit given over . . . to a maiden, a foolish girl, to do with what she will?

He had not known. He had not understood. But his own sire and dam, had they not let heroes ride them, to mutual glory? Did that not require them to be tamed? Why had they not told him the way of it? He had put faith in man's myth of taming. Since so many others were true in Goloth, why not this one?

It was always such a little hope—that he would find one worthy. But the one who had come was . . . just a girl.

That thought slowed him at last, the land around him changing from a blur of speed into shapes. When Moonspill saw where he was, where his fury had taken him, he was surprised—but only for a moment. For the place where he now stood was where his foolish hope had begun. Where desperation had forced it to begin. In this valley of jumbled rock, up near the tree line.

The scars of the fight were still there, in the gouged earth and shattered trees, in blood upon the ground. His. Man's. His love's.

*Heartsease!*

This was where he had last seen her. This was where he had lost her.

His eyes closed. A unicorn does not remember. A unicorn . . . relives.

* * *

Together again. It is their time, so brief, a matter of man's months in a span of years. Twenty years since their last running. That time gone in his first glimpse of her. Has she grown more beautiful? They are both old. . . . Yet five hundred years dissolves when she takes his breath.

She speeds away, his love. She will not make it easy for him. And though he is bigger, his stride longer, she leads him onto ground where speed is no asset, into the rocky lands where the earth is rent with crevasses, gashed with pits, scattered with boulders, forcing him to tread softly while her nimbleness lets her dance. Yet he thrills in the pursuit, each of them five centuries old and as young again as foals.

The valley climbs, and narrows. Now he sees where she is taking him, where the chase will end. They have come together here before. She disappears. But over a less broken piece of ground, he surges forward.

Her call changes. Alarm! There is danger here, and his speed is terror-driven now, for she is calling him desperately. He drives over the crest—

Into turmoil!

A maelstrom of men and horses. A hedge of spears surrounds her. She lashes out, breaks some, men fall away. But others have nooses, sending them flying around her hooves, her neck. . . .

He sees it. Wants to charge, kill, lose himself in the killing. The red rage calls . . . but he has not lived five hundred years not to know himself. Know man too. One man especially. The Hunter. He was ever careful, and this trap was skillfully sprung. So Moonspill must be careful too.

Ropes around his love, her strength failing. More men are running at her, but these bear tall mirrors, not weapons. Behind them someone else, following slowly. He glimpses a white dress.

*Think!* While they are focused on her, he has his chance. The fight is near the line of forest. It is their hedge of spears that is forcing Heartsease to her reflection. If he can drive them into the trees, they will lose their advantage. Amid the pines, he can take them one by one.

He leaps forward . . . and a noose drops over his horn.

*Think!* A sudden twist of head, a flick, and the rope sails away. *Forward.*

Weighted nets are thrown and curl around his fetlocks.

*Think!*

He stumbles. Men shout in triumph, charge forward. His love cries as more rope flies. He rears, ripping away the bonds. One man, more eager than the rest, charges, slashes with his spear.

*Think! Try to thi—*

Steel cuts into him, a gash opened from shoulder to chest.

Red. It is all he sees. His eyes drown in the color of his own blood.

Lost to it. To the red rage. No thought now. There is only the killing of those who would bind him. Though his love cries still, he is beyond her. Beyond anything but the kill.

Men run at him through a red veil. Men who will die . . .

*   *   *

Moonspill started, looked around, found himself again, in the valley where it had happened. The red rage had taken him, but he did not know where . . . until cold water had shocked him and he'd woken swimming. He looked up from the river to the cliff the men must have driven him over. He'd swum to the banks, reddening the water with his wounds. He had tried to find the shortest way back up the valley, but it had taken too long. When he got there, the Hunter was gone.

Wound-weakened, he had sunk to the ground, tried to gather enough strength to follow. But he was too slow. He caught up with them when they were already crossing the bridge into their city. In their midst, trussed and powerless, his love.

He'd nearly run down anyway. Thrown himself upon the

spears, no matter the odds. But he knew that he would die and then she would—because he knew what the Hunter intended for her.

It was not the time for the red rage. It was time for thought. And as he limped away from the city of man, his first thought was of a maid.

"For what you have done for our family, our family will honor our debt . . . for all time."

The weaver's daughter was the only one he'd ever thought might be worthy.

And back in the forest, a member of that family waited. She had not tamed him . . . yet. But perhaps, somehow, they could still find a way. A way beyond the rage.

Moonspill turned and began to run.

•  •  •

It was totally dark before she felt the vibration. She rose from the bed of pine boughs that she'd gathered, facing the path, praying it was him coming up it and not . . . anything else.

He cantered into the clearing. After a moment, he thought/spoke. *The cave is shelter.*

"The cave has bats."

She heard a rumble in his throat, wondered if it could have been a laugh.

*Bats are the least fearsome creatures in Goloth.*

She rubbed her head. "Maybe . . . but at least manticores don't mess with your hair."

That rumble came again, louder, followed by words in her head. *Come. You must rest. For on the morrow—*

His thought cut off. She swallowed, spoke carefully. "Are we going to, you know, try again? The . . . taming thing?"

He stood looking down at her, his tail twitching. *I do not know. I do not know why I thought it would be simple. But perhaps there is another way. Perhaps it will come in the time we spend together. We must try. For if we do not—*

Again, the voice in her head ceased suddenly. She was only aware of the feeling—an enormous longing. She knew that feeling well.

"Look," she said, "there's something I need to tell you about me. About what's happening at home—"

*No more words.*

"But my father— Oh! Ahh!"

He was back in her head, in that way he had been before. She flooded with warmth. Her eyelids instantly drooped, and she found herself tottering.

*Rest. I will watch over you.*

"Keep the bats off," she mumbled, lying down.

*Yes.*

"And the manticores," she mumbled, and was gone.

Moonspill stared down, wondering.

*She is different from the other. The weaver's daughter was older, somehow, though the same in years. Calmer. This one's mind, how it flies around!*

With the other, the hope he'd had seemed possible. With this one? He looked again at the tree he had destroyed. While he was tearing it to pieces, he had imagined it to be a man. A king. His enemy. His wildness could tear enemies to shreds. One, ten, one hundred perhaps? But a thousand? Behind their steel spears, their stone walls?

Untamed, he had no hope against the city of the Lion. The red rage would take him, and he would be gone. But if he could think, and not just destroy . . . then perhaps, perhaps . . .

Bending, he used his horn to knock chunks of wood into the fire. Glow turned to flame again, warming her, his tiny hope. Perhaps she did not have the strength to do what he required. Or the will. He could talk in her mind, and sense her feelings, but he could not read her thoughts. He knew she was unhappy. That her father made her unhappy. And that she had a need to match his own.

*Perhaps that is why we have been drawn together. The strength of both our needs.*

He stared down into the flames. Glowing worlds rose and fell there, in white ash and fire-veined wood. He saw a burning tower, something moving at its base.

*Heartsease.*

He sent the word out, like a prayer. Waited. But there was only silence. His enemy had her drugged, deep in his castle. Potions, distance, and thick stone lay between them.

*I will come, my love,* he thought anyway. *One way or another, tame or lost to blood, I will come.*

# NINE

# THE GIFT OF TONGUES

They rode at half past dawn. When she'd woken from a long, dreamless sleep—whatever he'd laid across her mind would make him a fortune back home!—Elayne had gone to drink and wash her face and had discovered some wild grapes behind the spring. They were a little bitter, but her hunger took care of that. And so fed, rested, she was filled with questions—about Goloth, its people, its fabulous beasts. And about the taming. He'd said they must try again, but . . . how?

Yet Moonspill barely replied, kept out of her mind altogether. *Later* was his only reply. She was about to make a stand, tell him she would do nothing until he'd at least told her when she might go home. But she'd made the mistake of putting a leg over his shoulders while she framed her demand. In an instant, he was up and running at full speed. There was no getting off without dying.

The forest gave onto a vast grassland, and they headed

eastish, as far as Elayne could tell from the sun—assuming it rose in the east in Goloth. Heading away from the doorway between worlds, farther away from her dad. Moonspill was still giving her the silent treatment, so she clung tight, chewed her lip, and worried.

The landscape began to reflect her mood. They entered a steep-sloped valley whose floor and sides were dull gray earth, split by a brownish river. The wind that had driven against them was gone too, its sweetness replaced by . . . Well, if she hadn't been in Goloth, on a unicorn's back, Elayne would have said it was industrial. Sulfurous, it stank of metals, of things burnt. Burning.

"What is this place?" She shivered, partly because it was colder as well as darker, the sun that had warmed them for the ride sunk in cloud. Then the valley sides narrowed . . . and something moved. On one side, on the other, above, below. Everywhere.

She gasped. In the blur of the ride, she hadn't seen that the valley's slopes were covered . . . with animals. The sight made her slip and grab his mane harder. It was insane! Everywhere she looked, every square foot of ground was occupied with . . . fur, with hide, tusk, horn, feather. It wasn't one great mass of cattle or migrating wildebeest as she'd seen on TV. These were all . . . different animals. To her left was a large herd of deer, stags with great racks of antlers, does beside them, their smaller young pressed against their sides. Yet just next to them, overlapping their edge, was . . . a wolf pack! Some sat on their haunches, some on four feet, tongues lolling.

To her right was a copse of trees, each one tall, many-branched, but almost leafless, diseased-looking. That didn't stop every branch from being crowded with birds and beasts. Pigeons sat in rows, crows above them, smaller birds below. Interspersed among them were squirrels, weasels. . . .

Her gaze started to fly around, unable to settle anywhere. Here, a bear and her cubs sat next to a cougar. There, wild boar encircled a family of foxes. She looked up, seeking some sanity . . . only to see bats dodge swallows, and hawks hover with spiraling buzzards.

But the worst thing, worse even than the silence—because there was not a chirrup, not a growl, not a bleat—each and every bird, beast, and crawling creature seemed to be staring at her. At her and Moonspill, who now slowed to a walk . . . just when she wanted him to gallop.

"Go!" she screeched. She even kicked his sides. "Get us out of here!"

The unicorn did not react, just kept plodding forward. And his silence, the awful silence of all those around them, made Elayne silent too. She looked at her hands in his coffee-cream mane, tried to focus on them and nothing else.

*What are they all waiting for?* she thought.

His voice came again, for the first time in a while.

*Me.*

The track climbed beside the turgid river. Ahead, the valley narrowed to a gap where the two slopes almost met, like an entrance. Or an exit. Fifty feet away, forty, and she found herself leaning forward, yearning to be out of the terrible, staring silence. Then they were moving through the gap, into a kind of rock bowl. It was a dead end with near-vertical walls. Water gushed through a cleft in the cliff face and formed a large pool that nearly filled the space there. They'd left the animals behind, to her huge relief . . . until she saw what rose beside the pool.

A manticore.

She shrieked, pulled back on Moonspill's mane, trying to get him to turn and flee. The beast had risen on hind legs. The same one that had attacked her? She couldn't tell. There was the lion's mane framing the man's face with its triple rows of teeth, the swishing tail with its poisoned quills, rising now as it sighted the unicorn . . . and her! She yelped again; but the unicorn just kept moving forward . . . toward two manticores now. Another had stepped from behind the first. A little smaller, the jaws just as terrible in a face that was almost female.

*Can this get any worse?* she thought. And then it did. Because something screeched, pulling her gaze to . . . Well, it looked like a giant bird, the size of an ostrich. It had a bird's head too, a rooster's, with feathers, talons . . . but its body was like a giant reptile. Stretching out its wings, it gave a high-pitched caw. It was answered from above; there was a beating sound close by that made her duck—and another snake-bird swooped to settle by the first.

*Cockatrices,* came Moonspill's voice in her head. *Do not look into their eyes.*

"Why?"

*Death.*

"Oh, good!" she whimpered, focusing on the mane again.

90

*All creatures have agreed not to kill, to put aside all enmity, for the gift that I bring them. But the cockatrice has a poor memory.*

"M-m-must be tough!" she stuttered. From the corner of her eye, she saw the larger of the bird-snakes raise a leathery wing like a cloak. Both pushed their heads into it.

Still, Elayne was taking no chances. She looked away from one horror . . . to another. To a creature with two heads, one roaring, one . . . bleating! A lion's head on a lion's body . . . but with a goat's head coming out of the same neck. And its tail wasn't a tail at all but a snake, its head writhing up, craning around.

"What the hell is that?"

*Chimera.*

"It looks like some freaky Frankenstein experiment!" she gibbered, stole another glance, wished she hadn't—because right behind this Chimera rose another. Now six heads were roaring, bleating, hissing. The other creatures began to call too—both manticores singing in terrible, beautiful harmony. Both cockatrices crowing through their rooster beaks.

*In a moment. You have waited this long.*

She realized Moonspill wasn't talking to her when the six Chimera heads all snapped their jaws shut, the manticores stopped singing, the cockatrices fell silent.

"You . . . you understand them?" she said out loud.

*Yes. We each can understand the other.* At last, Moonspill halted. He craned his neck around, one eye looking at her. *Do you desire to understand them too?*

"No thanks!" Elayne felt there had been quite enough

weirdness without being able to converse with something that wanted her for lunch. "But, if I did, um . . . how?"

Moonspill gave a short cry. She wondered if he meant her to imitate him, the way Ms. Colbert did at school with French. But then she saw movement and realized that he'd called someone.

Something.

It came slithering down the slope. When it reached the pool's edge, the straight line became a circle, which spun toward them. It looked like a very large Hula-Hoop—until it stopped beside them. She could see it properly now, how it was much thicker than any hoop and made of . . . *scales*, in a blue-green diamond pattern. For a moment, it kept its circular shape until, at the bulge in its middle, a set of jaws opened.

It was a two-headed snake. Twelve feet long at least from head to . . . head, both of which now rose, stretching to where her ankle rested on Moonspill's flank. Four yellow eyes gazed up. She jerked her foot out of the way, fast.

A sound came from each of the heads, neither rattle nor hiss, closer to the sound the unicorn made when he called, only much, much softer. Moonspill responded with almost a whimper in his throat. And then the weirdness reached a new height . . . because one of the snake heads started talking. In English. Kinda.

"In sooth, Moonspill? The fair maid doth speak the tongue of the sea-girt isle? Marry, 'tis an age since any would converse with us in those harmonious tones. Prithee, damsel. Enchant us with a word!"

Yellow eyes stared. "Eh?" Elayne managed.

"'Tis a letter, not a word." It was the other head that spoke. "Match it with another and make of it a brace, I pray you."

She looked at the four eyes, at the two tongues flicking between scaly lips. Licked her own. "Um, sorry, guys. But . . . what?"

"Zounds!"—the first snake's head shook as it turned to stare at its twin—"but the language is much marred since the time of the bards, is't not?"

"Marry, 'tis," replied the other. "Yet if she would but speak on, we'll have the knack of it in a trice, I fancy."

The first turned back. "Aye, prithee, do, and let us hear of it."

"Um . . . M-M-Moonspill?" Elayne began.

His words came. *It is the amphisbaena. The teacher of languages. If you speak, they will listen and learn. But if you would learn from them, then let Amphis and Baena bring you the gift of tongues. They will learn yours too, which is their great desire.*

Elayne swallowed. "Um, OK?" she replied, nervous but intrigued.

One head dropped to the ground, while the first—she had no idea who was who—slid up Moonspill's leg and circled around her. The other followed . . . and she had to stop herself from screaming, because each snake opened its jaws and pressed its mouth to her ears, taking them all in—which was bad enough, until something flickered there.

"Eww!" she bleated, like one of the Chimera's heads. "Does the gift of tongues have to be so . . . literal? Can't they— O-oh!"

It was as if tuning forks had been struck, one high, one

low, instantly blending into one . . . which faded but did not vanish, providing a base for two more notes. While those still hung in the ear, more came. Single notes, sliding together, forming waves of sound that flowed through her ears, into her head, flooding her whole body.

Elayne's eyes snapped shut. She swayed. "Ugh" was the most complete sound she could make. The hum grew, as if a choir were doing the humming, in total harmony. There were no words. Yet it felt to her that it was *all* words. Every word, every *thing*, captured, held in sound.

It shifted. And then she was no longer *listening* to the waves, she *was* the waves, one part of the harmony. Words did come now, yet spoken by thousands of voices, hundreds of thousands, so many that words themselves were indistinguishable—and yet she heard every one. They weren't *in* languages. They were language itself.

It was overwhelming—and wonderful! She didn't think she'd ever been so . . . *in tune* with the world and everything in it. Even if that world was Goloth, and totally weird, this feeling was . . .

"Ohhh!"

She opened her eyes. She was on the ground, with no memory of how she got there. One of the heads hovered above her, yellow eyes fixed on hers. Moonspill stood, long neck bent down so he could look at her.

There were so many words in her head, in so many tongues, that Elayne found it hard to settle on any. Finally, she blurted, "That was amazing!"

One snake's head spoke. "Forsooth, 'twas a pleasure to bring, and to take, such delight."

The other head rose beside it, eyes gleaming as it spoke. "Awesome, huh?"

Elayne stared at him. It took a moment. "'Awesome'?"

"Totally!" he replied. "Language. It's, like"—if something without shoulders could shrug, it did then—"way cool."

She was stunned . . . and then outraged. She sat up. "I do *not* talk like that!"

"Do too!"

"Do not!"

"Nay, Baena, she doth not," interrupted the other snake—obviously Amphis. "Mayhap, for a time when she was in the grade of the six. Before Lederer's daughter spoke slander of her parentage and she left the Sisterhood."

Elayne's jaw dropped. Jayme Lederer *had* totally dissed her family in sixth grade. "You . . . you listened to my memories?"

"Uh-uh." Both heads shook; one spoke. "Only, like, when they relate to language. You talked like that because your friends did, and then you grew out of it and, you know, cleaned up your slang." The eyes narrowed in ecstasy. "Slang! Sweet!"

"Stop!" she yelped, putting her hands over her ears. "You guys are freaking me out!"

One head turned to the other. "Zounds! 'Tis a strange use of the word!"

"Whatever! She wants us outta here." The one nodded its head. "Got it. Gone. Catch you later, girlfriend!"

Amphis began to put his head in Baena's mouth. "Wait!" she said. "Can I speak to, uh, ordinary animals too?"

"Aye, you can—though, in sooth, most beasts are interested in little more than their desires. And their mouths are seldom shaped for conversation. But if you have something to offer, they may hear and respond. And now—away!" Folding into a hoop, they rolled off.

Another voice came. Or rather three—for three heads of the Chimera spoke as one. And Elayne discovered that now she could understand them all.

"Come, Moonspill."

"Do what must be done and let us be gone."

"There is danger here, so close to the works of man."

After all the beauty Elayne had just heard, the Chimera's voices hurt. Lion, goat, snake—not a choir that blended together well. Then another voice spoke—or, rather, sang. This one *was* beautiful—or would have been if she hadn't heard it first when it was about to eat her. "The Chimera is right, Moonspill," one of the manticores cried out, "for there is danger here. The Lion seeks prey, as ever."

Another noise—half cluck, half hiss—came from behind the raised wing. "Trrruth," whispered the cockatrice. "Let us drrrink and fl-fl-fly."

All the fabulous beasts started talking at once. Then, through the gap that separated the small valley from the larger one behind, came thousands of voices. All of the ordinary animals there began to call. Not speaking in words exactly, but each individual plea was clear. The cacophony hurt. Elayne put her hands over her ears.

*Your new skill comes at a price.* Moonspill's words sounded in her head; he didn't speak like the others. *You must learn not to listen to all, as you do not listen to all the voices in your world. It is a skill that comes with the gift, else Amphis and Baena would go mad.*

"Oh!" She forced herself inside—to *listen* inside her own head. All these voices reverberated there, and it was like . . . like pushing through a vast crowd of people who pushed back. Breathing deep, she managed to focus, narrowing down to words rather than the babel, then to words spoken by a few voices only . . . the fabulous beasts. The chorus from the valley became just that—a background clamor of desire and pain. It was there, but like the harmony track, not the main tune.

Moonspill moved to the small waterfall that surged out of a gap between two great stones. Since she'd been kind of preoccupied, Elayne hadn't really looked at the flow before, hadn't noticed that it was foaming . . . but not in that good way that rivers sometimes do. A yellow, brown-flecked froth floated here, clinging to the banks. Again she noticed the sulfurous, bad-egg stench in the air.

*Polluted?* she thought, rising to get a better look.

*Poisoned,* replied the unicorn.

*By what?*

*Man,* said Moonspill. *He has forges at the sources of these waters, to make the instruments he needs to pursue his lusts.*

Elayne thought back to the forest from the night before, its pool. *But there must be other rivers. Why don't all these creatures go to them?*

*Beasts, even fabulous ones, have their territories.* Moonspill was staring into the water. Now he dropped to his knees and laid his horn into the discolored foam.

A moan came—from the beasts who now pressed forward, echoing in thousands of voices from the valley below. Elayne had a flash of memory, of the museum, of a tapestry. . . . Had that been only yesterday? What was the word? She'd heard so many, in the tongues of so many beasts, it was hard to find the right one in her own. But then she got it. *Is this "the conning"?* she thought.

*Yes.* Moonspill plunged his horn deeper into the flood.

Foam crusted brown on his forehead . . . then vanished. From the point where the spiraling horn entered it, the froth began to lose its putrid, artificial colors, its metallic, chemical sheen. The water began to change from shades of brown to emeralds and blues. It spread, through the gap in the rocks, into the valley below.

*How far will it go?*

*Throughout the land,* replied Moonspill. *To the other streams that are the tributaries of this one, down to the ocean and the inland sea. For a brief time, all animals will drink of its purity— even man. Until he releases his foulness again.*

Forges, he'd said. Elayne thought they must be big if they were polluting water this badly. "Man" must have developed from the society Elayne had read about in her family book. *What are they like now?* she wondered. But Moonspill either didn't hear her question or ignored it. Lifting his horn, he stood, putting himself between her and the fabulous beasts, who now rushed forward, spitting and hissing at each other as they jostled for position on the pool's bank.

Elayne watched the mayhem. It wasn't just the different animals that competed, the multiple heads did too—with each other. The lion's head of the Chimera snapped at the goat, who bleated at the serpent. The twin-headed snake that had taught her the languages was trying to slither to different parts of the bank.

"Hither, varlet! I am the elder and, like, must totally lead."

"No way! We were, like, born e'en on the instant. Thou art not the boss of me!"

They seemed to have got a little confused! Then thirst overcame disagreements. Slithering between the two manticores, they settled, drank.

Moonspill led her to the gap between valleys, and they both looked down . . . on chaos! Animals struggled to drink, shoving and barging. Bison and bears stood four-footed in the water despite the strength of the current. Apes, deer, and wild dogs churned the earth banks to mud with foot, hoof, and paw. There were otters in midstream, dodging swallows that swooped and sipped and swooped again.

She looked behind at the fabulous creatures there—two cockatrices, two manticores, two Chimeras. "They are all in pairs," she said aloud.

*There are not many left. Man has seen to that. Each pair stays in its territory.*

"Don't you have a . . . a mate, Moonspill?"

*Yes.* The unicorn turned and looked her straight in the eye. *Her name is Heartsease. She lies in a cage in the city of man.*

Elayne was startled by that. But also by what she saw in

his eyes—a terrible yearning. It wasn't just for his mate—he yearned for something from her. For this . . . taming, she supposed. But she couldn't really believe she could help him.

She looked away from the eyes, up to his horn, still wet with the water from which it had removed all poison. It made her think of her father again, of the "poison" in his blood: leukemia. And she knew. There was yearning in her eyes too.

*Maybe* . . . , she thought, an idea beginning to form. An offer. But she only got that one word-thought out, before the world went mad.

## TEN

# HUNT

First there was silence, so sudden it terrified. One moment the animals were guzzling water, squawking, screeching, shoving each other aside. The next they all—and altogether—stopped. The only movement was the lifting of heads, every single one of them raised to listen. Just as Moonspill's was.

The silence was so total, Elayne couldn't break it with a question. But Moonspill answered anyway. *The Lion comes.*

"What—?" was all she managed before the screaming began. The two cockatrices shot up into the air, shrieking, and were gone in three flaps of their huge wings. The manticores cried out once in harmony, and loped through the trees. The amphisbaena rolled into a hoop and spun after them. The Chimeras, six heads snapping, sprang onto the cliff face and disappeared up it.

Then came a noise completely alien in a world recently filled with screech, snarl, and roar—one clear blast of a bugle.

101

It was followed by a howl, a terrible howl. Piercing, deep, unbelievably savage, it seemed to come from several throats, so loud it overrode all other screams.

"What the hell is that?" Elayne shouted, shivering.

*Cerberus.* Moonspill knelt, fast. *Mount.*

"But—"

*Now!* Elayne had just one leg half over and he was already moving, surging through packs, herds, flights of beasts, fleeing the way they'd come, back down the valley. Some creatures went up the gray slopes, scrambling to and over the peaks above. Elayne gripped Moonspill's mane even harder than before. She could tell he didn't have his usual attention on her.

His great flying strides had gobbled up distance; they were already close to the end of the valley, a cleft where two jagged spurs of rock almost touched. They had outdistanced most of the other fleeing creatures. Only some huge stags, which must have been drinking lower down, were ahead now. The first few of them reached the gap . . .

. . . and were bucking, twisting, screaming in high-pitched cries, trying to escape something that Elayne could not see. Moonspill tried to stop, but he'd been going so fast that his hooves just slid over the churned mud track, failing to get any grip. She screamed. They kept going, were nearly at the gap, about to slam into the terrified deer and whatever held them—

Rope nets! Elayne looked up, saw more looming there, gripped by . . . by gauntleted hands!

The gap was narrow, a few arms' stretches wide, the thrashing deer and poised nets right before them . . . then Moonspill got his balance and just took off, jumping almost straight up, hooves scrabbling for a hold on the steeply angled rock face.

"Help!" Elayne cried, sliding back, fingers entwined in mane, her legs dangling. Then, somehow, Moonspill got traction—two hooves! four!—and they were moving again up the impossible slope, her clinging so hard she thought she was going to pull out his mane by the roots.

Cresting it, they came onto a plateau, a wide, gently sloping bowl filled with grass that reached to her hips, high up though she was on Moonspill's back. Chest heaving, he took a step into the grassland— And a bugle brayed, a different one with a different tone. The call conjured flame—a torch flared to their right; another, almost immediately flaming on their left. Squinting against the glare, she saw that the torch was held above the grass by an arm. The rest of the body was hidden, the grass taller than any normal man. Then there were five torches, ten, twenty, more on each side, an arm span between each one.

Moonspill reared up, nearly dislodging her again. Then his front hooves landed, and he burst into a gallop. More torches lit up, like lightbulbs being switched on one after the other ahead of them. Hypnotic—if it hadn't been so terrifying! If that terrible howl hadn't come again from the pursuing pack.

The torch gauntlet ended with the grass. Immediately there were trees, a space between two oaks, like a gateway to another world. They passed through it into the forest, and bugles, several now, started to call again. Looking back, Elayne saw, from the trees on either side of the gap, figures charging onto the path. Figures on horseback.

103

"Men," she yelled.

*They pursue me.*

"But they won't catch you," she cried, exhilarated. She was still looking back, and Moonspill's great strides had left the horsemen way behind. "We're losing them."

That was when she noticed something running beside them. On either side of them. There, gone, there again. And then she saw what it was.

Beside them, a unicorn galloped with a girl on his back.

"Us! Reflections of us!" she shouted. For in every gap between two trees, on either side, there stood a tall mirror. She looked at herself flashing by. Watched as a unicorn's head turned, saw.

Immediately, Moonspill began to slow.

A great, triumphant cry came from behind them. That howl redoubled in ferocity. "What are you doing?" Elayne yelped.

The voice in her head was sluggish, like a wound-down film.

*Uni . . . corns. Tra-pped. By . . .*

He couldn't even finish the thought. She finished it for him. *Mirrors!* Hadn't the guide at the Cloisters said something about them? So much had happened to her, it was hard to pull out the memory, but . . . weren't mirrors the other way to tame a unicorn? To lull it with its own reflection?

She was suddenly breathless from more than the chase. *Is that it?* she thought. *Is he . . . tamed? Easy as that?*

The path had widened slightly, though mirrors still lined

the way. *Move left*, she thought, pulling that way with the mane. And he did, lurching left, the passing unicorns on that side growing larger. *Right*, she tried, pulling again, and he gradually moved back.

*Wow! He's obeying me!*

She couldn't believe it. For a moment, she was lost in the wonder of it, the power. . . . Until the trumpet came again, louder. She glanced back—the horsemen had gained on them. How was that possible? Still, there was an easy answer.

*Faster*, she commanded.

And nothing happened. *Faster*, she thought again, with a little jab of her heels.

Nothing! If anything, Moonspill slowed. The cries of triumph were getting closer.

And Elayne realized. *He's not tamed, he's . . . hypnotized. Like he's drugged.*

She was only disappointed for a second. Terror chased that away. Terror . . . and something else. No way was she going to see Moonspill captured. For him—but for her as well. She was terrified—but she had to do something.

Clinging with one hand, she grasped the neck of her sweater at the back. Tugging, she managed to pull it over her head, without letting go of the mane, then used her teeth on the wool to free her right arm. She switched her grip on the mane, freed the other arm with her teeth again. It helped that he was slowing down. Otherwise, she'd never have been able to inch up the neck just a little, just enough . . . to throw the sweater over his head. Most got rucked around his horn, but she'd kept hold of the material. Pulling it back, she threw again. This time the sleeves dropped down—and covered his eyes.

"Go," she shouted.

He went. Freed from his reflection, he went, all right—straight into a gallop.

She wasn't sure how she didn't fall off, how they didn't crash into things. Didn't think about it, just kept talking, as the howls and hoofbeats receded a little behind them, as her thighs cramped from squeezing his neck, as a hundred blinkered unicorns passed on either side. "Left a little! Gooood. Now, right. . . . Not that much! Back! Better. Ah! A log. Jump . . . now! Jeez! No, I'm OK. Yes! Good, go. . . ."

The path of mirrors went on, seemingly with no end. Then she noticed a fork, rapidly approaching, a path to the left blocked by a large mirror. Whoever set it obviously wanted their quarry to go straight on.

The quarry had different ideas. It was the decision of a moment. "Head down and . . . lefffft!"

Horn smashed into the mirror. Glass exploded, shards flying up all around them. A piece of frame spun and smacked her in the forehead. But then they were past, riding between trees down a different forest path, their reflections left behind.

Elayne slid back down the long white neck, every part of her aching from the strain. She just had strength to tuck part of the sweater into her kilt top. The cries behind sounded loudly for a moment, then faded rapidly, as Moonspill stretched, eating ground.

When she had her breath back—and that took a while—

she shouted, "We made it! Woo-hoo!" She was so buzzed—until she found herself almost flying over Moonspill's head, so suddenly did he halt.

*Chasm.*

They'd emerged onto open ground, which seemed to end in a straight line ahead of them. When they approached it, Elayne leaned forward . . . and felt dizzy. There was a fall of a hundred feet or more to rushing waters below. The land across was a fair distance away. "Go right," she ordered. "Come on."

Moonspill didn't move. *This rent in the earth goes on for a day either side. There is nowhere to cross that man does not own. Waterfalls. A river. Too wide, too cold to swim.*

"Well . . ." She looked to the left, to steeply rising land, crags. She could see the mountains. "So head up there."

*Too steep to climb. And even if I could . . . it is the realm of the griffin.*

Did she hear a touch of fear? She didn't have a clue what a griffin was. But if Moonspill was scared of it . . . She looked again at the chasm, reassessing. It didn't look that wide—for a unicorn. "Can't you jump it?"

*Alone, yes. With you, I fear not.*

Bugles sounded closer. The howling came again too, that terrible cry. What had he called it? Cerberus?

Moonspill turned. *Time to fight.*

"No!" Elayne had a flash of the tapestries again, the wounds, the spears, the brutal faces of the hunters. "I'll stay here. You go. Jump!"

*Leave you? I cannot.*

"You must. They're after you, not me. I'll be fine."

The drumming on the earth, that awful baying, grew. He dug at the turf before him with his hooves. *You are right. If I am free, we will meet again. We must meet again.*

"When? Where?"

There was a shadow of a thought. *At the rise of the full moon. Black Tusk rock. Can you find it again?*

She wasn't at all sure, but with the vibration of hooves getting closer, she yelled, "I will! Go!" She began to slide off.

*No. Stay.*

For one scary-happy moment, she thought he'd decided to risk it, to jump with her. But he didn't back up. Instead, he moved to a tree that was almost on the chasm's edge. *Climb.*

*Why?*

*Cerberus.*

On his word, that awful howl came again. It was all the impetus she needed. There was a branch just above her out-stretched arms. Rising to place her feet on his shoulders, she wobbled, steadied, jumped, clung, swung herself up.

He looked up at her. She saw something in his eyes, some-thing that floated between them in minds still linked. She knew what it was—a terrible longing. She knew it—because she felt it too.

*We will meet again,* Moonspill thought.

*I know,* she thought back.

Then something huge burst into the clearing.

Moonspill leapt to meet it, both beasts moving so fast that for a moment all was a blur. It was only when they crashed together, frozen in fight, that she saw . . .

A three-headed dog. It was entirely black and the size of a

small bull. Elayne screamed as two sets of jaws fastened in Moonspill's shoulder, one tipped back to let out that fearsome howl.

"Moonspill!" she cried.

He bent his head down, then threw it up, shooting onto his rear hooves, twisting his huge shoulders. The jaws released, the black beast hung in the air . . . and Moonspill swung his head sideways, smashing the side of his horn into the hound's flank, knocking it through the air. The monster sprawled, struggled to its feet, three heads shaking to clear them. Then six yellow eyes focused on the unicorn. Three mouths snarled.

But Moonspill had won enough time, and he'd fought far enough back from the chasm. He hurled himself at the edge. For a moment, he hung in space. He had no wings, didn't need them. Landing, he was in an instant gallop, making for the forest on the other side.

The three-headed hound ran to the edge as if it would follow . . . but pulled up short, snarling, barking, roaring its frustration over the gap.

Then one by one the heads quieted, lifted, sniffed. And, simultaneously, all three turned to look at Elayne.

## ELEVEN

# THE HUNTER

Three snarls came from three saliva-dripping mouths. Then the monster was running, leaping. . . .

Elayne's feet were dangling. She snatched them up so fast she nearly fell. One of the heads bit into wood, massive jaws crunching down. For one terrible moment, Elayne thought it was going to pull itself up! Then the tree's bark sheared off, and the dog dropped—but not before one of the other heads grabbed at the sleeves of Elayne's sweater, which dangled from her waist, jerking it free.

The animal landed on its feet, one head spitting splinters, the other two ripping her sweater to shreds in seconds. "Hey!" she yelled, and regretted it the moment the beast turned all three heads to her and crouched to leap again.

Bugles blared—and the clearing was suddenly filled with cursing men on rearing horses. Some of them charged at the chasm as if they would follow Moonspill, just now disappearing into the trees. Their mounts were big—but not that big. The hunters who realized jerked on their reins in time. Two didn't, and they were thrown to the ground with their horses' sudden halting.

While a dozen men screamed at the space where the unicorn had just been, shaking huge spears, waving bows, Elayne sat, knees pulled up, not moving. *Maybe they won't notice me,* she thought. *If I keep really still, they might ride off, and then I could—*

Three jaws flew toward her. Elayne screamed.

"Maiden!" a man shouted, as the hound missed the branch, fell again. For a moment, even the dog was still, staring up. Then three men ran forward with long poles that had nooses on their ends, slipped these over Cerberus's heads, drew them tight. The beast thrashed about, trying to shake off the snare. Gradually, it slowed until the men were able to lower the animal, each of its heads panting, to the ground. Three thick leather muzzles were put on, chains slipped through collars. Only then were the nooses removed. The monster leapt up immediately, straining to the length of the chains, glaring at her.

Several men were making an odd gesture: joining the tips of their forefingers and thumbs in a kind of pear shape and shoving it toward her. This went on for a while, until finally one whispered, "She rode him."

"Aye," said a second. "'Twas a wonder to behold."

"Look at her dress. It is most strange," said another.

111

"Yet comely."

"Aye. As is she."

They studied her, she studied them. As for "most strange" clothes, they should talk! The hunters wore quilted . . . *doublets,* she seemed to remember they were called. Thick wool leggings, riding boots. Each man had a wide-brimmed hat and a black cape, lined in white fur. When one man turned to gesture, the cape swirled, and she saw a figure picked out upon it in gold thread—a lion, in midleap. Their clothes went with their old-fashioned English. These men didn't seem especially friendly, yet after what she'd seen at the conning, there was something weirdly comforting in people.

The gray-bearded man who'd first spoken dismounted. Throwing his reins to another, he came to stand beneath the tree. He beckoned, then called. "Descend!"

"I'm good here, thanks," Elayne replied, drawing her legs up tighter.

"I tell you to descend, maid, and at once," he shouted back, "or we will bring you down."

They had called off the monster dog. And she supposed she'd have to come down sometime. But his tone pissed her off. "You could try 'please,'" she said.

The man let out a roar, and signaled to the three men who still held the noose-poles that had snagged Cerberus. "Fetch her down!" the graybeard commanded. The three men spread out, nooses raised.

Then someone else spoke. The new voice was younger, low, clear. "Leave her be."

Into the circle of men strode another—and then everyone was kneeling. He didn't look up; Elayne could see only the top of his hatless head, his long fair hair. "Sire," the gray-bearded guy hissed, "she rode upon a unicorn. *The* unicorn!"

"I saw the wonder," came the soft reply. "And where is the unicorn now?"

"Gone, sire." The older man gestured across the chasm.

"Ah! Now that is a pity." The disappointment in his voice was restrained, but clear. Then his tone changed. The soft voice had a bit more steel in it. "But then, huntsman, why do you all appear so afraid of this girl?"

The man looked down. "Sire, I—"

"Let be." The tone was enough to command silence. Then the man turned, came to stand beneath the branch, and, for the first time, looked up.

He was young, the youngest there, late teens, maybe early twenties. Clean-shaven, with hair that dropped, thick and blond, to his shoulders. His face was all sharp levels and planes, with deep-set eyes whose color was hard to tell from her perch but were on the bright side. The kind of high cheekbones you could rest a teacup on, a jawline to match. Elayne thought his lips were a tad thin . . . but they were better when he smiled. Which he did now.

"Would my lady do me the honor of descending?" he asked, reaching up with both arms.

She was quite high up. She'd climbed there from a unicorn's back. But he must have been tall because his arms weren't too far below. *And he did ask nicely,* she thought. So she swung her leg over the branch. "Here I come," she said, and dropped.

He bent a little to catch her. But he was strong and lowered her slowly. *Steel*, Elayne thought, as their faces drew level. His eyes were the palest of blues, with little swirls within them. She had time to study them because he held her aloft, studying hers. Then he spoke, in a whisper meant only for her. "Are you yet a maiden?"

"What?" Elayne felt herself blush, then remembered that she tended to blush blotchily. *Not attractive. Not that I am trying to be attractive* . . .

The thought made her blush blotchily again. She had a feeling that he could have held her up there for a while, so she wriggled, and he lowered her to the ground. His eyes still delved, the question hanging there, and for a moment she thought she'd have to answer . . . until more horses came cantering around the bend. The king—he'd been addressed as "sire," so Elayne supposed that was what he was—had not let go of her hands. Now he spoke so all could hear. "You can bear witness, lady, why I, who should have greeted you first, came last." He gestured to a new arrival who held the reins of a huge, white, riderless stallion. "My mount threw a shoe in the last stages of the chase. A farrier's carelessness with nails. Which shall be punished. Eh?" He said this while glancing at the bearded man who'd first threatened her. He nodded, and Elayne shivered.

The king turned back to her. "You are chilled," he said, the steel gone from his voice. "Here!" He flicked a clasp at his neck and swirled his thick cloak around her, engulfing her, her face buried in some rich, sweet-scented fur. He adjusted it, smoothing down the fur near the neck, before stepping back. "I am Leo, of the House of the Lion. Hunter of Beasts, Slayer of Enemies, King-Elect of Goloth," he said, executing a perfect bow, arm spread wide, bending from the waist. "May I have the pleasure of knowing my lady's name?"

"My name?" It took her a moment to remember it, after all his titles, all this formality. She was rather startled to find herself dropping into a kind of curtsy and speaking formally too. "Alice-Elayne."

Several men cried out—and every man there now made that weird gesture: tips of their forefingers joined to their thumbs, thrust toward her. Every man but one—Leo just stared, his face drained of color, his breath coming quicker, puffs materializing in the cool air. His voice was low and hard. "Do you mock me?"

"What?" she managed. "No . . ."

He took a moment, his voice a little softer when it came. "The letters A and E conjoined are forbidden in a name."

"I . . . I . . . didn't know. But . . . why?"

He raised his hand. The muttering, which had grown as she babbled, stopped, as did she. He smiled again—though this smile never reached his eyes. "You are not of our land, that is certain. Thus you cannot know the harm. Enough!" he said, glancing sharply around, silencing another murmur. "Fetch me here a mount for the maid," he said, turning away.

"Um, you see, I don't . . . can't really . . . er, ride?"

She was totally ignored. Leo went over to his men. "And so, Lucien," he said, "tell me now of the hunt. How was it that you failed?"

"The mirrors held him, sire," the man complained. Then he glanced toward Elayne, his lowered voice still traveling. "But when a devil rides the beast—"

A hand silenced him. Leo looked across the chasm for a long moment, sighed, spoke again. "Fortune is a fickle mistress and departed the moment she arrived. And yet"—he turned, looked back at Elayne—"perhaps another opportunity will arise." He tried to smile, though she could see he was hiding some serious disappointment. "Now, to our camp, to feast and then to an early sleep. For we must be up with the dawn if we are to reach the mountains by nightfall."

A groom rode a horse forward, reined in beside her. "You see, I . . . I can't . . . ," she protested again, backing away.

"Cannot? You who rode a unicorn?" Leo stared at her for a moment. Then he nodded at the groom—who reached down, picked her up as if she were a piece of paper, and lifted her onto the horse in front of him. She swayed, grabbed mane, steadied. Then looked, as everyone there did, at Leo.

A fresh horse had been brought for him. He vaulted into the saddle and spurred his mount straight into a fast canter.

The groom kicked. Closing her eyes, Elayne grabbed the leather in front of her, swaying, clinging on desperately despite the man behind her.

The horse was not Moonspill.

Elayne kept her eyes shut tight. But when the horse didn't go into an immediate bucking frenzy, and she realized that the

116

guy behind her, even if he was leaning way away so as not to touch her, was not going to let her fall, she allowed her fingers to unclench a little. She felt sick to her stomach, focused on the mane till the spasms passed.

If one thing was clear it was that she was a prisoner. So should she be trying to escape? Hop off the galloping horse, hightail it for the hills . . . Elayne shuddered. Leaving aside expert hunters chasing her, she'd seen what stalked those hills. She'd be dinner before breakfast.

*And speaking of food,* she thought, *I am starving!* Leo had mentioned something about a camp and a feast. She'd always found it hard to think on an empty stomach. Escape would have to wait till it was full.

The trees gave way to an open plain, the land rising, so the horses slowed as they labored up. They were climbing toward the mountains she'd glimpsed before, but nothing else looked familiar. How far had they traveled? Which way was the black rock, the tree that was some sort of door to her world? Moon- spill said he'd meet her there, the night of the full moon. But when was that? She'd seen the moon the night before. Half a pizza. So the full moon was probably nine or ten days off.

Closing her eyes, she thought *Moonspill!* hard, and waited. Nothing came back. She wondered if there was some sort of range to the telepathy thing.

Nine, ten days? Before she had even a chance of getting back to her dad? Anything could happen to him in ten days in the hospital! And anything could happen to her. . . .

She bit her lip—and drew blood, because the horse bounced her over some rocky ground. Then they crested a hill—and there below, in a valley beside a stream, was an encampment, shaped in concentric circles, smaller tents on the outside, bigger ones toward the middle. At the center of all the circles was a pavilion, a huge tent with pennants fluttering from its poles. One of them, caught by a gust, spread. A lion leapt.

They had to stop, pull over . . . because coming straight up the faint track that led from the camp was a wagon. It was small, had only two horses pulling it. The driver sat holding reins and a whip. The box of the wagon was made of lattice-work, strands of thin wood woven together, so tight Elayne couldn't see in. But she had the strangest feeling that someone was looking out. At her.

It passed quite close by her. And when it did, she got the strangest scent. . . . *That's . . . chocolate!* she thought, her hunger redoubling in an instant.

The carriage passed. They rode down. The other hunters slowed, spread out. Everywhere men stopped their tasks to stare, many making that strange gesture at her. It reminded Elayne of old movies, with people crossing themselves when they saw something evil. *That's it,* she realized. *"Witch . . . avaunt!"* How lovely!

Or maybe they weren't used to women. She couldn't see any.

Everyone was dismounting on a patch of open ground before the big tent. Grooms scurried out to take the horses. Her guy reined in.

"Maid?"

Elayne turned. Leo was there, both arms raised. "May I?"

he said, but didn't wait for permission to reach and pluck her from the saddle. He lowered her but did not release his grip, his voice coming low. "Tell me, maid," he whispered, "are you the prophesied one?"

"No! I mean . . . I don't know what you mean. . . ."

Their eyes were locked, and his pupils grew large, as if needing more light to study her by. His whisper, when it came again, was excited.

"I think you are. For you rode him, he whom I most fear. You rode him, he whom I most desire." His voice dropped even lower. "Will you bring him to me, Alice-Elayne?"

"I—"

"My lord?"

A man's call saved her from babbling her confusion. Leo stared at Elayne a moment longer before letting her go and turning to the older man walking toward them. He came close, his voice low, for the king-elect alone. "A maid, sire? It is taboo in a hunting camp. The Gods frown upon it."

"That may be true, High Steward. Yet how could I not bring what the Gods themselves delivered to me—upon a unicorn's back?"

The older man gasped, stepped back, hands beginning to shape the now-familiar gesture. "All the more reason to send her back to the city, sire. Let us call the carriage back. The hunt is no place for . . ."

He stopped, obviously unable to figure out what to call her. Leo looked down, smiled. "Nay, I shall keep her close. For now." He went on briskly. "Find her quarters. Set guards around it." He looked Elayne up and down. "By the griffin's claw, but she is strangely dressed. Find her clothes more suited to the night."

The other man sighed, bowed. "Sire."

Leo turned back to Elayne. "Follow this man. He will see you well cared for."

The man in question looked like he'd rather care for a rattlesnake. "But—" she began.

"You will see me soon enough. At the revels." He began to walk away.

"Hey," she called. "Your cloak!"

He swiveled. "Yours, maid," he said with a half bow. Then, ducking under a flap of the main pavilion, he was gone.

"Come," ordered the high steward.

"Hmm? Oh. All right." Pulling the thick fur tighter around her, she went in the direction his arm pointed. He and two guards followed from several feet away, the older man calling out when he needed her to change direction. When they came to a largish tent, he gestured her inside.

There were two oil lamps burning, casting rings of light. By their flicker, she saw the end of a wagon, its back boards down. Its contents were weird. There were some drums, what looked like flutes, and several stringed instruments like guitars but smaller. There was also an upright, rectangular frame with the words "Tavern of the Boar" painted on it. Dangling from that was a puppet, a marionette.

"What is this . . . ," Elayne began.

But the steward had been rooting in a chest on the floor and straightened now . . . clutching a dress. He threw it to her. "Here. For the revels." Without another word, he went to the entrance, talked quietly to the guard outside. The guard nodded. The tent flap dropped.

She was alone, in a tent, looking at a tent of a dress! Holding it up, she could tell she'd be swimming in it. Plus, it was brown, bulky, and . . . eww! smelled musty. "Not the gown *I'd* choose for my first 'revels' . . . whatever they are. And why have they got dresses anyway?" She was muttering aloud, to break the silence. "When women are so obviously *not* welcome." She considered various possibilities and, with a shudder, decided she'd rather not know.

Taking off the cloak, she laid it on the wagon's tailboard, then her white school blouse, followed by the kilt. She was in underwear and tights.

Sighing, she was just pulling the shapeless sack over her head when she heard a scraping sound. She looked around. Rats? Several hung out in her back alley and she had always hated them. Unhooking one of the lamps she stepped nervously forward, the circle of flickering light moving over the tent walls. She didn't spot any whiskers.

And then she saw them, sliding under the canvas. Fingers.

"Help!" she squeaked, the word sticking in her throat. She was just about to give a full-blooded yell, when a head followed the hands. The head had hair. Long red hair. Then, with a grunt, a body slid into the tent.

And a girl sat up.

## TWELVE

# PLAYER

Elayne ducked behind the wagon—but she didn't yell for help. *Who would I call?* she wondered. *The thug outside?* Besides, this was intriguing. She'd been given the impression she was the only girl in the camp—and that her presence was an outrage.

The intruder was leaning over, brushing dirt from her dress—which, Elayne noted, wasn't a shapeless brown sack but a full-skirted emerald-green gown. There was a flash of white petticoat as the girl lifted and brushed, rubbing at a particularly bad spot. She began muttering—and Elayne was surprised to realize two things: They weren't in any language she'd ever heard before. And she could understand them all.

"By the horn," the girl muttered, "Frederick will kill me for this." Throwing the skirt down in disgust, she straightened, sighed.

She reached for the second lamp—and when her face was

lit, Elayne was shocked. She had almond-shaped eyes, a delicate mouth, a "petite" nose. But these nice features were totally caked in makeup. Her eyebrows, which were bushy anyway, had been doubled with paint. Heavy shadows emphasized the hollows of her eyes, gold brought out the lids, her lashes were gloppy with mascara. Her lips were a startling shade of crimson. Powder had been put on with a spray gun.

Getting the lamp unhooked, the visitor turned away.

Elayne wondered whether she should speak. But if the girl was anything like her, she'd jump, shriek, and bring the guard rushing in—which, judging by her entrance, would be the last thing she'd want. Elayne had no loyalty to anyone in this world, aside maybe from Moonspill. But she didn't want to rat this girl out.

The intruder moved to the other side of the wagon. Elayne leaned around. There were barrels tied there, and the girl undid the big leather strap on one, lifted the lid, and began to remove cloths and scarves. Then she thrust her arm all the way in, straining to reach. She froze, smiled, then pulled something out.

She knelt on the floor, the lamp beside her. In its light, she unfolded a cloth wrap, untied its strings, and laughed. Elayne sucked in a breath. For there, on the cloth, were three of the biggest pearls she had ever seen.

"Are those real?" she whispered.

The girl did pretty well, considering. The vertical takeoff, from squat to standing, was impressive. As was the strangled "Gnarmpf," which was all that escaped her lips. What was not so good was the glitter that appeared in her right hand. "Who speaks there?" she hissed, in English, not the language she'd mumbled before. She waved the dagger before her, then jerked it toward Elayne, who stepped out, arms raised.

"Just me," she answered. The girl leapt back. "Sorry to startle you."

The knife lowered slowly, the jaw fast. "By the horn . . . ," she breathed, staring Elayne up and down. "How are you . . . ? Who are you . . . ? Where did you . . . ?"

Elayne was sick of being the one who got asked all the questions. "Those pearls are pretty. May I take a look?"

The girl bent immediately, scooping the pearls up and folding them away in their wrap. "You did not see them."

"But I did."

"If someone asks you . . ." She hesitated. "It would not be well for me if they were found."

"So you are stealing them?"

"No, not stealing." A slight smile came, her first. "Redistributing. From those who need them less to those who need them more."

"You?"

"Us." She nodded around at the tent, its contents.

"Who is 'us'?"

"The players."

"Players?" Elayne had studied Shakespeare. "You mean, like, actors?"

She frowned. "I do not know that word. We play for the Lion tonight, on the eve of the great hunt. We were going to perform a comedy, hence this dress." She gestured down. "But there has been a change, and that is the reason I have to . . . move the pearls from this barrel, for we will now need what it contains."

"A change?"

"The king-elect has called for the epic of the first slaying." She cleared her throat. "When Lustrous Lion first did roar / Upon our gentle, fated shore . . ." She was beginning to, well, *act*, her voice lowering. Suddenly she stopped, her eyes widening. "What are these . . . ," she said, in a normal voice, ". . . these garments?"

She was referring to Elayne's discarded clothes. "Oh, that's just my uniform."

"Uniforms are worn only by soldiers."

The girl had picked up the kilt, held it to her waist. Since they were about the same height, it reached to just above her knee. "But this must be an undergarment."

"No, no."

"Then beneath must be covered?"

"Sure. I wear tights." Elayne lifted the dress to her knee. "See."

"Ti-ights?" The girl bent, studied. "But the material? How it glistens!" She reached out a hand. "Of what is it made?"

Elayne dropped the skirt. "Uh, nylon. You know."

"I do not." She whistled. "All I know is that it is marvelous fair. But you cannot wear something as short as this. Even with ti-ights! It is forbidden. Forbidden!" Suddenly she was waving the skirt like a flag. "Why do we speak of this? When I know not who you are. A spy perhaps? No wenches are allowed in a hunting camp."

"Hey! Who're you calling a wench? And what about—Hey!"

The girl had stepped close, fast, leading with the knife. "Speak swiftly! Where have you come from?"

*Oh man, where to begin?* "Um . . . um . . . um . . . somewhere else."

"Glana?"

"No, I—"

"Even in that land, such things"—she waved the skirt—"would not be allowed." She stepped in again. "What is your name?"

She'd gotten uncomfortably close. Her voice was harsh now too, and deeper. She was taller, broader; a little older. Way more intimidating. "Alice-Elayne," she blurted.

Elayne didn't know why she said her full name again. But it had the same effect as before. "What?" It was as if they had been fighting and Elayne had punched her. The girl sagged.

"I really go by Elayne," she said, stepping forward, holding out her hand. "And you are?"

The girl made that strange finger gesture. "Your name is also forbidden."

"So I was told. But why?"

"The prophecy. All know of it."

"I don't. . . . Tell me."

She seemed afraid now. She recited, but not like before. This wasn't "acting." This was truth, and it came on a whisper:

> *Through weaver's art it is proclaimed*
> *A maid shall come, unknown to man,*

*With letters A and E she's named,*
*The one who'll end the tyrant's span.*
*A unicorn by the maid beguiled*
*Full tamèd now, he will obey*
*The one, who's neither dame nor child,*
*And with his horn the Lion slay.*

Elayne's head whirled. This "prophecy" had to be based on the tapestry! The one that her ancestor had woven to leave the people of Goloth some hope. The scene that had gotten him killed!

Then she saw it. *My God! He said he meant it as a metaphor. But they have taken it literally. They think a maid will come and tame a unicorn who will then slay the king. And—duh!—who just rode in on a unicorn's back, shouting out her name?*

"Oh hell," Elayne muttered. The girl had the same look of both hope and fear that Elayne had seen on Leo. So many questions were fizzing around in the panic of her brain. "This tapestry? Have you seen it?"

The girl's eyes shot wide. "No one has. No one knows if it still exists. Legend says that after the first weavers hung it, it stayed upon the castle gates for a day and then was gone. Whither, no one knows."

"Weavers." Elayne echoed the word.

But it was taken as a question. "It is the name for rebels," the girl replied. "They have, in times past, risen up against the tyrant—but he has always brutally crushed them." She lowered her quiet voice to a whisper, leaned in. "But the last Leo fell to a weaver's knife. And there is talk on the streets of danger to this new one, the dead king's son, who must yet be crowned."

There was a glow in her eyes that made Elayne ask, "Are you a weaver?"

The eyes instantly hooded over. The girl leaned back. "Nay, nay," she said. "I am a mere player." Then she looked around as if checking for listeners before she asked, softly again, "Are you the one, AE? Are you the maid foretold?"

"Nay, nay. No way," Elayne said, panic bubbling up. Now she'd heard the prophecy, she wanted nothing to do with it. Taming unicorns? Killing kings? All she wanted to do was go home—to New York City, where it was safe. To her dad.

Outside, voices were drawing near. Elayne swallowed, breathed deep. The girl's stare, almost hungry, was beginning to freak her out. "They must be coming for me," she said. "You better go."

"Yes. I have what I came for." She shook the pouch, then tucked it away within her dress. She went quickly to the area of tent she'd raised, bent, stuck her fingers under the canvas. Then she paused, looked back. "Yet I leave with something else also. Something far more precious perhaps."

"What's that?"

She smiled. "Hope."

She pushed her legs through as men's voices came again from the opposite side. It was Elayne's jailers, talking . . . while this person who was slipping away was, well . . . at least, she was a girl. "Wait!" Elayne hissed, trying to keep her there with one question among so many. "If no, uh, wenches are allowed in a hunting camp, why are you here?"

Only her head and shoulders were still inside the tent. She paused, smiled. "A story easily told," she said, and, reaching up, she pulled the hair from her head.

It took a moment, perhaps because of the makeup. The hair beneath the wig was almost as long, falling in fair curls. She had been an attractive redhead—but he was better as a boy. "Oh," Elayne said, which was all she ever managed to say to good-looking boys, really.

"My name is Marc," he said. "And we will meet again."

Then he was gone, just as the high steward called, "Are you clothed and ready, lady?"

"Give me a minute." She pulled the chain from around her neck. The dress had cleavage, even if she didn't have much, and she didn't think a piece of unicorn horn in plain sight would help her cause. There was a large hem on the dress, though, and she found a gap in the thread, ripping it just enough to insert the horn and shove it way down. Then, throwing the cloak over her shoulders, she turned to face the entrance. "Ready," she called, then added to herself, ". . . as I'll ever be."

# THIRTEEN

# REVELS

The table looked like a battlefield. Bones of victims were heaped along it in pools of congealing fat. The men of Goloth wanted meat, meat, and more meat, and various beasts were carried in, winged, furred, horned, split and stuffed, elegantly mounted on platters, to be torn apart with daggers and hands.

Elayne was no vegetarian—but she almost became one. Still, she was starving, and there *was* bread, so she managed to select some of the better-done hunks of what *could* have been beef but tasted gamier—bison?—and cram them into a roll. This amused those around her, once the wine they'd been drinking made them braver. She'd been met at first with a staring, hostile silence.

Leo had put a stop to that. He'd descended from the table to greet her, bowed, and led her to what was obviously the place of honor beside him. This, and buckets full of wine, did the trick. They went from fear to leer and then ignored her completely.

She was happy about that. Her only plan was to try to figure out what was going on, and ignored, she was free to eavesdrop. Most of the conversation seemed to be about hunting spears or the best way to break a wild stallion, but there were snippets of news—that their quarry had been sighted by scouts. *Was that Moonspill?* Then, that three weavers had been hanged. She presumed they meant the rebels Marc had talked about rather than simple workers. But she wanted the conversation to turn back to unicorns—and was annoyed when it didn't. Wasn't she the dreaded AE? She was tempted to get out her piece of horn and jab Leo with it. That would get their attention!

She took another swig of wine, made a face. Her dad's was much better than this sour stuff. But she didn't have much choice. There were no sodas in sight, not even water, and the food was salty as well as gamy.

Starved of any useful information, she tried to focus less on what they said than how they said it. She was certain now that it wasn't the snake's "gift of tongues" that made her understand. They *were* speaking English, though in a formal, old-fashioned kind of way. If the tapestries had been made in the 1490s, the English hunter, Adam, would have crossed into Goloth speaking Ye Olde English. If he made everyone learn it, since he was the new Big Cheese—which is what her family book had said—she supposed it could have evolved into this. Their clothes seemed vaguely medieval. And this dinner.

Development must have been slower here. Plus, no Renaissance. No Industrial Revolution.

*I know,* she thought. *I'll write a paper on it for Ms. Melcher.* She took another sip and giggled. "The Evolution of Language and Costume in the Land of the Fabulous Beast"!

She looked at Leo. He'd left her to go talk with men farther down the long table. She saw him in profile, his long fair hair held back with a silver clasp. He was wearing a velvet coat-gown of deep purple, a simple but thick gold chain around his neck. She had to admit it, he cleaned up nice, was definitely the best-looking guy there.

She raised her cup again . . . then froze, slammed it down, pushed it away. Starting to find kings in Goloth attractive told her that she'd had more than enough wine!

Her chin sank onto her chest—and she jerked it up. *Pee-yew!* Perhaps that was why Leo was keeping away. The smells her dress was giving off were rude! The tent was roasting, between the braziers that dotted the place, the steaming platters of meat, the crowd of men in thick wool and fur. She'd had no chance to do anything with her hair, a thick black tangle at the best of times. But she didn't want to comb it with her bison-greased fingers. Napkins obviously hadn't been invented yet.

She was just wiping her hands on her skirt under the table when Leo moved back beside her, put down his cup, and nodded. A man at the entrance must have been watching him because immediately he raised a drum and struck it three times with a stick. The hubbub subsided.

"My lords and hunters . . . and lady," Leo said, tipping his head toward Elayne. "Tonight is a joyous feast, and a sacred one. Tomorrow we shall put all pleasures aside and prepare for a holy act. We hunt one of the mightiest of beasts, second only to the unicorn in the danger of its trapping." He glanced slightly at her before raising his voice to shout. "Tomorrow we hunt the griffin!"

Elayne shivered. What had Moonspill said about the griffin? Nothing—except even he didn't want to venture near one. And if he didn't . . .

A roar came from the company, though. Goblets were raised and smashed down, wine spilled. Leo continued, "Now, it is our custom to amuse ourselves with revels on the eve of the hunt, some rude comedy to pass the tedious hour between feast and sleep." His voice went softer, more intense. "But tonight I have chosen something else. For there is a force abroad in the land, some power"—did he glance at her again?—"and the sacrifices made on this hunt and those to be made at the Games that will see me crowned should not now be marred with easy laughter."

Elayne was lost—but the men around understood, suddenly serious, showing it in their nodding, their whispered "Ayes." "And so I have called for an older work from the players, one rarely seen. One to remind us of the sacred duty we embark upon with the dawn. For was this land not once a terror to all mankind, lived in the shadow of the beasts? And did not the first Leo bring the light?" He looked around the room, nodded, went on softly, "So let us hear his tale."

He sat. Servants extinguished many of the torches that hung in metal baskets attached to the tent poles. Light dimmed, men's voices diminished to coughs, then whispers, finally to a silence that lasted long enough to get uncomfortable . . . and then the play began.

It was quite good—a bit like Shakespeare in the Park, Elayne thought. There was music—drums, flutes, some guitar-like thing—and some dancing, mainly when the actors performed animals, which they did a lot. Leo had said it was an old story, and Elayne realized quite quickly that it was probably one of the oldest in Goloth: the tale of Adam's arrival—the first Leo, or "the Hunter" as he was simply called here—and his slaying of the manticore who had terrified the Golothians. It was quite different from the version she'd read in her family book and that Moonspill had told her. No mention here of the weaver. He'd been . . . *What did they call it?* she wondered. *Edited out?* And "the Hunter" had come, not from Europe, but from "'cross mountains/distant lands/blah-dee-blah." There was no mention either of any tapestry doorway.

The unicorn did make a brief appearance—her friend Marc, in an elaborate metal mask, performing the movements rather well, she thought—but the narrator, an old bearded actor with a deep, bell-like voice, merely introduced him as something to be seen later, a "next week's episode" kind of thing, which brought out some nervous laughs and more glances her way. It all concluded with the first Leo's triumph, the grateful citizens offering him the crown, which the actor modestly refused then reluctantly took. It was showbiz politics, she thought. She'd seen stuff like it before. Almost anytime she switched on the TV news.

The play ended with a clash of cymbals and three strikes on the drum. The tent flap settled slowly behind the players.

There was a long silence.

Followed by noise. Lots of it—the beating of goblets upon the table, the roar of men acclaiming what they'd seen. Elayne clapped—which amused people as much as her sandwich making had. Some of them mockingly began to imitate her.

Despite the acclaim, the actors didn't come back for a curtain call. The flaps opened enough to admit just one—the bearded player, hat in hand, shy smile on his face. He came forward, as Leo descended from the high table.

"Well, Frederick." Leo frowned. "Straying from the tradition, hmm?"

The player was almost lying down, he was bowing so low. "The youth of the company, majesty," he groveled. "Demanding the new, as is ever their way."

Leo frowned. "With that weaver Marc demanding more than most, hey?"

*Weaver?* Elayne leaned forward.

"Not a w-w-weaver," the man stuttered. "Just a boy . . ." The player swallowed. "We hope our play did not . . . uh-hum . . . did not displease, lord?"

Silence returned to the tent. All watched the frowning Leo, who turned and slowly looked around the tent, as if taking in every face, before he spoke. "I know that there are those among my subjects—around this tent, mayhap—who grumble that the monarch cannot change. Who think that the new reign will continue only in old ways, that the young

Lion will be no different from the old." The soft tone hardened. "Know this: I am not my father. I honor him as I honor the traditions of our land that have made us strong, safe from the beasts within our boundaries, feared by our enemies beyond them." He lifted a hand. "But let those who claim that Leo the Sixteenth will look only back and not forward witness how he embraces the new. How he rewards it."

He beckoned. Three servants came forward. Each held, on outstretched palms, a thick gold bar that overlapped the flesh. The player raised his own hands . . . and the king-elect placed one bar in them. And another, to a murmuring from the tables. Took a moment—then placed a third, to a huge shout from the onlookers.

The player had sunk to the ground—with gold, with gratitude. Leo bent to help him rise and, because of the angle, Elayne could see their two faces close together. See the tiniest of winks that Leo gave. See the player's slight smile.

It was a setup! The whole thing.

The player bowed his way out. There was a yell of joy through the tent flaps before they fell. Leo returned to his seat, lifted his wine goblet, and roared, "To the hunt!"

"Hunter! Hunter! Hunter!" came the chant.

Then everyone started talking and slurping again—except for Elayne. She'd definitely had enough.

"What troubles you, maid?"

Leo's handsome face was all concern, his voice soft and low. Everyone else was engaged in their own conversations. She definitely had his attention now. But what could she say of her "troubles"? Where would she start?

She didn't . . . so he did. "My lords here—all my people—are simple. They choose to believe you come from a distant land. From over the mountains perhaps, though no man can climb them. From across the ocean perhaps, the land of Glana—for their people are dark-haired like you—and our bitterest foes."

"But didn't your ancestor . . . come from a distant land? Wasn't that what they just said in the play?" She was trying to act innocent. It didn't work.

A glow came into his eyes. "Nay, lady," he said, "you know where he came from. The same place as you. And by the same method, I'd wager."

Elayne took a gulp of breath. "Wha—" was all she managed.

He leaned even closer. "Come, maid. Just as the name *Leo* descends from father to son, so the first Leo's story is passed on from one to the other. Where he came from. How he came. Through what . . . woven doorway."

*A story passed on like all those Alice-Elaynes,* she thought.

He continued. "I'd always believed it to be just that—a story . . . until the moment I saw a maiden on a unicorn's back! So tell me, *Alice-Elayne*"—his voice dropped to a whisper, her name hissed—"are you my salvation or my doom?"

"Uh, neither, I hope!" She prevented his interruption, rushing on. "I came through, yes—"

"From the Nether Lands?"

"Yes. Well, close enough . . . But I don't know *how* I did . . ." She swallowed. "Look. I fell, I was attacked by a manticore, then rescued by a unicorn, who galloped away. . . ."

She realized she was letting her wine-wrapped tongue gallop away with her. "I just want to get the hell out of here, really," she finished lamely.

He studied her for a long moment. "'Rescued by a unicorn,'" he repeated. "Why?"

"I . . . I have no idea. I—"

"Yet you know of the prophecy?"

His eyes bored into her. She almost started babbling again, then pulled herself up. *Careful*, she thought. Took a breath. "Prophecy? What prophecy?"

He stared a moment longer before he spoke. "That a maid will tame a unicorn . . . who will then kill the king."

Her recovery continued. "Oh! Is that why everyone is afraid of me?"

He studied her a moment, then glanced around the tent. "Yes. My nobles have much to lose if the king should fall and the weavers triumph." He turned back to her. "Yet *I* am not afraid."

"No?"

"No. The prophecy was first made five hundred years ago, and my ancestors have always faced it boldly. If the legend tells that a tamed unicorn will slay the tyrant king . . . well, then . . . the new king must slay a unicorn before all his people to prove his worth and take the crown." He nodded. "I have one in my dungeons now. . . ."

Elayne held her breath. What had Moonspill said, just before the hunt began, and she'd asked about his mate? *Her name is Heartsease. She lies in a cage in the city of man.*

Leo continued. "She is a fine enough beast, if old."

*Aha! She!*

"I will kill her if I must." He smiled. "Though I do not desire it. There is not as much glory in the killing of a female. And my realm is restive." He looked above her, his eyes unfocused for a moment. There was sadness in them, in his voice. "My father was not . . . the gentlest of rulers. Nor of men."

Suddenly he looked so young. Looked his age, which was only about five years older than her. He had just lost his dad, "gentle" or not. It was something she knew a little about. She almost reached out to pat his hand.

He swallowed, turning his gaze back to her. "I have vowed to be different—once I have proved my right to rule." He smiled again. "Perhaps you can help me to be . . . different."

Behind the king, she saw the high steward hovering. He was obviously not keen to interrupt such a private conversation. But he looked as if he was about to. She gazed up at Leo. "What do you want with me?" she asked softly.

"Nay! What do *you* want, Alice-Elayne? Wasn't it to . . . 'get the hell out of here'?" He said it in such a precise way, she couldn't help but smile. "There may be a way to do that. Perhaps we can help each other."

"How?" she said, her heart accelerating.

He leaned so close now that his lips almost touched her ear. "Tame the unicorn and deliver him to me," he whispered, "and I will lead you to a woven doorway. For I know of another."

"What?" But he didn't have time for her response.

"Sire," said the high steward, hopping from foot to foot behind Leo. "You asked that I remind you . . ."

She watched anger come to Leo's face, watched him

master it. His voice was soft, though loud enough for all to hear. "I did," he said. "For on the morrow, I face a mortal challenge in the hunt, one that every Leo must face. And I must face it rested." He signaled the man forward. "Convey the maid now to her tent. And mark this! Let her be treated with all courtesy."

The high steward beckoned. Leo inclined his head to Elayne, then turned away. Dismissed! She might have minded—except she couldn't wait to escape. From everyone's suspicious stares. From the stench of beast grease, wine, and stale sweat. From her own whirling thoughts. She needed some time to think. Needed to sleep. She'd had a helluva day.

She stepped down from the high table. The steward walked backward, bowing. Elayne knew that if she tried it, she'd end up on her ass, so she strode to the flap, turned there, gave a quick bow from the waist, and left.

He led her to a small tent, not far away, but far enough so that the renewed hubbub in the main one faded to a murmur. It was next to a larger one, over which a lion pennant flew. There were guards before each of them, holding spears. *To keep visitors out or me in?* she wondered. Both, she figured. Not that she had anywhere to go. Not that she had the strength to go.

The steward raised a flap, gestured her in, dropped it behind her. There was a pot, a pail of water beside it, some moss.

"Wow!" she muttered. "En suite."

She washed quickly, briefly. The bed—the only other thing in the tent—was a pile of furs that she slipped into the middle of without taking off her dress. It was cold in the foothills of the mountains. She wondered what "the morrow" would hold, what this "mortal challenge" was that Leo would face.

As she lay there, the smell of canvas reminded her of camping with her dad. *Where are you lying now, Dad?* she thought. She tried to visualize him—safe, well, getting better. She just wanted to get back to him. "There may be a way to do that," Leo had said. Was that a bluff? Moonspill said all the other doors had been sealed. But maybe he was wrong.

A small lantern cast a flickering light around the canvas walls. As she watched it, her eyelids began to droop . . . but each time she'd nearly fall asleep, something that had happened in Goloth would jerk her awake. Images began to blur—a three-headed manticore, a unicorn with a steel horn, a two-headed snake whispering into her ears. Except one of the snakes had Marc's face. The other had Leo's.

The furs were soft, not too smelly, comfy . . . apart from the one folded as a pillow for her head. It was lumpy. She tried to smooth it out—and felt something small and hard underneath. Delving, she wrapped her fingers around . . .

. . . a small twist of parchment. She unraveled it—and a pearl dropped into her hand.

"Oh!" she breathed.

There was only one person who'd have left it for her. The one who'd written the single word on the piece of paper. A player who needed some makeup tips but did a nice unicorn impersonation.

"'Hope,'" she read aloud.

No longer quite so alone, Elayne fell asleep.

## FOURTEEN

# HUNTING THE GRIFFIN

"What *is* that?"

Elayne asked the question of herself. Her two guards—one of whom she'd clung onto during the day's ride to the mountains—had obviously been told not to talk with her. They'd exchanged one personal—and rude!—comment on her appearance in that language she'd heard Marc speak when she'd first met him. She resisted the urge to let them know she understood their insults. She wasn't about to give away that secret.

Luckily, they also had no orders to restrict her—aside from any attempt at fleeing, she presumed. So when the hunting party went off and did hunting-type things, she'd scrambled up a slope, and the guards had silently followed.

She was glad she'd done it. Through trees that screened the little valley from the mountains, she had a view not only of the peaks but of what soared among them.

A griffin, she supposed, answering her own question. It was what they'd come to hunt, after all. And when the flying beast turned, its parts became clear against the granite in the crisp mountain air. It had the head of a raptor, with its sharp, curved beak. Large wings too—which it would need to support a body not birdlike at all, with not two but four legs, each with paws. As it flew, it shrieked, a piercing call, uncurling its large claws. It also had a tufted tail.

"Half eagle, half . . . lion," she muttered. And even though it was hard to tell against the mountainside, it had to be huge. "How the hell is any man going to hunt that?" she said aloud, turning to the guards. They kept their silence—but below them, in the hidden valley, noise came from the returning hunters, reining in.

Leo was looking sharply around, sunlight glinting off the helmet he wore, a circle of gold around its brim. "Here," she called, and he looked up and immediately began to run up the slope, reaching her in moments. The climb that had left her gasping didn't even interfere with his anger. "What make you here, maid?" he said briskly. "You should have stayed below."

"I wanted to see what all the fuss was about." She reached back, parted a branch so that Leo could also see the griffin. It was just making a landing on a crag.

He looked for a moment, nodded. "So now you have seen. And it is time for you to see no more." He placed a hand under her arm. "Come. My men shall take you back to the camp. You will be safe there."

The camp was tempting—if no one was around, perhaps she could steal a horse and hightail it out of there? That hope

143

lasted the nanosecond it took to recall, first, that she *loathed* riding and, second, the number of strange creatures Goloth possessed. Like the one flying above her now.

She looked up at it. "Go? And miss the hunt?" She took her arm back. "No way."

"'No . . . way'?" he echoed quizzically. "There is a way. *There* is your way." He pointed downhill again. "Women do not watch the hunt."

"Yeah, but women do not stay in a hunting camp, and we've already broken that rule. Please let me stay. Just for a little." She'd put on her softest voice, lowered her face, raised her eyes. It was a look she'd perfected to get whatever she wanted from her father.

She saw him hesitate. She could also see it was something he rarely did. "There is yet a little time before the danger. But"—he raised his hand against her thanks—"there is no one to wait with you. All of noble birth are involved in the hunt. All their servants too. These guards. We bring no one we do not need. . . ." He shrugged. "Except for the players."

*Aha!* "Well," she said, as casually as she could, "you could send me one of them." She couldn't figure out how to ask for Marc without giving him away.

Leo considered. "It would be rare fortune to find one who is sober. . . ." A little smile came, then he nodded. "Very well. To oblige my lady, I will send you a player. Yet if I do, when he says to come away, you must come."

"No problem."

"'No problem' . . . for you, perhaps." He shook his head, then continued his slide down the slope to his men waiting on the level ground below. They wore armor—breastplates, leg guards, helmets, the works. Their breaths, and those of their mounts, plumed in the cool mountain air. Elayne, pulling her cloak around her, watched as Leo, who was being armed by servants, spoke to his men. The finger-thumb combo was flicked by several in her direction. As ever, though, he was instantly obeyed and a servant dispatched.

Men were checking harness and weapons. Some carried spears, some long poles with square wooden ends. On several of the mounts, rolls were strapped that looked like nets, their strands made up of twined rope, each about as thick as her wrist. Nets? She'd assumed "hunting" meant they were going to kill the griffin. But were they going to try to catch it? In which case, even those nets looked puny. Ropes couldn't hold an eagle-lion the size of an elephant.

The servant returned. Trailing behind him came... Marc. It was her lucky day! He knelt before Leo, who bent and spoke. The player nodded continually, then rose, bowed, climbed slowly up the slope. As he did, her guards started down it.

Marc looked like her dad would look once in a while, before he had to give up wine because of the illness. Hung-over.

"Maid," he said, lowering himself gently to the ground.

"Big night?"

"Big?" He frowned, which caused him pain. Then shook his head, which caused him more. "It was long, certainly. The king-elect was pleased with our performance. We were pleased he was pleased—and celebrated our pleasure. It was the first

145

time I was allowed to partake, because of my success in the role."

"And you . . . *partaked* too much?"

"Perhaps." He nodded, winced, closed his eyes. "Aye."

She studied him. He didn't have the film-star looks of Leo, but he was still cute, despite the pallor of his skin. "You were very good. In the play."

He perked up. "You think so? 'Twas my first time as unicorn."

"You totally got it."

"And perhaps you would know?" He licked his lips, glancing back down to the hunters. When he spoke again, his voice was soft. "Is't true, lady, what all speak of—that you were found upon a unicorn's back?"

"Is't." She nodded.

He leaned closer, his voice urgent. "Then perhaps you *could* be the one prophesied. The one—"

A voice interrupted. Leo had taken a few steps back up the slope. "Dost the player please, maid?" he called.

"Dost," she called, happy that she was getting the lingo.

"Ask and he shall tell . . . ," Leo called, looking at Marc, ". . . almost everything."

A servant ran up to him, knelt, spoke. Immediately, Leo returned to his horse. Elayne turned back to Marc—whose eyes, which had brightened as he whispered, had hooded over again. His voice was different too. Formal. "The king-elect has ordered that I tell you . . . all. What is't you would know?"

*Where to begin?* "Uh . . . Oh! Those guards were speaking some kind of language I couldn't understand. What was it?"

"Dramach?" He smiled. "'Twas the language in Goloth before the coming of the first Leo. He forced all to learn his tongue. Now all at the court speak only that. Though many others in the land speak . . . both."

"Like you."

"Aye."

*Useful*, she thought, but said, "You must teach it to me sometime."

"As my lady pleases." He raised an eyebrow. "Wouldst know anything else?"

"Sure—like, what's 'king-elect' mean? Isn't he just king?"

"Nay. He has yet to receive the Lion's crown. First there must be a period of mourning for his father. Then must follow the Games."

"Games? You mean, what do you call it? . . . Jousting? And, uh, archery?"

He nodded. "There are such contests the first two days. Yet such ones, and other feats of strength and horsemanship, are held every year. It is only when one Leo dies that *these* Games are staged. For the next Leo must *prove* his right to rule . . . by a hunt in the arena, before the people. Beasts are captured, brought to the city—"

"But they can't use nets to capture a griffin." She glanced back up to the mountain. "They're way too big."

"And only a madman would try. Nay, we do not capture the mother . . . but her chick." He parted the bush, pointed to the crag. "It sits on the nest up there. A nest lined in gold."

Squinting, she could just make out the griffin's eaglish

147

head above the rock. "The king and his men are going to climb . . . up there?"

"Nay, that would be certain death." Marc pulled the bush's branch farther back. "*They* are."

She followed his finger. In the valley between their crag and the mountainside, something was moving through tall grass. Something that flashed so much in the bright sunlight it made her squint.

"What's that?"

"Arimphasians. The worshippers of gold."

The glimmer in the valley moved into an open patch, and she could see it clearly for the first time. Him. It was certainly a him, which she could tell because he was totally naked. She blushed and raised a hand, not so much to block the view but because of the glare. The guy was golden, sunlight gleaming off him. At that distance, about two hundred yards, she couldn't tell if it was paint or dust. She could tell that he was very tall, had muscles everywhere, hands that scraped his knees, and long, gold-flecked hair, which, thankfully, covered his bare butt.

He had stopped at the edge of the open ground and now swung his head toward them. "He's only got one eye!"

"Aye," Marc replied. "The Arimphasians are called 'the Cyclops people.'"

"You mean th-th-that this"—she stuttered—"this one-eyed guy is going to climb up there and . . . do what? Steal for you?"

"Nay, not for us. They steal for themselves." Marc was looking farther along the valley. "Besides, this one is not a thief. He is for something else."

"What is he for?"

He licked his lips and gave a smile. It was not a pleasant one. "Bait," he replied.

Movement pulled her gaze back to the tall grasses that covered the ground halfway to the mountain. The one-eyed guy had moved to the very edge of that brush, the last cover before the rock face. Behind him, others were beginning to slip through the tall grass. Like him, one-eyed and naked, but not covered in gold. About twenty of them, she reckoned. They seemed to be clutching nets too.

"The griffin loves gold above all things," Marc said, his voice beginning to take on the tone of narrator-actor, "only equaled in its lust for it by the Arimphasians. They delve beneath the earth for it, extract it, render it—for they are masters at the art of the forge. What they create, the griffin craves—and steals to make her nest."

"So you're on the griffin's side, right? Brotherhood of Thieves and all that?"

His eyes went cold. "I know not what you mean."

*Sheesh! Sensitive!* "I . . . I meant to thank you. For the pearl?"

Marc jerked his head down the hill, to the men preparing there. "Shh!" he hissed, then continued in his former tone, "And the Arimphasians in their turn worship the griffin. It is their God. Like all Gods, sacrifices must be made to it."

"What? What do you mean?"

He pulled down the branch again. "Watch!"

The glittering Arimphasian stepped beyond the screen of tall grass. The sunlight sparkled on him, dazzling. And then he began to run.

From above came the same high-pitched shriek she'd heard before. The griffin left her nest, flying straight up, spreading her wings wide, then halting like a hawk, hovering. Another cry came, as she plunged toward the earth.

Elayne couldn't help it. She grabbed Marc's arm, gripped tight. "He'll be killed."

"Aye," he breathed. "'Tis what he seeks."

When the beast swooped low, the other Arimphasians burst from the concealing grass, sprinting for the cliff face. As soon as they reached it, they began to climb, moving like speedy bugs up what appeared to be a sheer wall.

The griffin's claws stretched for the golden runner, a reaching paw jabbing the man, knocking him down. But he rolled, was up again in a moment, running flat out. He was into another clump of tall grass in a blur of speed.

"He's fast," breathed Elayne.

"Fast, aye. But this chase can have but one end—an end desired by both," Marc intoned. "His sacrifice will not be in vain, though. For watch there!"

She followed his pointing finger. The climbers reached the crag, poured over it, all twenty of them as one. In less than ten seconds, figures were climbing over it again, but slower this time, a bunch of them heaving something big between them, scrunched up, bound in rope. She saw a tufted tail thrust out of the mesh; two paws, a beak—which, even at that distance, she could see was twined in rope.

"But . . . they are not stealing the gold!"

"No. Like us, 'tis the griffin's chick they desire. The first to arrive has the most perilous job—to halt, with a noose, the chick's cry to its mother. For if the lion-bird leaves its hunt and returns, all is lost. Others arrive to bind the beast fast in nets. And see how fewer climbed down than ascended? The chick-cub is only the size of a stag—but as a fawn is born able to walk, so a griffin is born knowing how to kill."

"But why do they want the chick?"

"Sacrifices must be made *by* Gods as well," Marc whispered. He halted her next question. "Shh! And look."

The Arimphasians almost flew down the sheer face, slowed only by their burden of feather and fur, which they lowered from one outcrop to the next. They were halfway down when two shrieks—one of terror, one of triumph—dragged her gaze away.

The runner had burst from the grass, was surging for a group of trees. He never made them. The griffin, swooping low along the ground, smashed into him. His body twisted under the lion claws, the terrible beak lifted high . . . and Elayne had to look away. She couldn't speak, didn't want to look when Marc's hand tapped her hand—which was still digging into him—and said, "See! The Arimphasians have nearly brought their prey to the ground. Now Leo's hunt may begin!"

"What do you mean, Leo's hunt?" she said, her voice choked. Looking back down the slope, she saw that all the hunters were mounted, gazing intently at a man crouching at the end of the small canyon. He was peering into the valley beyond and had his hand raised, as if he were about to signal the start of a race.

Then she got it. "Oh my God," she whispered. "They're going to steal the griffin chick from the Arimphasians."

"Aye. 'Tis the purpose of the hunt."

Elayne flushed red. "So Leo's not a hunter but . . . but a thief?"

"Nay, maid. He is a warrior," Marc said, anger in his voice too. "Men fight for many reasons. The Arimphasians never remember that we sometimes come to take their prize. But when they see us, they fight to keep it. And they are doughty fighters, sure. Many a knight will die this day. We make our sacrifices too." He rose to his knees. "Which the king-elect has ordered you must not see. Come!"

He reached out an arm. She ignored it. "What? I'm allowed to see . . . that"—she jerked a thumb behind her without looking—"and nothing else?"

"I told you the fight can be hard . . . and spread. There may be danger, even up here. Now come."

He stood, beckoned. She looked at the sentinel, whose hand was still raised. The last of the one-eyes were descending from the cliff, the chick among them. She didn't try to keep the disgust from her voice. "You're telling me all this . . . this *death* . . . is just so Leo can kill a baby at these Games to prove he is a man?"

His eyes went wide. "The king-elect does not kill the griffin! That is for the nobles. The merchant class hunts a cockatrice. The commons' quarry is the manticore."

"What? Why?"

"So all may partake in the ritual of the hunt. Each class proves again how man conquers beasts."

"Barbaric," she muttered.

In Goloth, this was obviously not an insult. "Aye, maid, is

152

it not?" Marc grinned, reached for her again, actually took her arm. "Now away, and swiftly."

She began to rise, disgusted, wanting to be gone now. But movement froze her. The sentinel below dropped his arm . . . and all the knights spurred their mounts out of the canyon.

The Arimphasians might have had only single eyes . . . but they saw their ambushers immediately. There was a faltering of steps and then a great surge forward, all of them sprinting hard for the woods. The knights were already at full gallop, but it was difficult to judge if they could cut off their prey. The only sound was the muffled thud of bare feet and shod hoof on the soft ground. "It's so quiet," she whispered.

"The one-eyes cannot speak. And we do not wish to disturb the griffin at its feast," Marc replied. "Now, for the last time, will you come away?"

"No," she replied, taking her arm from his grasp, looking him straight in the eyes. "Unless you want to carry me?"

He stared back for a moment—and then grinned. "Good. For I wish to see this too. And if anything goes amiss, you will tell the king—if you are able—that you refused me."

He threw himself back onto the ground, crawling up to the lip of the canyon. After a moment's hesitation—"*if you are able?*"—she joined him, looking first to the mother griffin . . . looking away fast, shuddering from the quickest of glimpses: a beak plunging, tearing. But in that one look away, the distance between mounted and running men had quartered. Then halved again. "They're not going to make it," she said.

"Nay."

The Arimphasians realized it too. Suddenly they halted,

lowered their burden, thrusting the blunt-ended staves some carried out before them like spears. Most didn't stop. Empty-handed, they began to run—not away, but straight at the charging horsemen.

"Did I not tell you they had courage?" Marc whispered.

Some of the men of Goloth had steel-tipped lances, some just poles similar to their enemies'. Some carried nets, which they whirled around their heads like lassos, as the gap between the enemies closed. Elayne felt as if she were watching an old movie with the volume off, or at least turned down low, for sounds *did* come—grunts as one-eyed men crouched and sprang, as mounted men struck, some with blunt wood, some with slicing steel. She didn't want to watch . . . yet couldn't look away. Many of the Arimphasians were cut down in the first rush; others were trapped under flung nets, riders throwing themselves off their mounts to cinch the nets tight.

"Why . . . why are you catching them?" she breathed.

"I told you, the one-eyes are masters of the forge. Leo requires them to work his metals."

She remembered the poisoned stream, bubbling with pollution, that Moonspill had conned. "Slavers and thieves," she hissed. "How proud you all must be!"

But Marc's attention was below . . . where the knights were not having it all their own way. The Arimphasians were huge, their shaggy heads level with the stallions' ears. Several had leapt past pole or spear, avoided flung net. One was across a horse's neck, facing the rider, huge arms reaching forward, wrapping around the helmet, twisting. . . . Elayne closed her eyes.

But when Marc gasped, she had to look again. Charging at the single largest Arimphasian, who was standing alone before the bound chick, was the king-elect, following just behind one of his knights. But this one was too eager or too unskillful; when he thrust, the Arimphasian dodged, grabbed the pole, twisted it, pulled down hard. The horseman wobbled in his saddle . . . and the one-eye, reaching up an enormous hand, plucked him from his seat and smashed him into the ground. Then he yanked something from the dead man's belt. The dagger he raised flashed in the sunlight.

Leo brought his stallion up on its hind legs, front ones flailing over the now-armed Arimphasian, who wove among the flying hooves. And then . . . then it was almost as if Elayne could read the one-eye's thoughts. She saw him look around at his fellows, all now either taken or dead. He stopped weaving. Leo threw his spear. The blade slammed into the naked chest. He fell backward.

Onto the griffin chick. A rope bound the creature's beak. The dying Arimphasian reached up . . . and slit the bond.

For a moment, a deeper silence came—a terrible, waiting silence. Marc was rising slowly. "Gods save us," he breathed. Then the chick opened its beak and gave out one long, high-pitched wail.

Elayne turned. Perched on her feast, the griffin raised her eagle head to gaze up the valley. A stand of trees blocked her view of the now-frozen men, both one- and two-eyed. Then, with a dreadful cry of her own, she launched herself into the air.

The silence, which had been broken by two screams, was

155

shattered by scores of them. Everything frozen was moving at once—men, Arimphasians, horses. Another knight joined Leo, and together they thrust their spear poles through the chick's net, lifting it between them. Setting spurs to flanks, they raced back toward the canyon. The melee was no more. Hunters and hunted had merged into something else now.

Prey.

"Fast!" Marc shouted, grabbing her arm, pulling her into a slide down the slope. Now she didn't resist. Horses were tethered there, his and one other.

"But I can't r-ride," she stuttered. "Can't I ride with you?"

"Too slow," he yelled. He saw her face, spoke softer. "Come, I will aid you."

He hoisted her up into the saddle, where she grabbed the reins, pulled hard—which did nothing to calm a horse already panicked by screams. It reared up, almost throwing her. Marc mounted his horse, reached, snatched her reins, pulling them over the horse's head. Somehow she found the stirrups with her feet.

"Yah," he said, kicking his own mount's flanks. Both horses took off down the canyon.

Within seconds they were overtaken—first by men on horseback, then by Arimphasians on foot, their huge strides gobbling ground, enemies united now in terror. Elayne couldn't look back, all her attention focused on the mane in front of her, holding on by will as much as by grip. But she could hear—the pounding of hooves, the desperate breaths of men and mounts, the continuous wailing of the griffin chick.

And then something else, something under it all—*foo, foo, foo*—a beating in the air. Getting close, fast.

At last they were galloping full out, starting to overtake the running one-eyes, being overtaken by the hunters, passing without a glance.

*Foo, foo, foo.* Getting closer, closer . . . then ceasing, suddenly, replaced by a terrible scream. Despite her terror, Elayne had to look back—in time to see a man being jerked from his saddle, yanked out by talons sunk into his neck. The griffin tossed the man up, caught him in her beak. The screaming stopped, a body fell. *Foo, foo, foo.* The flapping began again. "This isn't happening!" Elayne yelped. "Can't this thing go any faster?"

There was a wood ahead. Men were already reining in there, safe under the branches. But it was a long way off, and the wingbeats came again, louder, nearer. *Foo, foo, foo.* She scrunched her neck down . . . and then her horse took off. They were flying, she could see the ground beneath flailing hooves. Her horse whinnied in high-pitched agony. A shadow was over her. She looked up, saw . . . vast, spread wings. Hideous claws, six inches long, sunk into her mount's rump. An eagle's head, twice as big as the horse's. She watched the curved beak part in a terrible cry . . . then snap shut, jab down, into the mane above Elayne's hands. The horse shrieked, twisted. But it couldn't shake loose. Wings flapped. . . . She was being lifted higher. She thought about jumping—but couldn't ungrip her fingers. "Help!" she screamed. Then she was falling forward as the griffin tore its beak out of the horse's neck, the cry coming . . . the cry changing to a screech. They sank, a little. And Elayne forced her eyes open.

A man clung to one of the beast's lion legs, his own swinging beneath him as he was flung this way and that. He was holding on with only one arm, because in the other he had a short sword, which he plunged into the animal's furred thigh, blood spraying into the face of . . . Leo!

The griffin swung her head around, jabbed down. Leo parried razor beak with sharpened steel. The beast was gliding again, huge wings spread wide. Big as she was, she was carrying Elayne, a horse, and an armored man. They sank, and horse hooves skimmed the ground.

"Jump, maid!" The shout came from right beside her. Marc was there, stretching out an arm. "Jump. Now!"

Somehow Elayne's fingers unclenched, though she took some mane with her as she released. Somehow she got her feet from the stirrups. She stretched out an arm, Marc reached, missed, reached again, gripped . . . and yanked her from the saddle. She crashed onto him, nearly toppling them both. But he held tight, jerking his reins to the left, away.

Immediately, he reined in. Both gasping, they watched as man, horse, and beast flew on. Free of her weight, they began to rise again, the griffin flapping, the horse screaming, the man being flung this way and that, stabbing all the while.

"Oh, why doesn't he jump?" she cried.

"Too high now. And look! Look!"

The trees were dead ahead. They were approaching them fast. The beast was struggling to rise above them. She released her talons; the horse fell, cartwheeling down. Leo dropped his sword, wrapped both arms around the animal's leg. Lighter, she rose higher, higher . . . not high enough.

Man and beast smashed into the woods.

The force drove them deep into the canopy. They splintered many branches before they stuck in the top of one tree. For a moment, there were only a few sounds—the snorts of horses suddenly reined in; the wail of the griffin chick, sinking to a moan; the creak of the tree bearing sudden weight. Then it snapped and they fell, other branches exploding like kindling, crashing to the ground. Elayne looked but couldn't see him. Leo was lost in leaves, feather, and fur.

Marc, everyone, spurred their horses forward. Men dismounted, ran in, spears leveled. But the griffin was still, her wings broken, her neck bent back. Dead. And it looked as if the man was too. He had ended up on top, and they pulled him gently from the beast's feathered chest.

"My lord!" cried a knight. "Speak!"

No one breathed. The silence extended. The knight looked up, shook his head.

Then Leo groaned. His eyes fluttered open. "The maid?" he croaked.

The knight glanced back, saw her. "She lives, lord," he said.

"'Tis well," Leo said, and closed his eyes.

Sobbing, Elayne buried her face in Marc's shoulder.

# FIFTEEN

# RIDING

On a cliff far above the carnage stood a unicorn.

It had not been hard to find them once he had made the long journey around the gorge that cleft that part of Goloth in two. Man left a trail easy to read, of dirtied streams and desecrated groves. He had caught up with them as they took their positions for the hunt. From across the valley, he had watched it all. With his keen eyes, he had even seen *her*, where she watched. But he had not come near—for this was the land of the griffin.

The two fabulous beasts must not meet. If they did, one of them would die. The griffin did not allow any intruders into its domain—beast or man. A unicorn was intelligent enough to avoid a meeting, intelligent enough—when calm—not to seek to kill purely on instinct. A griffin had not that restraint. If it saw a unicorn, it would attack. If they fought on the ground, the unicorn had a chance. But if the winged beast stooped from the air . . .

He had just witnessed again the power of his ancient foe. And yet a man had killed it. A man with a circlet of gold on his helmet. It was not hard to guess who that man might be. Another enemy, more recent.

Leo.

Moonspill snorted, tearing the dirt before him with one hoof. He had watched in dread the danger the Summoned was in. He had thought to plunge down the mountainside himself and attempt a rescue. But the griffin would have seen him and, in an instant, attacked. If, by a miracle, Moonspill had survived that, then man would have had a chance to do what he had failed to do before—and take him.

Torn, as ever, like the ground he tore before him— between what his instincts urged, what his duty demanded, what his heart sought.

His instincts were centered in his horn—a weapon more powerful than any sword or spear of man, wielded with far deadlier skill. He felt the urge to use it, to fight. Yet he held back, knew he must choose wisely, where and when—if he was to do all he must do.

His duty, first. When the last unicorns that survived in Goloth chose to leave it, his duty made him stay. Fifty years before, at the gathering at Black Tusk, the decision had been made. Since man had become more skilled at the taking of their kind, the unicorns would forsake Goloth just as they had forsaken the world of men. They would risk crossing the mountains—at night, when the griffin slept—to reach a world the eagles had told them was free of humankind.

All agreed . . . save one. For he was the one who, through his foolishness, had let the Hunter into Goloth. He had introduced that evil. It was his duty to remain, to do what he could against it.

All left . . . save two. For Heartsease would not abandon him. She would not be parted a second time from her only love. Together they remained, running separately for much of the time, for such is the solitary way of the unicorn. They had met twice since the other unicorns left, and each time, two foals were born. When their young were strong enough, the parents had seen them over the mountains. Each time, Heartsease had asked him if he would stay. Each time, he had returned. And she had returned with him.

Two unicorns had tried to do the work that all the unicorns had done before. Keep the waters clean for beasts to drink. Keep beyond the traps that the Lion set. Harder to do each year.

*We are both old,* he thought now, gazing down upon men scurrying to their king's aid. *This was to be our last time, perhaps, wasn't it, Heartsease? Before Leo ended that hope. Before he took the mare and not the stallion.*

And now the Summoned, his faint hope, was in the Lion's grasp as well.

Moonspill threw his great head up and down. His horn bade him charge down into the valley. But it would achieve nothing, this instinct of his, this desire, nothing save his doom. And besides, though she had shown courage when she helped him escape the Hunter's mirrors, she had not yet done what he needed her to do. She had not proved herself worthy to be borne as anything other than a burden.

Perhaps this Elayne, this descendant of Alice-Elayne, would do that in what lay ahead for her in Goloth. Perhaps if she kept the rendezvous they had agreed . . . ? He would wait for her in the moon-shadows of Black Tusk. If she came, his faint hope still lived. If she did not . . .

Moonspill reared, front hooves flailing, horn thrusting toward the sky. He let out a roar that echoed around the crags, crashing into the valley below, causing all there to look up. Yet all any saw, be they one-eyed or two-, was a blur of white, dissolving in sunlight.

*At least,* he thought, *I do not have to wait standing still.*

* * *

Riding. How she hated it. Partly it was being led, always some guy holding her reins, guiding her along. She felt so helpless.

Mainly it was her bottom.

If the first day after the griffin hunt had been bad, the second day . . . At least, before, they'd gone at a walk, keeping pace with the slowest wagon, because Leo was lying hurt inside it. But that second morning, he'd emerged, arm in a sling, mounted . . . and they'd spent the rest of the day in a new form of torture—trotting! She kept going down when she should have gone up and vice versa. Despite the initial terror, she much preferred the canter and even the occasional gallop. She didn't have to steer; her horse just followed the guard's.

The few times they walked, she even tried standing in the stirrups—bliss!

Someone must have noticed her ungainly style and pain-racked face. *Leo?* she'd wondered. He'd not come near her, though, stayed at the head of the column while she was toward the back. It seemed odd. Why didn't he come and accept her thanks for saving her life? But that second night, a ceramic pot had appeared in her tent, containing a thick paste. There was a note, one word: "Rub." Rub she did, despite the pungent scent . . . to almost instant relief. She didn't know what the miracle ingredient was, but it took away all the pain—and for the first time allowed her to think of something other than her butt. Such as . . .

*What the hell am I going to do?*

She'd slept badly that second night, tormented by dreams—of a rendezvous she couldn't keep because she was facing backward on a horse; of sharing a golden nest with a griffin chick; mostly of running down endless, empty hospital corridors, never finding the room where a machine was beeping faintly. Wearily, that third morning, she pulled on her increasingly stinky dress and limped from her tent. Her usual silent guard wasn't there. Someone else was.

"Maid!"

Marc was mounted, holding her reins and his own. Her horse was nipping at his. Elayne felt like doing the same. "Well, thanks for all the company!" He looked puzzled, so she continued, "You could have come and seen me before. I've eaten alone in my tent every night."

"Ah!" Comprehension came. "Alas, a man cannot spend time alone with a maid."

She put on her best "Southern belle." "What, sir, because of my reputation?"

She knew she wasn't very good at fluttering her lashes. It tended to look as if she had an eye condition. But he got the point, if not the impersonation. "Aye. And mine. Meetings between young men and women are strictly controlled, lest—" He broke off, blushing.

"So why are you taking the risk now?"

"We are in company." Marc gestured. It was true; horsemen were mounted and moving out all around them. His voice rose. "And Leo, our mighty and generous leader, thought there might be questions you would like answered before we arrive in the city."

"We're close?"

"Aye. We will see it from the next hill."

"What? So why didn't we make it last night?"

"The king-elect wished to discuss with the elders of the city the best way to receive you." He gestured to her horse. "Shall I aid you?"

"I can manage," she replied, still annoyed with him. She did, just, though he had to pull her reins to stop her horse's circling. Once she'd found her stirrups and got a good grip on the mane, Elayne looked ahead. Horsemen and wagons were already stretched out in a column along a wide dirt track that ran between cultivated fields. They'd been in farming country for a while now. There'd been the occasional village where a few inhabitants would pour out of the stockade that surrounded their houses to kiss the king-elect's feet at his stirrup, to gawk at the griffin chick, caged on a wagon—and to gawk at the Manhattan chick. Messengers had ridden ahead, and rumors must have spread. The villagers either made that "Begone, witch!" gesture at her or gaped—quite a lot of them toothlessly.

There was another village on that hilltop up ahead. It was still a ways off. Definitely time to get some answers. But where to begin?

He heeled his horse forward, hers followed—and his fading blush prompted her—that and the thought of the villagers she'd seen. They'd all been clothed in almost identical dress—coats or aprons for the men, long smocks for the women, who also had their heads swathed in scarves. It made it hard to tell their ages, but even the youngest female there looked like a woman and not a girl. And that's what had got her—there'd been no teenagers. Back in her world, if a king rode past with a griffin, packs of teens would be hanging out, trying to look cool while they stared.

She had a feeling that *teenagers* was not going to be a common term thereabouts. "So where are all the younger maids?" she asked. "And the lads too?"

"They are being . . . educated."

There was something in the way he said "educated" that sounded ominous. "Where?"

"At twelve years of age, maids and lads are separated and sent each unto their own place," he replied. "They are then educated according to their needs and skills. Boys who are apt

166

are taught the arts of battle—for we are often at war with a race across the great water, those of Glana, a dark race, like you—" He broke off, looked around, whispered, "Is't where you are from? Glana?"

Elayne tossed back her long black hair and smiled, she hoped, mysteriously. "And what do the girls get to learn?"

"The skills *they* need, of course. To cook, to sew, to weave if they have the aptitude. To look after the household and raise the children."

She restrained the urge to stick her fingers down her throat. "Lucky them. How long does this last?"

"For the lads? Three years or more, till their skills are proven. Some then go into the king's guard; others apprentice to the hunters. Most return to the fields—where near all villagers are now, 'tis harvest time—or to their family trades." He preened. "Now I can make a blade dance with the best and would have made a fierce warrior. But I come from a lineage of players, so I returned to the theater."

He tossed back his head, shaking his long blond hair, and she had to smile. "You were very good, Marc."

"Think you so?" He tried to look modest, failed miserably, leaned forward. "You should witness my Ice Queen, in *Semericon*. Or Phoebe, the country lass I assay in *'Twas Greener in My Youth*. Or indeed—"

"Uh-huh. Can't wait," she interrupted. "So what happens to the maids?"

"The maids?"

"Aye. When they have learned their 'skills.'" She had a pretty good idea. But she wanted to hear him say it.

167

"When they come of age they are married, straightaway."

*There are no maids in Goloth,* Moonspill had told her. And there seemed little point in asking if the maids had any choice in the matter. Or in the husband. "So the kings are taking no chances, eh? What was that prophecy again? The one you told me about in the tent?"

He did the opposite of blush—went white, looked around. "I know not what you mean," he muttered.

Elayne thought she'd said it softly enough, but he signaled her to be quiet with a palm driven down, eyebrows up. But even if he wouldn't repeat it—she remembered enough. Certainly the bit about a maid—initials *A* and *E*—taming the unicorn and the tyrant falling. It was pretty clear now why everyone treated her as such a threat.

Except for one man. She looked for Leo again at the head of the column, and as she did, it halted. A man was riding back along it, and she saw it was Leo's steward. He stopped beside her. "You are to come with me, lady," he said. He didn't even wait for a reply, just snatched her reins from Marc, turned his horse, led her forward. Glancing back, she saw Marc's concerned look. She was led right to the front. From the timber walls of the village, a few people stared down. The head of the column was just beyond it, halted on the last part of the hill's upward slope.

And there was the king-elect. The steward released her horse as they drew level. Leo reached and took over the reins, drawing her mount to the side of his. "You will ride with me now," he said.

"Sire," Elayne said. "I'm underwhelmed by the honor."

She was ticked, tired of being pushed and pulled around. So she grabbed hold of her reins, yanked. He didn't let them go, and the leather went taut between them.

Anger sparked in his eyes. "You question—" he said, then broke off. For a long moment, he stared at her. Then he released the reins, and Elayne dragged them across. *Good going, Elayne*, she thought. But her horse was docile, and it must have looked as if she kept it under control.

Leo nodded, spoke. "As you have seen in the places we have passed, rumors of you and the manner of your coming have already reached my people. They will be curious to see this . . . wonder." He smiled. "And I would have such a wonder beside me. Come." He tapped his heel on his horse's flank. Luckily, hers followed. They moved to the crest of the hill . . . and she gaped.

She wondered if she'd ever seen anything more extraordinary.

## SIXTEEN

# CASTLE OF SKULLS

She'd flown into New York many times. She'd always loved it, seeing those skyscrapers springing from an island, the rivers surrounding it, the bridges crossing them.

She was looking at an island now. There were towers too, and one bridge. But this was nothing like Manhattan.

"Whoa!" The horse stopped. "Uh, not you." She tapped heels to flanks, and it lurched forward, catching up to Leo.

He noticed her expression. "What is't, lady? Have you never seen a city before?"

"Not one like that!"

Her horse happily followed Leo's down the slope. That left Elayne free to stare—and marvel.

The island seemed taller than it was broad, but that could have been an optical illusion because the buildings were jammed together, some at crazy angles, leaning into the ones next to them, with what looked like rope walkways swinging between, and rickety staircases joining them at different levels. There were smaller buildings too, attaching larger towers to each other.

*What nutcase designed this place?* she thought.

"It is magnificent, is it not?" Leo said proudly.

"That's one word for it," she replied. A wall, crowned by battlements and punctuated by military towers, circled the island. Facing them, a continuation of the roadway they descended, was the solitary bridge. It had buildings on it too, as higgledy-piggledy as the ones beyond crowding the passage on both sides. A passage further narrowed by hordes of people.

Elayne peered. They were a couple of hundred yards away, but she could see soldiers in helmets with some kind of spear held horizontally, pushing the crowd back. "What are they all waiting for?" she asked.

"The Hunter and the Unicorn Maid," Leo said, and leaned toward her. "May I?" he said, gesturing to her reins. "I would be seen leading you in."

Feeling relief, feigning indifference—and knowing she had no choice—she released them to him. Just as well, for the next second, he rose in the stirrups, waved his hand . . . and a blare of trumpets behind them made both horses dance. Immediately, the crowd surged against the soldiers, and a chant began, a single word: "Hunter! Hunter! Hunter!"

A dozen men came forward. They were better dressed than the bulk of those behind them, who all wore some variation of apron and clog. These men had doublets that flared out over their hips, striped tights covering their legs, brass-buckled shoes on their feet. Each had a cap with a feather in it, swept off as they approached.

"Hail, King-Elect!" cried a gray-haired gentleman, stepping from the throng. Glancing at Elayne with a look that was a mix of intrigue and alarm, he continued, "Have you been blessed in your hunting, lord?"

"Witness that I have."

Movement behind her. Six soldiers were bearing the cage forward on poles. In it, slumped against the bars, was the griffin chick. Its eyes were wide, staring at the crowd. Its beak, thrust out as if seeking better air, had been retied with a strip of rough cloth to prevent its terrible scream. It couldn't stop the low croon of pain.

The crowd pressed up against the soldiers' spears, silent now, watching. Leo drew his sword and moved to the cage. For a moment, Elayne was scared that he was going to hurt the animal. But he just slipped the weapon between the bars, slid it along the animal's beak, and suddenly jerked the blade up, severing the cloth. The chick opened its beak and screamed, in terror, in fury, a sound that had her clutching at her ears. No one around her did, though. Their hands were all raised in acclamation, their voices too, yelling out that one word again and again.

"Hunter! Hunter! Hunter!"

Leo took the acclaim for a few moments more—then gestured for silence. He was instantly obeyed. "And here is an even greater prize perhaps," he cried. "For here is the maid who was delivered to me . . . by a unicorn!"

172

There were more cries at that, though these were varied—shocked, amazed, fearful, joyful. Elayne knew all eyes were on her—and lowered her own to the horse's mane. Then Leo started forward, and the better-dressed men put on their caps, bowed, stepped to the side. She was led across the bridge, the last section of which was attached by thick chains that ran into the walls of the vast gatehouse ahead.

Passing under it, they emerged into an even narrower roadway, just as crowded, soldiers again holding back a jostling crowd. It was dark, and Elayne looked up, thinking the sun had gone behind a cloud. She saw sky—but only a tiny strip of it because the tall, narrow houses on either side leaned in so much they almost touched. It was like riding up a tunnel.

They climbed, their horses' hooves ringing on stone. The streets were cobbled—and filthy! A narrow gutter ran down the middle of the lane, water—well, liquid anyway—swirling down it, bearing things she decided not to study too closely. As the lane twisted up, the houses got a little larger, the scent in the air a little less pungent, and the clothes of the people leaning out their windows or lining the street a little better. And then the road suddenly ended, opening into a large square.

There was a building within the square—a castle within a castle. It had arrow slits for windows for most of its lower frontage. In its middle was a huge gateway, a raised iron grille dangling above the entrance. Battlements ran the length of the walls. In each corner was a tower with a conical roof.

There was a structure with a sloping roof behind the battlements. Elayne thought it could almost be a house, because it had windows, not arrow slits, and drapes in those

173

windows. She saw movement, a curtain that must have been held back suddenly dropping. It fell . . . and it was only then that she noticed what was just below it.

A metal pole thrust out beneath every window on the front. Each one must have had a curved end, bent up. She couldn't be sure. But something had to be holding the head that was impaled on each.

Elayne shut her eyes—too late!—turned her head away. "Eww!" she moaned.

Leo leaned over. "What ails my lady?"

"What . . . ? Who are . . . ?" she squeaked, waving, not looking.

"Weavers," he replied.

She glanced up, looked away again fast. "Shoddy workmanship?" she muttered queasily.

"Pardon?" He stared at her for a long moment before he spoke again. "And you know why they are called 'weavers,' do you not?"

She recognized a loaded question when she heard one. And of course she had a pretty good idea. But he didn't need to know that. Being "AE" was obviously bad enough. Descendant of the original "weaver"? Not good. "No . . ."

"They are named for the very first, and foulest, of traitors," he said softly. "Weaving was his trade."

He studied her for a moment, silent. She tried to keep her face blank. Then he turned his horse's head away and began moving across the square toward the castle. Her horse followed. When he halted just before the entrance, the iron grille poised above them, she said, "Really, I—"

She got that much out before he reached, took her arm in a strong grip just short of painful. Pulling her over, so close he only had to whisper. "What you *do* know, maid, I would find out—and will, before long, I fancy." He paused, staring into her eyes. "For now, look up and know this: the first weaver's treachery was discovered—and punished. His treason continues to this day . . . and is punished still."

He shook her arm once, then released it. Elayne decided not to take his advice—*Seen one skull, seen 'em all*, she thought, gulping breath. But there was something else she'd seen in his steel-blue eyes, for all their determination and threat. *Could it be fear?* she wondered.

Eyeless sockets followed her as Elayne rode beneath the spiked iron grille.

They passed from the large courtyard to a smaller one. There was an entrance to a tunnel straight ahead, a downward slope, torches on walls. The men bearing the griffin chick—whose cry had sunk again to a low moan—marched past them bearing their captive. Grooms rushed from the tunnel to take their horses. Leo dismounted easily . . . but Elayne found she couldn't. A horse suddenly seemed the best place to be.

*Maybe I can kick in my heels, charge through the gate, gallop back the way I came—back to where I met Moonspill.* The full moon was still four or five days away, judging by the globe that had waxed above them every night. Perhaps there was somewhere she could hide and wait for him. *Anything's better than this Castle of Skulls!*

But she didn't, of course. She'd have fallen off in the first twenty yards.

Leo, with a murmured word to a servant and a short bow to her, disappeared up a staircase. She just couldn't figure him out. He'd avoided her on the ride to the city but wanted her at his side now because . . . Because why? He'd said rumors about her would already have reached the town. How was he going to explain her? And with all that stuff about the prophecy? She knew she had to be a threat to him. And she had just seen what happened to threats—their heads were spiked on the front of his castle. But he had saved her life. Nearly lost his own doing it too. Why hadn't he let the griffin take her?

She swayed in the saddle. She was getting light-headed with worry; with hunger too. The last smoked bison sandwich had been the night before.

Two servants stood beside her, one holding her reins, the other with his hands raised. "My lady?" he said.

Prying her fingers from the mane, she let him help her down. But as soon as her feet hit the cobbles, she teetered. The servant held her till she steadied, then moved away, gesturing to a different doorway than the one Leo had taken. Elayne hesitated. *What if it leads to a dungeon?* But with the grooms waiting, there was nothing she could do.

She was led up, not down, which she hoped was a good sign. Up a huge stone staircase, its walls lined with tapestries—ordinary ones, not very exciting even to her inexpert eye. On the fourth floor, she was guided down a corridor. Halting before a door, the servant reached past her, pushed it in. "My lady," he said, gesturing.

Taking a breath, she stepped through. As soon as she did,

the door slammed behind her. "Hey," she said, reaching for the handle, turning it. The door didn't open. She was locked in.

She faced the room, almost not wanting to look. But it was an ordinary room. An ordinary room in a medieval palace, she reminded herself. The stone floors were covered with thick rugs, the walls with a better class of tapestry. A four-poster bed stood against one wall, drapes hanging from it. Exploring further, she discovered a fire in the hearth opposite the bed, a door in the wall beside it. She pushed it open and stepped into a small side room.

"Oh. My. God!" She couldn't believe it! It was possibly the most amazing thing she'd seen in her whole time in Goloth—and that included all the fabulous beasts.

It was a bath! A long tub, made of beautifully smoothed wood. Steam rose from it. She stuck her hand in— *Yow!* The water was intense.

They'd only ever given her the one dress. It was pungent when she first put it on, and she had just spent four days on horseback. The best she'd gotten was a basin of icy water.

Desire drove all fear from her mind. "I am going to take a bath," she declared to the walls, "and if they split my skull afterward, at least I'll die clean!" She returned to the main room, was about to rip off the dress when she thought, *What if there is, like, a spy hole and they're watching me?* So she went to the bed, slipped between the drapes, which hung to the mattress. It was tentlike in there. The first thing she did was take the unicorn's horn out of the hem. Staring at it for a long moment, she wondered where Moonspill was.

She hesitated—then lifted an edge of the heavy mattress and shoved the horn beneath. Then she wriggled out of her dress . . . but left her underwear on. She hadn't seen the equivalent of Macy's on her travels. And she was pretty sure she wouldn't like the local idea of undergarments. She suspected there weren't any. So she thought she'd give hers a scrub in the tub along with herself. Poking her head out of the drapes, she looked around . . . but there was nothing she could do, "spy holes" or not.

She made a dash for the bath. It smelled amazing, of lavender and rose. It was so hot, though, it took her quite a while to lower herself in. Finally settled, the water at her chin, she looked through the sweet-smelling steam, noticing what she hadn't before—a chair with huge carved arms, draped with blankets, which she supposed were for drying herself on. *They can wait*, she thought. This was the best she'd felt since coming to Goloth, and she wasn't in a hurry to do anything but wallow.

Elayne dozed. But thoughts intruded as the bath cooled. She had to assume they weren't going to leave her there all day. A bath at the end of a journey was great, but food was probably going to be next up, and she had better be ready.

There was a little tray attached to the side of the bath. On it was a square of soap. She lifted it, sniffed more lavender and . . . *sage*, she thought. Tipping her head back, she soaked her hair, scrubbed it, scrubbed the rest of her, scrubbed her underwear.

The water was tepid when she climbed from the tub. Hanging her underwear in front of the fire, she used the soft blankets to dry herself, wrapping one around her, rubbing her hair with the other as she went back to the bed—

"Hey!" she called.

Her dress was gone! She looked around everywhere, fast, ran to the door—still locked! Someone had sneaked in, taken her clothes, sneaked out. . . .

"Great!" she wailed. Whatever was to come, she didn't want to face it in a blanket.

And then she saw the dress.

It was laid out on an armchair . . . and totally gorgeous, she discovered as she lifted it up. Sort of a pale teal in color, embroidered with leaves and flowers of a darker green. The material was a rich, fine wool, though lined in silk that showed where the skirt rucked up in the front. It had long bell sleeves, which were rimmed with some kind of white fur. The bodice was fitted and split by a modest plunge down the chest, edged with thick gold braids.

Beside the dress was a white linen undergarment. She put on her still-damp underwear, then slipped the shift over her head, found it reached from shoulders to knees. Then she pulled the dress over. It was a little large, though far less bulky than the players' hand-me-down. On the chair was also a long, heavy chain studded with semiprecious stones. It seemed too heavy for a necklace. . . . A belt? Cinched around her waist, it pulled the dress in. There was one last item on the chair—a crimson velvet head scarf, attached to a black band. It went on like a headband, and she could push her hair up inside it.

Something moved, to her left. Elayne jumped . . . but it

was her moving, in a mirror she hadn't noticed before. Tucking in the last stray strand of hair, she stepped forward. A woman from the Middle Ages stared back. "Not too shabby," she said aloud. She looked very pale, regretted that she didn't have any mascara or blush. *Oh well*, she thought. *Hard to know what to bring when you're snatched through a tapestry by a unicorn.*

Which reminded her . . . She went and dug out the piece of horn from beneath the mattress. There was no pocket in the dress—but this skirt also had a deep hem. Using the horn as a pick, she managed to make enough of an opening to shove it inside. There were some shoes by the mirror, and Elayne slipped them on. They fit, almost perfectly. Someone had guessed her sizes pretty accurately. It wasn't just a bath that Leo had sent ahead for, it appeared. She stared at herself, nibbling at her lower lip. Leo! What was all this dressing up for? What was his game?

She was still turning this way and that—staring, admiring, wondering—when she heard the laugh.

She started, looked quickly all around the room. Nothing moved, except flames in the grate and her reflection in the mirror. She swallowed, called, "Who's there?"

The laugh came again. High-pitched and on a series of notes, like a musical trill. As far as she could tell, it came from the wall to the left of the bed, where a tapestry hung. On it a woven hunter raised his spear above the stag he chased.

She took a step. As she did, the tapestry bellied out toward her. Grabbing an edge, she pulled it aside.

There was a door behind the tapestry. And it was ajar.

## SEVENTEEN

# QUEEN BEE

She pushed it, leaned out. Faint light spilled from barred windows onto a long, narrow room. Almost a corridor, except it had some furniture in it, a few chairs, a table. It was paneled in wood and lined with portraits. Men and women stared down, unsmilingly. Fat or thin, bald or hairy, they all had a similar look to them, in the eyes.

*Leo's eyes*, she thought.

She'd stepped through to study them . . . then she heard that laugh again. Definitely a girl's laugh. It came from the farthest end of the corridor room. She could see a door swinging shut there. "Hey," she called. "Wait!"

She ran. The door had closed before she got to it, but she pushed her way in—

And was almost blinded. There were torches everywhere, burning in metal holders on the walls. Then she realized that they were doubled, quadrupled—because there were mirrors everywhere too—standing ones, hung ones, dangling ones, all shapes and sizes. Moving, she saw a dozen Elaynes shielding their eyes.

Mirrors weren't the only things hanging. Gauzy cloths floated in the air, held on invisible wires. One billowed, stroked her face. . . . *Silk!* Some reached all the way to the floor; some hovered above, reflecting in all the mirrors, multiplying every way she looked.

Another laugh came, closer this time. Definitely in this room, somewhere ahead. "Who's there?" Elayne asked again, pushing aside the cloth that brushed her face. "Where are you?"

"Here." The word was whispered, followed by another giggle.

"I don't want to play this game," Elayne said, annoyed.

"Come, then," said the voice.

Elayne moved forward. It was hard, turning in to mirrors, pushing aside silks. There was nothing in the room to get her bearings on. She didn't know if she was moving straight forward or going in a circle.

"So close," the voice said, and it *was* closer. Elayne turned toward it, stumbling away from her reflection. She took a breath, managed to suck in silk, spat it out. . . .

A huge bed was before her. It was circular, covered in pillows, all of such varied colors and patterns they almost hurt the eyes. She squinted—and realized that the bed was occupied. For right in the middle, as colored and patterned as the surroundings, sprawled a girl.

A very fat girl.

"Salutations," she said brightly, her voice high-pitched. She patted the bed. "I would esteem it a high honor if you would sit with me."

Elayne was stunned. This was the first girl of about her own age she'd seen in Goloth. All of "maiden age" were either off at that finishing school for wives Marc had talked about or were, no doubt, up to their eyeballs in the "duties" they'd been trained for.

At least Elayne *thought* she was about her own age. It was a little hard to tell. She wasn't particularly "petite" herself, but this girl was huge! Hamster cheeks, fleshy arms, and cleavage that bulged out her bodice, making her dress look about two sizes too small. Her hair was braided, twisted, and pinned up, which only emphasized the full-moon quality of her face. Her eyes were small and dark, sitting in her face like two raisins on a cookie.

They stared at each other for several seconds—until the girl patted the bed again. Elayne sat, on the edge. "Sweet-meats," the girl said, producing a tray from behind her back.

Elayne's eyes went wide. On the platter was a variety of candies in all shapes, textures, colors. Many were coated with sugar. But there were also lumps. Dark brown lumps. Elayne pointed, too excited to speak in case she drooled.

"Cacao?" the girl giggled. "It is rare, traded with the Glanasa for much gold." Picking a piece up, she leaned forward . . . and popped it into Elayne's gaping mouth.

"Umph!" she mumbled. The piece of chocolate was huge, and mouth-floodingly delicious. She'd been living on hunters' fare—heavy on the meat, even for breakfast. After much begging, she'd finally scored some of the carrots they fed to their horses. So this? Her eyes rolled into her head in delight.

"Aye! Aye!" The girl clapped her hands, gold bangles chiming at her wrist. "That's my favorite too." She studied the tray. "I should resist but . . . a feast of welcome, like this? It would be churlish not to. . . ." She swooped, snatched. "To your health!" she cried, toasting Elayne as if it were wine before popping it in her mouth.

She was a sucker too—the best way to eat good chocolate. And this was great, thick and dark and almost bitter. After a while, the girl tried to speak. "Um-a-yah-yah," she muttered, pointing to herself.

"E-uh-mm," Elayne ventured, and they both giggled.

Another minute and the girl swallowed. "Amaryllis," she said, licking her fingertips. "Will you be my friend?"

She stretched out a hand, nails up as if seeking a manicure. Elayne took it, shook it—and the girl cried out, surprised. *Oops*, Elayne thought. *She probably expected me to kiss it.* There she was, after all, in a palace, in a room of silk and mirrors and . . . sweetmeats. *She has to be a princess.*

But Amaryllis's shock changed swiftly to delight. She slapped her other hand on top and began to shake Elayne's vigorously, jerking it up and down, laughing all the while.

"Uh. Ow! Yeah." Elayne managed to pull her hand free, but the girl was wearing large rings, and the stones on one scratched the back of her fingers. Sucking it, she spoke through a mouthful of skin and a little cacao-flavored blood: "My name is Elayne."

"I have heard of you. Heard too that is only one-half of your name." She stared for a moment, then raised the tray. "Another?"

Since she was still licking chocolate off of her fillings, Elayne declined. "Ah!" Amaryllis said. "You show restraint. Is that why you are so thin?"

Elayne was about to say that she wasn't really when Amaryllis pounced like a hawk, snatching up another dark piece. "Celebration!" she declared. But she didn't seem to enjoy it so much this time. She chomped it, finishing it quickly, while her eyes never left the study of Elayne's face. "So you are she," she said, "who was borne on a unicorn's back."

"Well, not 'born' exactly— Oh," she interrupted herself. "You mean I *rode* one." Elayne shrugged. "Oh, sure." *Jeez*, she thought. *Talking to my first Golothian teenager, and already I am trying to act cool!*

The other girl didn't care. "'Tis a wonder," she said— somewhat glumly, Elayne thought.

"And you are, uh, a princess? That must be . . . um . . . nice?" she asked, smiling encouragingly.

The girl wasn't encouraged. "I am not yet. And mayhap I will not be if—" She looked down at the tray of sweets, raised her hand . . . then jerked it back, turned her head, listened.

Elayne heard them too. Footsteps. "Who—?" she began.

"Swiftly," Amaryllis said, scooping up the tray, shoving it under some of the pillows. She gestured frantically. "Conceal yourself!"

Elayne looked around. *Where?* Well, anywhere, she

185

supposed. She had no idea where the door was she'd come in, or if someone was approaching that one or another. So she just took a few steps through some silks and went behind one of the tall standing mirrors. The footsteps halted. Elayne breathed, counted. Got to ten before they started again, moving away. She decided to wait for a call. When it came, it was from the other side of the mirror.

"Ee-layne!"

She peered around. Amaryllis was turning this way and that, studying her reflections. "They try to take away my pleasure, my only pleasure," she said. "You grow too big, they say. But I do not think so." She looked at Elayne. "Do you?"

Elayne stepped around. "I . . . I think you should be whatever size makes you happy."

Amaryllis looked at Elayne for a long moment, biting her lower lip. "Perhaps it does not make *him* happy. He does not say so. But when he comes, the rare times he comes, he seems—" She broke off.

"'Him'?" Elayne asked.

The small eyes narrowed further. When she spoke, her tone was different. Colder. "Do not mistake me for a fool, Ee-layne!"

"I . . . don't. I—"

The other girl spun around, moved away, silks pulled by her passing, a flowing trail back to her bed. "Mirrors," she shrieked. "I hate mirrors."

*OK!* "Then why do you have so many?" Elayne asked, following.

Amaryllis crawled to the center of the bed. The tray of

sweetmeats was out again in a flash, her fingers hovering. She looked sharply up. "You do not know?"

"No."

"So," she said bitterly, "all tell me of you. And yet there is none who tell you of me? Not even him?"

*Him again.* "Do you mean—"

"Leo," she yelled. Her voice dropped. "Well, since no one else does, I will tell you of myself," she continued. "I am a maiden, just as you are. Do you know what that means?"

*Careful!* "Uh . . . not sure."

"It means, *Ee*-layne, that I am just like you." The girl rose to her knees, threw her arms wide, and cried out, "For I am also a tamer of unicorns."

# EIGHTEEN

# THE CHOICE

"From the day I was taken from my family three years ago," Amaryllis continued more quietly, "to this very day, I have lived with mirrors. To burn my reflection into the glass, so that even when I am not before them, yet I am there. A maiden pure and chaste can do this, and it is the first part of my duty. But it is when the unicorn, seeing the glass that I am now living within, slows, halts, freezes, that my real task begins. Then I can come forward, put my arm around his neck, whisper in his ear. And then, when he lays his horn across my breast, ah, then"—she gave a groan, clutching herself there— "then is the beast tamed. Then may the hunters come and bind him with fetters not even a unicorn may break."

Amaryllis's eyes were glazed, staring into the room, almost in the trance Elayne supposed she'd get herself in when she went taming. "So, you've, uh, done this?"

The other still stared, into her past. "Aye! When the old Leo was killed, my time had come. And the king-elect courted me, as is the way, bringing me presents, speaking soft to me. His trackers had found the unicorn's hoofprint. The one he desired more than any other, the strongest, the most fabled!"

*Moonspill*, Elayne thought.

"Traps were laid, mirrors set. I was brought to the valley. . . ." She closed her eyes, her face relaxing.

"Yes?" Elayne lowered herself onto an edge of the bed, eager to hear. "And did you . . . ?"

"Yes," she breathed. "The unicorn was held by my double in the glass. I came, spoke softly." A frown disturbed the serenity. "It was not as I had been told. The unicorn was not, on the instant, tamed. But held enough anyway for the men to come, to bind the beast." Her eyes opened. She looked angry. "But once the beast was bound, I found . . . I found . . ."

"Yes?"

She looked straight at Elayne. "It was the wrong unicorn. I had tamed the dam and not the sire."

*Right*, thought Elayne. *No wonder Moonspill is so desperate!*

"It was not my fault, but the hunters'," Amaryllis continued, staring hard at her now. "They had found the wrong print. And the law would still be served—a unicorn could be slain by the new king; it matters not whether it be stallion or mare." She looked down. "Yet it matters to my Leo."

She turned again to the tray, grabbed another chocolate, crammed it in, chewing angrily. The scent of it came to Elayne . . . and she suddenly recalled the sealed carriage that

189

had left the hunters' camp when she'd arrived after Moon-spill's escape. That same scent of chocolate coming from it! They'd got rid of Amaryllis to make way for her. *Careful,* she thought. *Be double careful here.*

With mouth full, Amaryllis spoke. "Leo's heart was fixed upon that mightiest of males. He would kill it, to quiet the people, grown restive with his father's rule. And so he does not come to me now but sends servants with excuses in his stead." Her tone got shrill. "I have kept my part of the compact. Now he must keep his. He must take me for his third wife! It is the law!"

"Whoa!" Elayne couldn't help the exclamation. *Wife? Third?* "He has two wives already? What is he—a Mormon?"

"More man than most, perhaps."

Elayne coughed. Amaryllis's eyes were welling up as she continued. "It is the custom. I have tamed the unicorn! I should be his wife!"

She began to sob into a silk sleeve. Elayne reached forward, touched her shoulder gently. "Well, why wouldn't you be? Kings keep their . . . their 'compacts,' don't they?"

The sobbing stopped. She raised teary eyes again. "But what if another maiden were to tame a unicorn? The unicorn of his heart's desire?"

*Ahhh!* "Hey!" Elayne said, leaning back, arms lifted in surrender. "Trust me, I would never . . . I mean, Leo? Come on! He's cute and everything, but—" She broke off, hardly believing she was talking that way. "He's all yours," she finished lamely.

Amaryllis stared at Elayne, sniffing. Behind the tears, her

eyes had gone cold. Then she shook her head. "You may not have a choice," she said.

"Of course I have a choice." Elayne laughed. "I mean, they can't just force you to tame a unicorn and marry some guy." The other girl stayed silent. "Can they?"

The silence lasted an uncomfortable moment longer—until Amaryllis lifted the tray. "Sweetmeat?"

Elayne ignored the offering. "Can they?"

Amaryllis dropped the tray, leaned in, whispered, "He is the king-elect. He can do anything he desires. Besides"—she raised her voice—"you are 'Alice-Elayne.' If you are the prophesied one, he will need to deal with your threat. One way or another."

Elayne didn't like the sound of that. She swallowed. "But I am not . . . prophesied. I am just . . ." She was about to say "an ordinary New York girl" when she realized how absurd it would sound.

Amaryllis wiped her eyes. When she spoke, her tone had changed, the whine gone. "Do you desire to see them?" she said, in a friendly way. "Come." She slid off the bed. "I'll take you to them."

"What? See what?"

The girl had walked through hanging silk, stopped now, looked back. "Why, the tapestries, of course."

"Tapestries?" Elayne echoed. "Do you mean—?" She broke off. It had all begun with tapestries—her ancestor's weaving of the hunt of the unicorn—in *both* worlds, according to her family book. And at the revels, Leo had hinted that there was another "woven doorway" between the worlds. . . .

What if this other doorway was in the Castle of Skulls?

Trying to keep the excitement off her face, Elayne rose too. "OK," she said. "Lead on."

Amaryllis smiled, beckoned. Elayne followed, and they wove through billowing silk and moving reflections to a door. Putting a finger to her lips, Amaryllis opened it a crack, peered, then opened it wide. She went through, Elayne close behind, into another corridor. Not the same one she'd come in by, with all the portraits. This one had staircases going up and down, four of which they passed. At the fifth, Amaryllis paused, listened . . . then lurched across, threw open a door there, dragging Elayne into a closet, yanking the door shut behind them.

They pressed into a musty pile of blankets. Barely able to breathe, Elayne also held her breath, as footsteps came nearer, voices too. People passed. Amaryllis waited for a long while— too long!—but at last she pushed out, and, gasping, Elayne followed her for a few yards, then down a staircase.

At the bottom was a set of double doors. Leaning out from the last step, Amaryllis looked both ways, then scooted across. She turned the door handle, and, just as voices came from somewhere down that corridor, they stumbled in.

It was dark, too dark to see. Something flickered, and Amaryllis moved to it. Flame grew, brightening the room. She was holding an oil lamp, turning its knob. Her shadow rose on the wall, where it danced against . . . a tapestry.

The lamp didn't give out much light. There were long, bright cracks on one wall. When her eyes had adjusted a little, Elayne realized they were shutters, covering windows. Ignoring Amaryllis's warning hiss, she went to them. She was too excited. She had to see the tapestries. She opened a shutter. Evening light filled the great stone hall and lit walls lined with woven unicorns.

She could have been back in the museum in New York—except this was the real deal, a real dining hall in a real castle. She rushed straight to the wall opposite the windows, aware of the unicorn's horn in the hem of her dress, banging against her shin as she moved. She knew—from her family story, from Moonspill—that it was the magic of the weave that created the door. She searched now for that magic . . . and was instantly disappointed.

The huge panel before her was of a hunting scene, hounds and men chasing a unicorn, just like in the Cloisters. She was no expert—but even she could tell that this one wasn't close to being as good as the ones she'd seen before. There was none of the "movement" the guide had described. The hunters' faces were flat and lifeless, their clothes dull. And the unicorn? It had none of the grace of the one in New York.

She ran along the wall, ignoring Amaryllis, who was beckoning her from the far end of the hall. But the next tapestry was just as disappointing, just as lacking in life—and she quickly discovered they were all like that. They were the same scenes as the ones in the Cloisters—the unicorn conning a stream, leaping from it. But it was as if someone who had seen them maybe once or twice had tried to re-create them.

One thing was clear. Either he'd had some really off days . . . or her ancestor had not woven these tapestries.

Elayne stopped dead in the center of the hall, looking at

each of the panels in turn, confirming something else she'd suddenly realized. Not one of these tapestries had the letters A and E.

She wanted to cry. *No doorway here,* she thought, biting her lip.

"Ee-layne! Come!"

Amaryllis was still waving from the room's end. She was standing in front of a huge fireplace. The chimney stack rose above it, disappearing into the ceiling. On that stack was another panel.

"Oh. My. God," Elayne whispered, walking slowly forward.

It was a panel from the Cloisters. *The Unicorn Is Killed and Brought to the Castle,* Elayne thought it was called. And she remembered from her family's story that François had woven a great panel for Adam's—the first Leo's—coronation.

This had to be it! As she got closer, she could see it was a far superior work to the ones that lined the walls. The faces were of different people, and bright with emotion. The trees appeared to move in a breeze; the unicorn—well, it was being stabbed in one half of the panel and was dead in the other, slung across a horse's back. But it was certainly a much younger version of Moonspill.

It was François Robochon's work, all right. Only one thing was different, she saw at once. In all four corners, the work looked kind of blurred. Peering closer, Elayne could see that they were patched, and not particularly well. But she knew why that was.

The letters A and E had been chopped out.

A hand reached out, fastened on the front of her bodice, dragged her forward. "Swiftly," Amaryllis said, pulling her almost into the grate. Reluctantly—Elayne was sure she must have missed something—she allowed herself to be pulled. The other girl was standing right against one of the chimney's supporting columns, which was made of big square blocks of stone.

"Have to leave, right?"

"Not yet," Amaryllis whispered. "Not before I show you a secret that Leo shared with me when he was . . . fond of me." She chewed at her lip. "Now I share it with you. Only a very few have ever seen this." She put her finger to her lips, then turned and pressed a stone rosette in the center of one of the great blocks. It slid in, to a distant rumble. Immediately, the middle of the tapestry to the right of the fireplace was sucked into the wall. Something had opened behind it.

"Here," she said, lifting the end nearest her, handing Elayne the lamp. "Lead and I will follow."

Elayne led. She used one arm to push the cloth out, leaning into it because it was so heavy. After three paces, she felt the draft of an open space and her light spilled onto a stone doorway. She looked back. Amaryllis was right behind her. "I pray you, enter," she whispered.

The door was so low, Elayne had to duck slightly. Stepping beyond the entrance, she straightened, looked back. "Amaryllis?" she called.

The only sound that came was the stones sliding into place behind her. Sealing her in.

Elayne jumped, way too late. "What are you doing?" she

screamed, banging the flat of her hand against the smooth stone till it hurt. She stopped, listened, breathing fast. Then, beyond her gasps, she heard it. Very faintly.

"Help! Help!" came her cry. "The girl! The witch!"

*Bitch!* Elayne thought. Though it didn't come as a huge shock. That came when she turned around . . .

. . . and saw The Doom of Kings.

The secret room was small, and the tapestry was too, smaller than the others in the hall beyond, but it filled the back wall. When she lifted the lamp, she saw that it was just as Alice-Elayne Corbeau had described. There were two stories in it. The first was smaller and on the left, and showed a maid with the letters *A* and *E* tied to her belt with a tasseled rope. One hand was around a unicorn's neck; the other pointed to the center of the panel, and the action there. . . .

To the unicorn plunging his horn into the man's chest.

She brought the lamp closer. The man looked a little like Leo but older, not as good-looking. Though she was sure not even movie stars would stay handsome when they were dying so horribly. The detail was intense: she could almost hear the howl of agony, see it in the twisted lines of a face in shock, in the body doubled over by the smashing force of bone on bone. The horn had driven through the velvet doublet, the hole it made lined in split threads, giving an almost 3-D effect. And the blood! Elayne was sure she was going to feel wetness. But the weave gave under her touch, crackling like a crust.

She snatched her fingers back, wiped them on her gown. This was the tapestry she'd read about. Her ancestor had meant it as a symbol of hope, but it had morphed into a prophecy: that a maid would tame a unicorn who would kill the tyrant king.

She shook her head. From that misunderstanding, a whole society had been shaped. Girls were married off young so there were no "maids," except one, who would . . . not "tame" a unicorn—Elayne knew that was a lie now—but trap it, at least till it could be shackled and then killed by a new king in an arena.

She looked at Moonspill's younger self. Looked at the horn thrust into the king's chest. Why would a tyrant keep this thing around, even hidden? Surely it was still a threat? Then that memory came again—Leo, leaning into her at the feast, telling of another doorway. It had to be here—in the last tapestry her ancestor had woven. That was why it had never been destroyed.

Beyond the chamber, Elayne heard shouting. She knew she didn't have much time. So, reaching down, she plucked the necklace from the hem of her dress. Moonspill had said—to her, to her ancestor, the original Alice-Elayne—that a touch of the unicorn's horn was the key to the door. Now she just had to find the lock to slip it into.

More shouts came from outside. *Come on, Elayne!* Her gaze roved over the tapestry, settling on Moonspill where he stood to the left, the maid's hand resting on his neck. His horn spiraled up to the sharp point that would soon end the life of the tyrant.

The point! The tip she held in her hand! Moonspill had given it to Alice-Elayne as a talisman—and as a way back if the need was ever great enough.

"That's it," she said, reaching the horn up. And then she stopped, holding it just above the weave. *Come on,* she thought, *I'm no one's prophecy. I've done all anyone could expect of me. Besides, I'm needed elsewhere.*

Stones grating, sliding back. They were coming—and she could escape them. Escape to her world. To New York and all she knew. To her father, so sick in the hospital.

*Dying in the hospital.*

The thought shocked her. Was that the first time she'd admitted it? That he was dying? That all the talk of radical treatments and new therapies was just that—talk? If she rushed back to him now, what would she do?

*Nothing—except watch him die.*

A draft of air hit her. They were lifting the tapestry outside. Someone hissed.

*Move!* She pushed the real horn to the woven horn. It was one half inch away.

*Unicorn's horn!* Not an old yellowing piece of it. The whole white shaft spiraling from Moonspill's forehead. He had placed it in a poisoned stream and turned the waters sweet.

He could do the same again.

It had been a fantasy of hope. Now it seemed . . . possible. But she had only a moment, just one, to decide.

So she did . . . and used the moment to tuck the horn back inside her hem before three guards, swords drawn, ran into the room.

## NINETEEN

# PERSUASION

They put her in the armory. Only the king could condemn prisoners to the dungeons—or so she'd gathered from the debate the guards had as they pushed her along corridors with much "witch, avaunting" and the waving of swords. Leo was about "royal business" in the city. She would await "his pleasure."

Elayne didn't like the sound of that. And she didn't like where she was. If it wasn't a jail, it would do till the real one was ready. A cold, windowless cellar, made colder by all the metal lying around. Swords, axes, pieces of armor, bows, and blades.

*Huh*, she thought. *They probably think that since I'm just a girl, I won't be able to use any of these.* To her annoyance, she discovered they were right. Trying to lift one of the lighter-looking swords nearly dislocated her shoulder.

She sat there getting colder, thirstier, hungrier, the thought of the piece of chocolate she'd declined tormenting her . . . but not as much as the thought of what she'd done—and not done.

She kept thinking about the moment she'd stood there, horn in hand, with her world and all she loved perhaps just a push through the weave . . . and she hadn't pushed! It didn't matter that in the long, cold moments since, she'd questioned whether it could have been a door at all. Her family book hadn't mentioned it—and why would François have summoned Moonspill to get him and his daughter out of Goloth if he'd woven another exit?

But that was logical hindsight. In the heat of the moment, she'd *chosen* to stay. *Oh yeah, and what was the plan again, Elayne? To kidnap a unicorn and take him back to New York to heal my dad?*

Elayne started . . . to laugh! It was that or cry, and she'd shed enough tears lately. This whole world was crazy. What could she do except be crazy too? Everyone had plans for her—Moonspill, Leo . . . probably these "weavers" ever since "Prophecy Girl" came to town.

"You know what?" she said out loud. "At least I made a choice for myself!"

She had! It felt good, after everyone else's choices for her. And now she had to try to somehow—*somehow!*—make her way back to the only door she knew existed for certain in Goloth. Under Black Tusk.

Shaking with laughter reminded her of something else— she really had to pee! She was just considering which helmet to invert when the key in the lock turned, the door opened, and a young man stepped through. "Maid!" Leo exclaimed, coming straight to her. "I am desolate that I was not told sooner. Alas, cares of state!" He bent closer. "You are chilled!" He flicked the clasp of his thick woolen cloak, sweeping it around to engulf her, before turning to the door. "In!" he called.

Servants entered. Two brought a brazier, coals glowing behind a grate, which they set down. Another man brought a platter of bread, cheese, and sausage, while a fourth carried in a tray with a pitcher that steamed and two goblets.

"Out!" said Leo, and the servants bowed their way to the door, closing it behind them. He hunted around, dug out some kind of camping stools from a pile, unfolded them, waving Elayne onto one. He sat on the second, picked up the pitcher, filled the goblets, handed one across. The wine was heated, smelled of sweet spices. She sipped. It was delicious. "I—"

He raised a hand. "Eat," he said.

*Well, when the "king's pleasure" coincides with my own* . . . She began to cram in cheese, sausage, and bread, alternating mouthfuls with gulps of wine. Leo watched her, smiling. She was warm again, her hunger was passing, and her need to pee, she realized, had been largely cold and terror. When she smiled back, he leaned close to refill her goblet, spoke softly. "Why were you in the prophecy room?"

*Here it comes*, Elayne thought. Wiping her mouth, she replied, "Amaryllis said she wanted to show it to me. Then she trapped me in there."

"Amaryllis? She should not have come to you nor taken you there." He shook his head. "And that is not the tale she told."

"Not surprised. But it's the truth."

"She is not given to lying."

"Well, maybe since she's been lied to—" Elayne bit her tongue, then tried to soften her tone. "She mentioned a possible wedding. . . ."

His eyes narrowed. "It is . . . complicated, maid."

"Oh, I'm sure it is." She meant to say it sympathetically but it came out a tad sarcastic. *I blame the wine*, she thought, taking another gulp.

"Amaryllis does not matter here." He studied her. "What matters is the tapestry. Did you . . . seek to pass through it, perchance?"

"Pass through? No, but . . ." Elayne put her goblet down. *Careful*, she thought. "But I . . . I was curious, of course, ever since you mentioned there might be another doorway."

"I did, aye," he replied. He was staring hard into her eyes. Then he looked up, away. "But the tapestry is not it."

It was the looking away that did it! She'd played enough poker with her dad to know—Leo was bluffing. There was no other door. It was both disappointing—and liberating. Now she truly knew what her only option was.

Leo looked back. "I offered to lead you to one—in return for a certain service."

"Taming the unicorn," she blurted, instantly regretting it.

But he didn't pounce on it. Instead, he stared a moment longer, then stood up, turned his back, picked up the sword Elayne had barely been able to lift before. Flicking it into the air, he caught it one-handed, gazed along the plane of the blade. "Perchance your coming is not what it seems," he

202

continued in that soft voice, not looking at her. "Perchance the prophecy will be fulfilled . . . but differently." He laid the weapon down, turned back to her fast. She could see a glow now in his eyes. "For are not prophecies usually stories that mean something else?"

Elayne swallowed. "What do you think it means?"

"Well . . ." He smiled. "Could the 'death' of the king be not a real death but the death of all that is old and burdensome? The death, mayhap, of tyranny? Of . . . my father?" He stared above her for a moment. "I revere his memory. However, he was a hard man, and cruel upon occasion. He did not see how his people desired change." He looked at her again, stepping closer. "Desired one who could bring that change. Someone strong enough, who had proved his strength."

He had a smooth voice. His tone was so impassioned. He'd get lots of votes—not, she was sure, that they *did* vote in Goloth. And he had very blue eyes, in which reflected lamplight flickered. She was held by them, found she couldn't look away, couldn't stop it when he leaned even closer . . . and kissed her.

She'd been kissed before—well, sort of. This was different. Slower. Weirder.

*I really, really shouldn't drink wine*, Elayne thought, not responding . . . but not quite moving away either.

He pulled back slowly, his eyes seeking hers, his deep voice coming softly. "Perchance *that* was the true prophecy," he said. "That you would come and bring change to this land, death to the old, life to the new. Help me to bring about a new world. Help me to prove myself strong. Bring me the means to prove that strength." He nodded. "And what a reward you can have, Alice-Elayne. Tame the last unicorn for me, and you can choose . . . whatever you desire. A return to your land or"—the smile came again—"the reward the maiden-tamer gets—a place beside me on the throne."

The king-elect of Goloth was leaning in for another kiss. But it was his fast-approaching smile Elayne really saw. It never reached those entrancing eyes, was only on the lips—which she noticed again, from about six inches away, were really, really thin.

He swooped; she turned; he got a mouthful of hair. Part of her wanted to tell him what a sleaze he was. But she resisted it, resisted a very strong urge to slap him. Because she realized anger wouldn't help her—but the sleaze might.

"Oh! Sorry," she said, pulling her hair from his lips as she slid off the stool.

"Maid . . . ," he said, rising too, following.

She lifted a hand to halt him. "Give a girl a chance to think, would you?" She was blushing, no doubt, so she added what she hoped was a girlish laugh as her mind raced. She took a deep breath. "So if I help you catch M—" She stopped herself. "Catch this male unicorn, you'll guide me to this other door and let me go home?"

"Aye, that. Or . . ." He took another step closer.

She stepped a pace away. "Or . . . Yeah, sure, let's think about that option too." She smiled—probably too brightly—and looked at him for a long moment. He was offering to get her to Moonspill . . . After that, well, she'd figure something out. The first step was to get there. "OK," she said. "Deal. Let's do it."

He tipped his head. "You will aid me to capture the stallion?"

"Aye."

His eyes narrowed. "How exactly will you aid me, maid?"

"Uh . . ." Options whizzed through her head. "I think . . . no, I *know* where he will be, the night of the full moon. So we go there, you bring your mirrors, presto!"

Maybe she wasn't that good at poker herself. He didn't look convinced. "The Games begin the day after the full moon. I must be here, in the city. Unless . . . how far away is this rendezvous?"

"Uh, not far."

"Then perhaps we can go there sooner, maid. Return in time for the Games." That no-eyes smile came again. "A unicorn in the arena. You beside me in the royal balcony. Beside me, perchance . . . everywhere."

He'd already played that card. It hadn't worked so well the first time but the man was used to being obeyed. Leo lunged at her, hands groping, eyelids lowering, thin lips looming. Perhaps she'd drunk too much wine on an empty stomach, but all Elayne's schemes, all her desires, went—except one.

She slapped him.

"Back off!" she shouted.

For a long moment, he just stared at her, stunned. Then he was roaring. "You dare . . . dare!" He grabbed the sword again, raised it high. Elayne shrieked, threw up a pathetic arm. . . .

205

No pain came. Nothing happened. After a long moment, she peered from under her arm—to see him slowly lowering the weapon. Laying it down, he crossed to the door, stopped, turned. He'd gotten control of his voice, if not his coloring. "You are obstinate, maid," he hissed. "Yet I think you *will* do all that I ask . . . when you have time to consider the alternatives." Throwing open the door, he bellowed, "Guards!"

There was nothing she could do, nowhere to run. Two huge men came in, each seizing an arm. Leo tore a torch from a wall bracket and strode out the door. The guards, Elayne between them with her feet dangling, followed. Along stone corridors, down spiraling stairs they went, till they had left all other light behind. Deeper they descended. She could feel the dankness, smell the cold stone. At last they halted before a wooden door. Leo grabbed a key from a hook. The lock gave with a rusty squeal. Pulling the door open, he cried, "In with her!"

She was flung through the doorway. The door slammed shut. She threw herself against it. All her defiance was gone. "Please!" she begged. "Please! Wait!"

His words came muffled through thick wood. "We will talk again when you have had time to consider, maid. Much time. Then I think you will decide to aid me. To give me . . . everything I desire!"

Footsteps moved away, disappeared. The cell had not a trace of light in it, and the silence was so complete her whimpers sounded like shrieks.

# TWENTY

# DUNGEON

Elayne leaned against the door, too scared to move, knees drawn up to her chin, arms wrapped around them. *He'll come back,* she thought. *He just kissed me, for God's sake! And he needs me. Anyway, who would throw a fifteen-year-old girl into a dungeon?*

Then she remembered—a tyrant would. About the only movement she made was to reach up and wipe her lips.

After a while, she shook herself. She didn't know how long she'd be there. "Much time," Leo had threatened. What was that in Goloth? An hour? A year? She should at least get a sense of where she was.

There was zero light, absolutely nothing to get "accustomed" to. "Hello?" she said loudly. There was no echo, so the cell wasn't enormous. It smelled musty, the air stale. With an effort, she heaved herself up, took a step, another, her hand thrust out before her. Counted ten before she hit wall.

She flailed her hand above her. *Nothing.* Jumped. *Ouch!* Stubbed fingers on the ceiling; so it was low, about two feet above her head.

Squatting, she ran her fingertips across the floor. The surface was quite smooth until . . . *Yes!* She found a groove. She followed it. . . . It joined another, three more radiating out. "Flagstones," she murmured, pressing her fingertips down. Not earth. There was something below her. She wasn't at the very bottom of the world. It was strangely comforting—until she thought what *could* be below a dungeon in the Castle of Skulls.

She rose, walked sideways, arm out—and hit wall about four steps away. Crossed back the four steps, two more . . . wall! Then she began to follow it all around.

There were no alcoves, no tunnels leading off. It was a stone box, ten steps long, six across, eight high. *Nice tomb,* she thought, and began to laugh, stopping herself immediately. Hysteria wouldn't help. She wasn't sure what would, but . . .

She continued her shuffle to complete the square—and something swished at her feet. Crouching she felt—straw.

"Oh, goody," she said aloud, "a bed."

Flopping down, Elayne immediately thought of her own bed—the cotton sheets, the pillows, the down comforter. She started shivering. . . . No, she realized, the shivering hadn't stopped since she hit the cell; it was just coming in growing waves. "My bed," she groaned, tasting the salt of tears running into her mouth. Tipping over sideways, pulling as much straw over herself as she could, she rocked herself to sleep.

She woke suddenly, violently, hand swinging to the right

beside her, trying to find the bedside table, the lamp—neither of which were there. She had no idea how long she'd slept. Ten minutes? Ten hours? *How do you keep time in a tomb?* she wondered. Her left arm was bloodless from using it as a pillow, hand and fingers numb. She sat up and shook it. Then stopped when she heard the scratching.

*Rats?* she wondered, and shuddered. There were enough of them in the alley behind her loft, and she hated them. But castles must have thousands! She squirmed back into the corner of the cell, drew her legs up, listened harder. The scratching had a regular scrape to it. Could rats keep rhythm? Maybe it was . . . someone. Another prisoner, trying to make contact? "Hello-oh?" she said, her voice wobbly.

The scratching stopped . . . then came again, faster for a few heartbeats before stopping again. A different sound— grinding, stone against stone. Then . . . *There!* From the middle of the floor came a flash of light, a line of it, a square of it. A flagstone rose into the air, then scraped across the floor. It was pushed by two gloved hands.

The light, in that complete darkness, was like the sun at noon. She shielded her eyes and, through splayed fingers, saw a lantern rising through the hole. Something rose with it, and when she saw what that was, Elayne screamed.

It was a grinning skull, lipless mouth spread wide in a terrible smile. It made a hissing death-rattle noise, but her screams drowned that.

Beyond the noise of scream and hiss, she heard feet thumping down the corridor outside. The skull turned sharply to the sound, then as fast back to her. As she took breath for the next yell, words came. "Silence! I am here to aid you."

The mouth did not move—and Elayne realized that it wasn't a real skull. It was a skull mask.

There was pounding on the door. A gruff voice shouted, "What ails you, maid?"

"Answer him gently. Make him leave," the skull whispered.

"Take off the mask," she said.

"I—"

"Take it off now!"

A hand grasped the bony forehead, jerked.

"Marc!" Relief and fury fused in a whisper. "You scared the shit out of me!"

They heard a jangle of keys. "Maid!" the guard shouted.

Marc jerked his head. "A nightmare," Elayne shouted. "I am afraid. Light, please!"

Marc gave her a "What the hell?" look. But the guard just laughed. "You will bide in the dark, as the king-elect commands."

His footsteps moved away. Marc beckoned. "Come!" he said.

She scrambled over. Lamplight spilled into a narrow tunnel, smooth walls curving out of sight. Marc offered a hand. "Be swift!"

"Down there?" She swallowed.

"You would rather stay here? Come! And wear this." He pulled a piece of cloth from under his doublet, shook it. It was another mask, of a cat or something. It had a slightly goofy face.

210

"You couldn't have worn one like this?" she grumbled.

"We were rehearsing a new play when I heard what had befallen you. Come!"

She looked down. The tunnel hadn't become any more inviting. "Why do I need a mask at all?"

He made room and pulled her in. It was a tight fit, their bodies pressed together, faces only a few inches apart. "'Tis musty down there. Spiders have made webs—"

"Oh, this just gets better and better. . . ."

"So it is best to be covered. Turn around," he said, gesturing her down.

"Face-first?"

"The walls are slick with moisture. And there are few ledges. It is easiest to find them, and hold yourself, on your hands."

There *was* a kind of ledge a few feet below and Elayne slid down to crouch on it. Marc passed her the lamp, then reached back and grabbed the flagstone. Stone scraped, followed by a clunk as it dropped into place.

He knelt beside her on the ledge. As he did, the light, which had been flickering, began to shrink until only a little core of flame held to the wick. "Ah," he said, "I was afeard of that."

"You were afear—" she managed, before the flame vanished.

"Come," he said.

She felt him slide ahead of her but didn't, couldn't, move. "Are you rescuing me?"

"Aye."

"Why?"

"Maid, we must hurry."

"Why?"

He sighed. "Because I am a weaver."

"Really?" she breathed.

"Aye. Now come! Brace your arms so you do not slide too swiftly."

She heard him begin his descent. Sticking her hands out, she slipped a little ways, caught herself. The sides were pretty smooth.

"What is this tunnel?"

His voice rose from the dark below her. "Tyrants usually like to kill their enemies in the sun for all to witness. Yet on occasion someone offends whose death must be concealed. So they murder him in the room above. Then drop him down. Now come!"

Her arms had begun to shake with the bracing. Yet she found she couldn't let go. "Where does this end?" she called.

His voice came from still farther away. "In the lake. 'Tis how we found it. Some years past, a weaver, an eminent man of the city, was stabbed up above, thrown down. But he was not quite dead. A fisherman, one of us, saw him as he emerged, heard his dying story. We suspected it would be useful one day."

"We?" She still didn't want to let go. Chatting seemed nice.

"The Weavers' Council. Now, come, maid! We needs must hurry."

"But—"

She'd meant to follow him slowly. But her hands were

numb, and her arms buckled. She began to slide. "Whoa!" she cried.

"Do not—" he managed, just before she hit him.

He tried to brace them both. Failed. "By the horn!" he wailed as they were launched downward.

"Oh-oh-oh-OH!"

It couldn't have been that long a fall. It just felt like it. Banking around a corner, shooting down a straight, one moment she was half on Marc, then totally on top. A series of bumps drove the air out of them both in shuddery shrieks—*uh-uh-uh-uh!* Then a longer, straighter, steeper stretch sent them faster, faster. . . .

"Quiet!" Marc yelled, though he'd been making as much noise as her. She sucked in some mask—*Disgusting!*—and then a slight upward slope slowed them, a little, not much, not enough.

They shot out into the night air, still joined, a two-headed octopus with eight flailing limbs. They passed over a small sailboat, its mast so close Elayne could have touched it. Then it was almost as if they stopped, velocity ending, gravity taking over. Separated at last, they tumbled toward the moonlit water.

*Smack!* The surface slapped Elayne, and she lost the little air she had left. She floundered, not sure which way was up, then saw some moonlit bubbles and kicked along them.

"Ahh!" she gasped as she sucked in air. Her mask had been ripped off by the impact of the water—but she yelped as a skull broke the surface beside her.

Marc tore off his mask. "There!" he pointed. The boat

they'd flown over was a black shape, silhouetted against the denser blackness of the city's walls. A lamp glimmered at the bow.

"Swim," Marc commanded.

*Easier said than done*, she thought. Her dress was wool and instantly waterlogged, the weight dragging her under. Treading water, she ripped, pulled, yanked, somehow made enough room to slide from it. She let the dress go . . . and just as she did, she remembered.

"No!" she shrieked, and dove beneath the surface, powering herself down, hands snatching before her. One hit material; she dragged the dress to her, frantically feeling for the hem. She found an edge and felt along it, pulling, twisting, her air failing. She was kicking hard, but there was no way she was going to make it back up with the weight of the dress. Then, just as she began to panic . . . she felt the horn's shape and tore it free. Striking out for the surface, she broke it with a huge gasp.

"Maid!"

Marc was beside her, looking nervously down into the swirling water. "I thought one had taken you."

"One what?" she spluttered.

"Kraken."

"What?"

"Water dragon."

"Oh, fantastic."

She hadn't needed much encouragement anyway. She slipped the horn's silver chain over her head, struck out. They reached the boat at the same time. Arms stretched down, and she was hauled aboard like a tuna, lay wheezing like one on the deck, shivering in her shift.

Marc lay beside her. Blankets were thrown over them both by bearded men in loose shirts and leather aprons. Commanding them was a man dressed differently, better, like the guys who'd greeted Leo on his return—a velvet doublet that spread into a sort of skirt, above striped . . . tights, she supposed. He wore a hat, a cloak. "Swiftly now," he said, gesturing to a tented shelter at the back of the boat, glancing up to the battlements, where lights moved. Sentries, presumably.

They staggered over, slid under canvas. There were nets, crates; it was some kind of fishing boat. There was also a small wooden bench, which they dropped onto, shivering. The better-dressed man pointed to some clothes there—boys' clothes. Doublets, jackets, some baggy type of trousers, short boots, cloaks. "Dress swiftly, maid," the man said. "Your disappearance will be soon noticed. We have but little time."

*Before what?* she wondered. She was happy to be out of that dungeon, happy to have dry clothes, but she suspected these weavers would want something from her—just like everyone else in Goloth.

The man stepped out onto the deck. Marc snatched up clothes and followed him. The canvas dropped, but they didn't move far away. Presumably because they began to speak in that other language, one she would not understand.

So Elayne leaned closer to listen.

It was a guttural tongue, a lot of it spoken in the throat. But she could make it out clearly enough. *Thanks, snakes,* she thought.

"Is all else ready?" Marc asked.

"Aye," replied the other. "Matthias waits by the water gate. He will take her . . . to another, whose name is unknown to us both. For if the tyrant was to take one of us—"

"Yes," said Marc, "and spies may move among us. . . ."

"Indeed. And then the plan will be as the Weavers' Council decided."

"What was the decision?"

"To keep her safe—till the last morning of the Games. Then an officer in the palace guard will smuggle her into the depths of the Castle of Skulls." Even through the canvas, in this strange language, Elayne could hear the man's excitement. "She will . . . tame the unicorn imprisoned there, ride her out before the people where—"

Marc's voice interrupted, as excited. "Where there will be enough gathered together to overwhelm Leo and his men. Tyranny will fall!"

She had heard enough. More crazy plans for her. But she only had one for herself. Now it was time to put it into action . . . and see if what everyone believed about her could help her and not them.

Running her fingers through her wet hair to make it wild, she took a deep breath . . . then threw back the awning. "I have seen a vision," she intoned, in English, not their language, and in what she hoped was a prophetess-like voice. "I have had a dream."

She saw the older man and the two crewmen join their fingers together; saw even Marc's hands twitch. "The tyrant will fall on the last day of the Games. But he will not fall to the dam of the unicorn. The sire will come. The sire will kill."

The men all took a step back. The older man began to stutter. "D-d-do you mean, maid—?"

"Aye! I have a rendezvous to keep with Moonspill, the last, the greatest, of all unicorns. Once together, we shall not be parted—until the prophecy is fulfilled. Until tyranny dies!"

She thought she might have gone too far. But suddenly Marc gave a cry. "Look," he whispered.

He was pointing at the unicorn's horn. Elayne had leaned forward, and it had popped out of her shift. "Yes," she said, lifting it up. "He has given me the key to the door of worlds, and—"

She stopped herself. She had said enough. More than enough, judging by the looks on all their faces. There was another sharp inhalation of breath, a staring silence, as she hid the horn again beneath her shift. Finally the well-dressed man spoke in an awed whisper. "Do you speak true? Can you do this, maid?"

"I do," she replied, then added for emphasis, "I will. For I hate Leo as much as you do."

"'Tis all our prayers answered if you succeed, maid! Weavers are now in every level of society. Others support us, just waiting for a chance. All will be there, in the arena on the last day of the Games. And if they witness the prophecy fulfilled—they *will* rise!"

She nodded. *Bizarre,* she thought. *Everyone in Goloth wants me to "tame" Moonspill—including Moonspill himself.* But enough was enough. A night in a dungeon had cured her of all bravado. She was just a girl . . . and she was going home. To New York. To her father.

The man leaned in. "But how will you journey to this rendezvous?"

Elayne sagged. She'd gotten to the end of her boldness. Fortunately, someone else took up the slack. "I will accompany her. I will be her guide and companion," said Marc. Elayne turned to him, smiled.

"'Tis well spoken, lad," the man said. "We will drop you at the fishing village upon the landward shore. You will need this." He pulled out a bag that clinked. "For horses and provisions. How long must you travel, maid?"

The tree was to the northwest, Elayne was sure, beneath that distinctive black spire. Moonspill had ridden fast from it, first to that cave-glade, then to the conning. From there, the hunting party had gone up to the griffin mountains, then down from them to the city in three days. It was, as far as she could tell, a rough triangle. She guesstimated. "Three days?"

"Then you will arrive there when the full moon sails the skies. While here in the city, it will be the eve of the Games, which last three days—time enough, I warrant, for you to ride the unicorn back to Goloth"—the man's eyes went wide with excitement—"and slay the king!" He focused on her again, his voice more urgent. "We will spread rumors of your sighting in the streets. Perchance you will get away clean, if you ride fast and sleep little."

*Great*, Elayne thought, an anticipatory soreness already in her butt.

"Come," said the man. "The maid must change."

He and Marc stepped away, and Elayne heard orders being softly given, felt the ship turning about as she ducked behind the canvas again. Quickly she stripped off her shift, rubbed herself down with a rag that was there—it smelled a little of fish, but what could she do? Then she slipped into the other clothes, which didn't fit too badly, pulled on the boots—which were way too big, so she took them off again and stuffed the toes with more fishy cloth. Not exactly comfy, but she'd be riding more than walking anyway.

Tucking her hair up under a cap, she stepped out of the shelter. The boat was already pulling into the docks on the far shore. The waxing moon was low in the sky, so it had to be quite close to dawn. There was no one around. Marc was in serious conversation with the other man. Noticing her, he came over, nodded his approval. "You make a good boy," he said.

"Thanks," she replied. "So do you."

They were dressed almost identically, two peas in a pod. Almost the same height too. "If we are questioned," he said, "we are brothers returning to our village. We have sold our produce for the feasts that will take place at the Games."

"Farm boys, eh? Okeydokey!"

Elayne slapped her thigh. Marc looked pained. "And you are simple," he said.

"There's no need to be rude."

"Nay, maid. I mean you are to let me talk for us both."

Elayne was tempted to surprise him with a burst of Dramach but held back. She watched the boatmen tying up at the dock, turned away, and grinned. She was nervous, still, of course. But she was out of that terrible dungeon. She wasn't going to be starved, tortured, chewed on by rats, or . . . God knows what else! She was going home.

She began to whistle under her breath. At last she'd said no to others and yes to herself. What could go wrong?

## TWENTY-ONE

# REUNION

Mist and silence. Nothing moved except the mist itself, swirling gray, chill, and damp before her, against her, all around her. Marc had gone to see if there was any end to the freezing cloud that had engulfed them three hours before. She'd told him not to. Apart from the mist, night was falling fast. How would he find his way back?

"My little friend does not need sight to guide him," he'd said, reaching down to stroke the fur between eyes that peeped out of his shirt. "Only leave the fish there upon the rock and he will find it."

A weasel! Just one of the many things Marc had bought— or stolen—for the journey. Aside from horses, exchanged for fresh ones in every village they'd passed through, some food, a rod to catch fish, and blankets, he'd mostly acquired weapons. A sword—"For man," he'd said. A bow with a sheaf of great

221

barbed arrows—"For the manticore." A long spear that had a small metal plate halfway up the shaft.

"For cockatrices," he'd replied when she'd questioned it. "If you stab one, its poison can go through the wooden shaft and kill you. Yet steel captures its venom."

"Cockatrices." She'd shuddered, remembering the half rooster, half lizard from the conning of the stream. Moonspill had told her not to look into its eyes, nor get close enough to sniff its breath. Death from both, apparently. "We are not going to meet any, are we?"

"Marry, I hope not. But if we do, there is this"—he'd hefted the spear—"and, more importantly, this!" Like a magician going "Ta-da," he'd opened his shirt. Two brown eyes had stared out.

"A rat!"

"A weasel," he'd said, rolling his own eyes. "Its bite can kill a cockatrice."

She'd pictured the huge chicken-lizard again. "That seems . . . unlikely."

"Nonetheless, 'tis true," he'd replied. "For every poison, there is an antidote. For every beast that kills, there is one that kills it."

*So here I am, with the weasel's treat of a stinking whole trout as my only companion.* Elayne shivered violently. She was wearing two cloaks—Marc had gallantly given her his—but it still wasn't enough. She'd considered stealing one of the horses' blankets, had already pressed herself against a warm flank for a while until the beast got spooked and backed off. *No,* she thought, *all I can do is sit, shiver . . . and curse.*

Because they were so close! When they were alone at the

fishing village, she'd told Marc their destination. He knew it—ancient hunting country, apparently—and for the next three days had led them toward it. She'd even seen the rock—Black Tusk, Moonspill had called it—in the distance before the mist swamped them.

She leaned down to peer at the trout on the rock. The trout peered back. Marc had caught three the day before. They'd eaten two, sushi-style. No fires, he said, in case of pursuit. She could still taste it—and wished she couldn't.

Crunch! A twig snapped, all thoughts washed away in sudden terror. Stumbling forward, she grabbed the spear. She wouldn't be able to see a cockatrice's eyes, so she was probably safe that way, and she tucked her mouth beneath her collar to avoid its exhalation. But if it was a manticore, she knew she was in deep—

Something ran up her leg. She gave a little shriek. But the weasel didn't stop. He leapt onto the rock and began to tear apart Elayne's companion, the trout.

The weasel had a harness attached to him. A leather lead ran off it. At its other end, ducking under her raised spear, came Marc.

"Could you call or something before you sneak up on me?" she hissed.

He sat. She'd thrown off his cloak when she grabbed the spear. He picked it up, covered himself, drew up his knees, shivered. "I did not call for fear that not only you would hear," he muttered.

"Good point, nicely presented." Elayne lowered the spear and her voice. "Well?"

He was a vague shape in the mist, but she could still see the shake of his head. "Nothing. I followed the stream a ways, thinking it might come out near Black Tusk. It vanished into the ground. Then I thought I heard . . . something. So I returned."

"Something?" She leaned forward. "That something could be Moonspill. Perhaps we should try a call?" She'd been calling him with her mind for ages now. No reply.

"Do not, maid. You may call upon a unicorn . . . but mayhap another beast will answer."

"Well . . ." Elayne chewed on her lip. "Do you think this mist will clear anytime soon?"

He shrugged. "It may, aye. But I have heard hunters tell of the mist that swallows these parts for days. It is said to be the first exhalation of cockatrice breath. The second is when he finds you, breathes again, and you are no more."

"Nice. Thanks." She'd discovered that Marc tended to really get into any mood he was in. An actor committing to the part, she supposed. So if he was happy, he'd frisk around, cracking jokes. Worried, and he'd get all serious and have this far-reaching stare. After three days, she found it pretty irritating. "So whaddya think, O great hunter? Do we just sit here and become a beast's breakfast? It's already dark. Somewhere up there, the full moon's on the rise. We have to do something."

Her tone riled him. "What, milady?" he said with false politeness. "For unless you can see through mist . . ."

"Well, at least if we move through it, we won't freeze to death," she snapped in return, raising the spear she still held, slicing its blade through the mist. "And furthermore— Oh!"

Elayne staggered, Marc dodging the spear that slipped from her fingers. It was the suddenness of it, as if someone had thrust a finger straight into her brain. But it wasn't painful, more a caress than a poke. It was just a word.

*Well.*

"Moonspill," she gasped.

Marc took a step toward her. "Is he here?" He looked spooked. "Did you hear something?"

Elayne felt before she heard—the vibration upon the turf, four cloven hooves taking off and landing, taking off and landing. "The unicorn," she said, her legs suddenly weak.

Then Moonspill split the mist, was there, rearing above them. It wasn't something she'd ever get used to—that incredible stallion's body, those eyes of fathomless blue, the horn pointing at the sky, piercing the mist.

"Moonspill!" she cried joyfully. But the boy beside her didn't. He knew they were there to meet a unicorn—and yet he shrieked, raised the spear he still held, lifting it high, its long blade and razored tip only a few feet from that huge white chest.

"No!" Elayne cried—to both of them, for Moonspill let out a roar, brought his horn down, smashed the spear aside, hooves raised instantly over Marc. She leapt between them, arms up. "No," she shouted again. "He's a friend. A friend!"

For a moment, Moonspill's hooves hung there, threatening still. Then he turned aside.

*No man of Goloth is a friend to the unicorn.*

Marc sagged behind her. *This one is. He guided me here.*

225

Marc was staring at her, jaw dropped. He could not hear what she heard so clearly. "I can . . . ," she began to explain.

Moonspill had backed away, tail swishing. He gave a snort, and thought-words interrupted her.

*Come. Mount. There is danger here.*

She took a step toward him. *Cockatrice?*

*Worse. Man.*

"Man?" she replied aloud. "Are you sure?"

*I am. Come.*

She'd reached Moonspill's flank when Marc cried out. "Maid, where do you go?"

She wasn't even going to think it. Not yet. "Goodbye," she called.

"But . . . maid!"

She turned back to Marc. He looked upset. *Of course,* she thought. *He expects me to tame the unicorn, ride it to the city.* "Don't worry," she said. "I'll . . . be back."

She hated lying to him then—but what could she do?

He ran to her. "Fare you well, Ee-layne," he said, using her name for the first time ever. "I hope . . . ." He blushed. "I hope that I have been of some service."

Instantly, she felt even more guilty. She wouldn't have made it without him. The prison break. The journey. He'd led her on a rein the whole way. And he was nice too, despite his moodiness. She turned back to face him. "Of course you have! Thank you. I—"

He shocked her then. He'd never so much as touched her hand. It just wasn't done between boy and girl in Goloth. Now, though, he threw his arms around her and held her in a great hug. "Fare you well, maid," he whispered close to her ear, patting her back.

"You. Too," Elayne replied, a little awkwardly. "Uh, gotta go!"

Marc nodded, sniffed, released her.

Moonspill had stooped, not even knelt. Elayne flung a leg across—and he was up, had her centered, was galloping in moments. And Marc was instantly forgotten as she gripped the mane in front of her.

The mist parted before them, clearing fast, like someone pulling back a veil. Elayne saw boulders, an expanse of green—and then, as if it had just been thrust up, that spire of rock, a great black finger pointing into the sky. At its knuckle, and on the rise, was a bulbous full moon.

*Yes!* From the moment they were joined, flesh to hide, mind to mind, Elayne was ecstatic.

She'd made it! Escaped from Leo, and the weavers too, from what people expected of her, demanded of her. She'd kept her rendezvous with Moonspill. And though she still had her fingers dug into his mane, gripping tight, she didn't even feel that scared anymore. Because anything was possible now. Anything—

Then the howl came. A breath-stopping, skin-chilling, mind-freezing wail. It came in three voices because it came from three heads.

"Cerberus?"

*Yes.* Moonspill slowed to a canter.

"But . . ." She managed a look back. Their gallop had taken them into a steep-sloped, wooded valley, shreds of mist hanging in the branches like blossoms. "What's it doing here?"

*Tracking you. The beast can track a sparrow through a forest in flames.*

A blast of horns came—and there was no time for Elayne to wonder, to question. No time to worry about destination. Not when scores of horsemen, each man bearing a torch, came pouring down the slopes like so many flaming comets. Every direction was afire—except straight ahead.

"On!" Elayne cried.

Moonspill needed no telling. He reared, plunged his forelegs down, was galloping in an instant. The valley narrowed. . . . There was something like an entrance ahead, where two boulders nearly touched.

They did not make it. A flaming wagon was pushed across, cutting it off. Behind it, men waved spears and shouted.

Moonspill swerved. There was the faintest trace of a path up the steep slopes, through the bracken, one only a goat could take. Or a unicorn, with a goat's cloven hooves. Up they flew. Once more she saw that huge thrust of rock. The top was lost again to gray, to the growing darkness—but they were approaching the base of Black Tusk for sure. Farther along it she knew that a forest path led down to the place she most wanted to be.

Elayne laughed. It was just like the time they'd eluded the hunters before. They were going to make it. They were going to—

Then a thought came, ending her laughter: *Surely hunters learn?*

They crested the slope—and she saw instantly that they had. There was the path, dropping steeply down, winding between tightly packed trees. They were on it before they could stop . . . and plunging along an avenue of wood and glass. For in the gaps between every trunk, mirrors had been set up, and their reflections now gave chase on either side.

*He is clever, the hunter-king.*

She felt the dullness of Moonspill's thought, felt his pace slacken, heard the hunters' cries double at the sight. The path was so steep here, she knew that if she tried what she'd done once before, tried to climb his neck and block his sight, she was sure to tumble straight over Moonspill's head. But she hadn't come this far to be stopped now. Grabbing fistfuls of mane, she lifted both heels and jabbed down hard. "Go!" she screamed.

It was not his top speed. Perhaps he was only as fast as a fast horse then. But for a few moments, Moonspill's hooves flew, powering them down the path, which leveled now, went straight. She looked ahead and saw . . . the dead oak, recognized its silver, blackened trunk from that brief glimpse before. It stood over a fork in the path, two lightning-withered branches like arms, pointing two different ways. One led to the left, away to open country. She and Moonspill had taken that path before. Now it was blocked by the largest mirror yet. The other path led slightly up, into a bowl of land. It was unblocked. It was where the hunters wanted them to go.

Even at Moonspill's reduced speed, they would be at the fork in moments. But Elayne's mind was weirdly calm, moving slowly, as if she had all the time in the world.

A fork in the path. A choice. The ground was more level here, so perhaps she could manage to climb his neck, block his sight with her hands, guide him through the mirror, smashing it aside with lowered horn. They'd outrun any pursuit in the wilds of Goloth.

But Elayne did not move. She let him shy away from the large mirror and his double there, let him go straight on where the traps of the hunters directed them—into the bowl, the scoop of land she remembered, with sides so steep not even a unicorn could climb them. For once, the hunters' wishes and her own were the same. Because, at the bowl's far end, one last tree stood. An oak tree.

*The* oak tree.

She knew where she was going. But it must have been a shock to Moonspill, coming drowsy from the avenue of his reflections. He drove his hooves into the earth, halting his charge so suddenly that Elayne shot forward onto his neck, lost her grip, tumbled onto the leaf-strewn ground. Winded, she lay there for a second, before struggling onto her knees. *Up,* she thought. *On.*

And then she found she couldn't stand, couldn't move. Because the walls of the bowl began to ripple and shift. It took her a long moment to realize why that was.

They came sailing down, unfurling. Veils: One. Ten. A hundred. Blanketing the slopes, covering every part of them. Elayne saw a thousand moons reflected in the tiny mirrors that were stitched onto the hanging cloths. Saw a thousand Moonspills with drooping heads. A thousand Elaynes.

It was too bright. She tried to look away from it, but there *was* no away, trapped as they were by mirrors and moons and unicorns.

Then a man spoke, and she could hear the laughter in his voice.

"They claim I will not change things. That I will not bring the new. And yet see my newest invention! I did little think that I would find such a perfect place to use them."

Elayne turned back to the way they'd come, to the one way in and out of the bowl. At first, she thought there was something wrong with her sight, that three armored men came forward, two of them walking backward. Until she realized these two were held in mirrors—reflections of the one man facing forward, the one who had just spoken.

Leo.

He gestured. A servant stepped up and threw something that landed with a jingle at Elayne's feet. "It is bridle, blind, and mask together," Leo continued. "Bewitched though he is, he is not yet tamed. None but a maiden may put it on him, and live. Do so, maid." He stretched out his hand toward her. "Do so—then come and claim your reward."

She couldn't help herself, stunned as she was. She bent, picked up the leather, cloth, and metal apparatus. She saw that it would enclose his head, thrust steel in his mouth while two raised cups would cover his eyes. Inside them she saw mirrored glass, knew that the little light that came through slits in the top of the cups would show him to himself, would bind him, finally, completely. The length of heavy canvas, the size of a jacket, would trail down his neck once the hideous device was in place. This had more straps, where reins would no doubt be fitted.

She lifted it . . . and the beginning of an idea came. She moved around to Moonspill's huge white shoulder. She paused there, looked back at the king and all his reflections.

"Why do you wait, maid?" Leo's voice had lost its smile.

Jumping, she gripped the mane with her left hand. She had the muzzle in her right, and she used the momentum of the jump to fling its canvas end around, not over, Moonspill's head. She pulled the material tight, blinding him . . . and at the same time jabbed her left heel hard down into his flank. She may have hated riding—but she had spent most of her time in Goloth on horseback.

Moonspill lurched, turned. "Yah," she yelled.

Leo bellowed, "Take them! They cannot escape from here."

But he was wrong. There was another way out. It needed only a touch of a unicorn's horn. Not the one around her neck. Not with five feet of ivory thrust out before them.

*Straight,* she thought, and Moonspill went straight, fast, covering the last few yards of the gully in a heartbeat, plunging into the oak tree.

For a microsecond there was resistance, and she thought she'd got it wrong, thought that they were going to crash, die. But then the resistance melted. The void they leapt into was dark, as dark as any dungeon. They flew, or fell, she couldn't tell which, plunging on, through branch, leaf, wool, spun silk . . .

. . . into New York.

# TWENTY-TWO

# A UNICORN IN MANHATTAN

*None but the unicorn knows the true power of reflection.*

*There! In the glass, in my eyes, they are waiting. All of them are waiting.*

*I have heard it in the thoughts of those humans I have been close to. In the blue depths of my eyes, they see a universe, a million stars cascading into infinity.*

*I see history.*

*In the mirrors of my eyes, the stories wait. A thousand tales of adventure, of love, of despair and triumph. The tales of every ancestor that ever raised horn and roared a challenge to the world. These are not just remembered. If they were, how easy to simply look away?*

*These stories live.*

*In the glade of the oak tree, a Lion seeks to bind me. What do I care? When I look into my thousand reflected eyes, he is gone. Everything is gone. For I am there.*

*I am there, I am Bucephalus, with Alexander the Great upon my back, horn plunging, hooves flailing, shattering the Persian ranks.*

*I am there, I am Ambrosius, lowering the spear-struck Arthur into the hands of those who would bear him to Avalon.*

*I am there, I am Salvia, waiting as the Maid of Orleans lays down her scythe, lifts her sword, mounts me, and drives the English from France.*

*I am there, I am myself, the last unicorn, climbing the mountains of the world, in search of legends.*

*All this in a mirror. If I could choose, still I would not look away. Why would I, when I am lost in wonders?*

*Every beast that breathes has one flaw, one weakness. This is the unicorn's. To be trapped in glass, truly lost in reflection. The Lion who hunts me, with his armor and bright spear, is gone. They will bring cords to bind me. They will kill me in their arena. All that is slipping away. Because there, in my eyes, I ride as Bucephalus. . . .*

*But then something comes between me and my reflections. I want to shake it off, to be drowsy with stories. Yet, in the part of my mind that returns now, I remember who is upon my back.*

*It is the girl. The Summoned. My small hope lived in her, even when she was lost. And now she has found me again.*

*She found me. So I will choose to heed her. I will go where she guides me.*

*Wherever that may be.*

* * *

Elayne felt cloth, parting before her face. *No*, she thought, *not parting*. But they were jumping through it anyway, through some gap, some slit in the warp and the weft.

Then she was flying—over Moonspill's head! Grabbing the horn with both hands, she clutched desperately as his hooves skittered on the wooden floor. He jerked to a stop, and Elayne released her grip, crumpled onto the floor, gasped, looked around.

The room was lit by a single red bulb high up in the ceiling. Moonspill was standing before one of the tapestries, a vast whiteness in the room. His thought came. *Is this the Duc de Carisac's castle? It was for him these tapestries were woven.*

"Castle? No, no. This is the Cloisters."

*Cloisters?* He swung his head. *Where are the monks?*

"Not 'cloisters' like that. I mean . . ." She faltered. How do you explain a museum to a unicorn?

He shivered. *But we have crossed back into the world of man?*

"Yes."

He turned to stare at her, his eyes narrowing. The question took a while to come. *Why?*

There was no single answer—and no way she could answer any questions now. "Look," she said, "we have got to get out of here."

*Why?*

"Because there are hunters here too," she said desperately.

Where could she take a unicorn in Manhattan? It was obviously nighttime, it was dark, and there was no one in the galleries. Yet the whole place had to be full of alarms, didn't it? She wondered why none had gone off yet. Maybe they

235

were only on the outside doors? There had to be security, though, and they hadn't exactly been quiet.

She felt something was missing. *The muzzle*, she remembered. But it must have been ripped from Moonspill's eyes in their passage through the tree, because it wasn't there. "Come on," she said softly, rising shakily to her feet. "Let's get out of here."

She hadn't paid much attention when she'd come there with her class. "This way," she guessed. She went up to the doorway, Moonspill following, his hooves clacking on the wooden floor. "Can you be qui—?" she started to say. But then she heard voices. "Shh!" She halted, listened. They weren't close, but they were definitely there. Taking a breath, she peered around the doorframe.

She was gazing down another hall, another beyond that. They were both quite dark, lit by single red bulbs. But beyond the second one, there was more light. That's where the voices were coming from. *The Main Hall*, she thought. She vaguely remembered a high-roofed room with columns, a ticket desk, a bookstore on its far side. It was the way her class had come in.

She hesitated. But it was the only way out she knew. "Follow me," she whispered, then remembered. If she couldn't do anything about his hooves on the floor, at least she didn't have to speak. *Slowly*, she thought.

She led, he followed. They crossed the first room, paused at the doorway that led to the second. She could see it was a longer hall, with statues, other tapestries on the walls. And she could also see into the Main Hall.

There was one guy crouched on the ground, wearing overalls that said "Watchdog Systems." Another man, in a black uniform, was standing above him. *Security guard,* she thought.

"So can you or can't you?" he said.

The crouching guy scratched his chin. "By opening time? Jeez, I don't know."

"This was supposed to be fixed last week."

"And it was—this is a different internal circuit. I just gotta track it down. Don't worry, exterior alarms will be fine." He laughed. "No one's going to be breaking in here."

*But what about out?* Elayne thought.

"OK," the guard sighed. "I guess I'll have to check everything on foot. If I'm not back, just make sure you lock the front door and reset the alarm before you leave here."

"Sure, sure."

Elayne held her breath . . . but the guard went the other way out of the hall. The crouching guy began searching through his toolbox. "Damn!" he cussed, stood, called, "Hey!" He waited but got no reply. He hesitated. Then, shrugging, he turned, headed the opposite way from the guard . . . out the main door.

*Have we just got very lucky?* she wondered. *Quick!* She began walking on tiptoe between the statues. Moonspill clacked behind her. Halting, she peered out into the Main Hall at the various exits to other parts of the museum. No guard. She looked right. Stairs led down. A cold breeze was blowing through an open door.

"Come on!" Her excitement made her say it out loud. She

ran down the stairs, unicorn close behind. A stone passage sloped down about twenty feet, three tall stone openings on its left. An icy wind blew through them, and beyond was the forecourt of the museum . . .

. . . covered in snow! Deep snow, banks of it, with more falling. When she'd left New York, a blizzard had been forecast. But the city must have been hit by a series of them while she was gone.

Elayne spotted a gray van, with the alarm company logo on it, and she could hear objects being pulled around inside. There was a low stone wall beyond it. Her feet silent on the snow, Elayne crossed to it, climbed up, beckoned Moonspill nearer. When he was close, she scrambled aboard.

A curving drive descended before them. She thought she remembered seeing cobbles, but if she had, they were now covered in snow, so Moonspill's hooves would make no sound. The man must have heard something, though. "You there?" he called.

"Let's ride," she whispered.

*Whither?* he thought, moving slowly toward the road.

There was only one place she wanted to be now. *Home.*

They were moving down the drive. But at its bottom— where would they be? She lived in the Meatpacking District, way downtown. The Cloisters were far uptown, at 190th or so. That was . . . 175 city blocks, minimum. A long way, even on something that moved faster than a Harley.

Thick flakes of snow were driving against her, borne on that icy wind. She was still wearing the boy's clothes she'd put on in Goloth. It was freezing!

At the end of the drive was a roadway. Across it, trees.

*Which way?*

"Um . . ." She'd lived in New York all her life. But the night and the snow were confusing her. She knew she wanted to go south—but which way was that?

Moonspill turned in a circle, hooves plowing up the snow. As they spun, she glimpsed some lights. A car approaching? They couldn't just stand there, waiting to get caught in its beams. "There!" she said with a confidence she didn't feel.

Across the road, a path on the other side went down, switchbacking through a wooded park. For a few moments, she felt they were safe, hidden by trees and falling snow. But then the path ended, at a playground, a road beyond it.

Moonspill halted. Elayne looked up and down. Where the hell were they? It had to be the middle of the night; in a snowstorm, so there was hardly anyone around. Then to her right she saw a dark figure moving slowly up the sidewalk. Since she had no better ideas, she thought she might as well go the opposite way.

Moonspill followed her thought—which was just as well, as she really had no idea how to steer him! She sought through the falling snow for a landmark, a street sign, any- thing to give her a clue where she was. She bit her lip— which, in the cold, bled instantly.

And then she saw the signs. A big one first, which at least told her north and south, the 9A highway going either way. Then, as they got closer, she saw a much smaller sign beneath the big one—and the words made her heart accelerate: "NYC Greenway."

The greenway! It was a cycle and pedestrian path, and she had biked it a few times with her dad. Not this far uptown, though; she'd never have guessed it ran all the way up to the Cloisters. But she knew it ran down the west side of Manhattan, along the Hudson River.

*Go up there.*

They climbed steps . . . and then they were on a path, the highway running beside it. *Now just go,* she thought. And they went, snow and darkness shrouding them. Hooves ate distance. The path ran down to the water, then soon passed beneath a huge structure in the sky.

*What is that?* came Moonspill's voice in her head.

*Bridge,* Elayne thought, as they galloped beneath it. *George Washington Bridge.*

His thought replied, *And what is upon the bridge? What are these creatures that follow their lampshine into the night?*

*Creatures? Oh, you mean the cars?*

How could she explain cars? Did anything have a motor back in the medieval times he was used to? A windmill? She was trying to think—when Moonspill suddenly rose up on his rear legs, roaring a challenge at another creature with a lamp, this one hurtling toward them.

They'd come to a narrow section between the river and a railway track—and along that came a train, its single bright beam a monstrous eye, piercing the falling snow. Elayne didn't know if the driver saw them, but a horn sounded immediately, a deep roar that had Moonspill almost leaping the fence for the fight.

"Stop!" she shouted. "No! It's not a creature; it's . . ." The train began to pass them. Freight, fortunately. She didn't know how she'd have coped with scores of peering passengers. "It's like . . . like a cart, but it drives itself."

She knew it was lame. But Moonspill's forelegs dropped back onto the ground. *It does not threaten us?*

"No." She shivered as the cars trundled past. "It's just a machine. Can we move again? Keep on this path."

He took off, straight into his gallop. The path went under tracks and bridges, widened into parkland and basketball courts, narrowed to a track close to the water. Above, apartment towers loomed on the tops of cliffs. They sped through the snowy silence. The cold, the speed were making her giddy. *I'm home from my vacation,* she thought, *and I've brought back a unicorn!*

They emerged into more open ground, and the big river piers began. She saw signs. "Twelfth Avenue." "Fifty-seventh Street." Cars were creeping along both. She sensed a "Whither?" coming.

*Straight. And, Moonspill?*

*Maid?*

"If you can go any faster, um . . . do?"

*Hold fast.*

*It's a funny thing with speed,* she thought to herself. *The faster you go, the slower it seems.* She could only really tell by the way the snow now stung when it hit her. The few faces she saw were a blur of features. She could only assume she looked the same to them, that anyone who saw them was shocked enough by a huge white horse galloping past. The horn would have been a blur too. Elayne clung tight—and

241

shook her head. She'd had some surreal experiences recently. Riding a unicorn in New York City was right up there.

Piers passed, ships at dock, a huge liner. There. Gone. Moonspill flicked his head at the sudden, unmistakable scent of horse manure . . . and she remembered, from bike rides, that the police had stables on the Hudson. As the road angled left, she saw it, the huge bulk of the Chelsea Piers on their right. "Slower!" she yelled. Moonspill obeyed but didn't stop, slowing enough for blur to become substance.

"We're close," she yelled. A door opened in a store, someone backlit. "Not close enough. Go!"

Elayne counted to twenty. Figured it was enough to cover eight blocks. "Slow!" she shouted. Moonspill dropped into a canter, and she saw the sign. "A little farther. Now . . . left!" Moonspill swung across the wide avenue . . . and into Gansevoort Street.

Her street. They were going down it the wrong way, but she didn't think that mattered too much at this time of night. On a unicorn.

There were still a few places where people packed meat in the Meatpacking District. Mainly, it was a place for New Yorkers to come and party—and for people like her dad and her to live. He'd been an architect on a warehouse conversion project and had liked it enough to buy a small apartment for them. But no meatpackers, tourists, or residents were around this snowy night. Guiding Moonspill into the alley at the back of her building, she stopped him halfway down and slid off.

"Whoa!" Her legs had gone boneless. Leaning against his

heaving flank—*Wow!* she thought, *even he's tired!*—she gradually got her breath, her legs, back. Then she staggered over to the big metal-slat gate. It was padlocked to the ground. Her keys, and everything else she'd had, had been lost when she was sucked into Goloth. But long ago Elayne had acknowledged her amazing ability to lose anything she owned. So even though it was forbidden, she had a fallback.

Kneeling, she dug her finger into the decaying mortar between two bricks. There was just enough space there for . . .

The key dropped into the snow. She worked the lock with her frozen fingers, then threw up the iron gate. It rose with that distinctive clanging as the slats rolled up. She stepped inside. Stood there for a moment, taking deep breaths. She couldn't believe it. She'd never been happier to be home. And she hoped that maybe, just maybe, someone else was too. "Come on!" she cried, heading for the stairs.

He didn't follow. She turned back. Moonspill was watching her. And Malachi was watching Moonspill.

## TWENTY-THREE

# HOME

Malachi.

He wasn't always there. He called at least three alleys home. But theirs was his favorite on particularly cold nights because the Lebanese restaurant that backed onto it stayed open late, had a kitchen vent that pumped out hot air and an Arab chef who was generous with leftovers. Malachi had one of the more interesting diets among the homeless in the city, mainly consisting of hummus, stuffed grape leaves, and kebabs.

Malachi looked at the unicorn, Moonspill looked at Elayne, she looked at Malachi. For a while, none of them spoke. Then Malachi did.

"Shoot! Ain't seen one of them in a *lonnnnng* time."

Moonspill had turned to the threat, head lowering. Elayne stepped hastily forward, thinking, *Might as well take the bull by the horns . . . horn . . . uh, unicorn.* "Where did you last see one, Malachi?"

He scratched his thick, curling beard. "Over there, princess." He waved vaguely. "Damn thing was pink, though."

"Pink? Uh-huh." She shivered. "Listen, Mal—"

*My mother's sister was a shade of pink.*

Moonspill thought it. Elayne heard it, of course. But, to her immense shock, it was Malachi who replied to it. "Was she? She was real friendly. Promised I could stroke her next time." He rose from his cardboard nest, started to shout. "She never came back!" He glared. "No one ever comes back!"

Malachi was harmless. But he saw things others didn't, including pink unicorns, and sometimes they made him angry. He'd yell for a long time. "Hey," Elayne called gently, stepping forward, raising a hand to calm him.

*You can stroke me, if you will.*

Elayne stopped. Malachi squinted. "For real?"

*Yes.*

"Moonspill, you don't have to—"

*He is wounded, is he not?*

"'Wounded'?" She shrugged. "Yes, I suppose he is."

*Then let him . . . stroke.*

She didn't know if Malachi heard them. But he tottered forward, suspicion in his eyes, a dirt-encrusted hand thrust before him. It fell on the white flank.

*Peace.*

Elayne remembered how Moonspill had once said that to her, during her terrifying arrival in Goloth. Remembered how it had helped.

It helped here. "Good boy," the homeless man mumbled, his hand moving up and down. "Good old boy!"

He began to hum. Elayne vaguely recognized some old soft rock song from the radio. "'Take it easy,'" he sang.

More snow fell. Then Malachi suddenly turned, lurched away, tumbled again into his nest, pulling cardboard and old blankets over himself until only his head, topped by the woolen ski cap her dad had given him, peeked out. "Take it easy," he called, closing his eyes.

They looked at him for a moment. *Should we not bring him to shelter?*

Elayne shook her head. "He wouldn't come. We've tried before—even just inside for a shower. He won't do it."

Moonspill's great head nodded. *Then let us find some. For I am cold.*

Elayne was surprised yet again. She'd thought he was coldproof. But she wasn't. The unicorn followed as she turned back into the bay that was the lower floor of their home. She pulled the slatted door down, padlocked it. They didn't have a car; they just used this space for storage. There were stairs to the side, and she led Moonspill up. She knew from the Cloisters that stairs were not his favorite thing. But he managed.

Outside the loft door, she hesitated. If her dad was there, she didn't want to startle him awake by knocking—and startle him again with Moonspill. So she reached up above the doorframe. She had another illicit key stashed there. "Home," she said, opening the door, stepping through.

He followed her in. Elayne could see right away that the place hadn't been lived in. It was exactly as she'd left it, cereal box out, dishes in the sink. Still, she checked her dad's bedroom just in case. He wasn't there, and his bed hadn't been slept in.

Though she was cold and wet, she went straight to the kitchen, to the light flashing on the phone. Dreading it, she picked it up, dialed the number, tapped in the code. She expected there to be a gazillion messages.

There were just four. The first dated from over a week ago. It was a woman's voice. She was from St. Vincent's Hospital and was asking her to please call Dr. Sadowski immediately. The second was a day later, same woman, same message, more urgently delivered. The third was two days after that and from a man—Dr. Sadowski himself. He asked her to call ASAP. He sounded pissed. And he added that her father's condition had worsened.

"Worsened?" Despite all the treatments, the leukemia was steadily poisoning his blood. It had affected him in different ways. He'd lost a lot of weight; he ached. And the chemo had been rough. He'd been bad the last time he went in, hallucinating. Some people reacted to the new drugs that way, apparently.

The final message was dated yesterday. Another woman, different voice. Gentler, calming. "This is a message for Elayne. This is Caroline, from the Compassion Hospice. We have made your father comfortable, and he is sleeping a lot. But when he is awake, he is asking for you. Would you please call me just as soon as you get this message?"

She dictated a number, but Elayne didn't hear it. *Hospice? Wasn't that where they sent people to die?*

*What is that?*

"Uh, a moment." This wasn't the time to explain a telephone to a unicorn. And her brain was numb. She managed to replay the message, write the number down, dial. After three rings, it went to a recording. "You've reached the Compassion Hospice. We're so sorry, no one can take your call right now. If you'd like to—" She clicked, hit Redial.

*You are sad.*

*Yes.*

*Your father is wounded too.*

*Yes, he is. He has cancer. His blood's . . . poisoned. He's in . . . a kind of hospital. I am trying to call—*

She stopped, stared at Moonspill, his flanks still heaving. Listened to the ringing.

"We're so sorry, no one can take your call right now." She clicked the receiver off.

Her dad had been in the hospice less than a day. Chances were that he might have deteriorated but he wasn't—she swallowed—dead.

The phone was still in her hand. She put it back in its cradle. Though part of her wanted to just rush to the hospice, she knew there was no point. Not unless . . .

All her trials in Goloth had brought her to this moment: to a unicorn in Manhattan and her father dying. So now, clearly, slowly, Elayne thought her desire.

*Will you take the poison from my father's blood?*

He stared at her for a long time, tail twitching, breathing shallow. *Is this why you have brought me back to the world of man?*

She decided to speak rather than just think it. It felt as if he wasn't in her head so much that way. "Well, I . . . I *was* trying to get you away from . . ." She faltered, remembering her choice back in the valley of the tree, then blurted out, "My father's dying."

The loft had a high ceiling . . . but his horn scraped it as he rose on his rear legs, smacked into the hanging lamp, sending it swinging wildly, the light passing back and forth over them. And even if the loft was big, it was not big enough to contain the roar that had Elayne clutching her ears in a pathetic attempt to shut it out. But her hands could do nothing to stop his words.

*You . . . brought me here? Dared to return me to the world I'd left forever? Dared to take me from the world where I am so needed?*

If thoughts could shout, they shouted now. . . .

*You dared to interfere with destiny?*

Terrifying though his anger was, Elayne had had enough. "*You* dared!" she shouted back. "Dared to yank me from my world, where I am just as needed as you are in yours. And as for 'destiny,' who are you to decide *my* destiny?" Her voice sank. "The only thing I care about is my dad."

For a long moment, they glared at each other. Till he dropped onto four hooves, lowered his horn, looked away. It took a while before his next thought came. *It is true. I summoned you for my need. A similar one to yours, it seems. For we both desire to save the one we love. And we both believe it to be near impossible.*

The words in her head were colored with incredible sadness. Her anger vanished, and she couldn't stop herself. She went to him, laid a hand on his shoulder. His tail flicked, but he did not back away.

"You never told me what your . . . your need was," she whispered.

*The opportunity never came.*

*Tell me now,* she thought to him. *It's to do with your mate, isn't it?*

He took a breath. *What do you know of her?*

*Not much. Leo told me he had a female unicorn in his dungeons, ready for the Games. But that he'd prefer to kill you.*

Moonspill lowered his great head. *He would. I had thought of offering myself in her stead. But I know man. He would take me, bind me . . . then kill two unicorns instead of one.*

Elayne thought of Leo and knew Moonspill was right. *So what was plan B?*

*Pardon?*

She had to smile. *What did you think you'd do?*

*Think . . . is what I had to do. I could not storm a city. I knew that if I got close, and any tried to capture me—and they would—the red rage would take me. I would be lost to it. And if I could not think, however great my strength, however many I killed, I would die in their streets and my Heartsease would die in their arena. I had to find something beyond the rage.* He looked at her fully again. *And then I remembered a maiden, and a promise she made, not just for herself but for the centuries: to come if my need was dire. I remembered what I had felt in her.*

*What was it you felt?*

He paused. *Someone worthy of kneeling before.*

"Kneeling before?" She spoke her thought, remembering when she'd first got to Goloth, how he'd knelt and laid his head on her chest, seeking . . . "You thought the answer lay in being 'tamed.'"

*Yes.* He gave a snort. *If other myths of man's world were true in Goloth, why not that one? Surely that was what my ancestors must have permitted when they had allowed themselves to be ridden for a time?* He sighed. *I thought that if one like her tamed me, with her mind and spirit and my strength and daring, then perhaps together . . .*

Elayne shook her head. *But taming wasn't what you thought, was it?*

*No. It was not even the surrender I feared it to be. It was not . . . anything.*

*And anyway, I wasn't my ancestor, was I? I wasn't . . . worthy?*

He didn't reply. Didn't need to. She turned away from him, from his disappointment. She stood by the window, watching the snow fall.

*Yet there were two promises made that day,* Moonspill thought. *And if the one cannot be kept, perhaps the other can.*

She turned back, fast, flushed, blurted it out loud. "Do you mean . . . ?"

*Yes. One love saved . . . perhaps. I am not at the height of my powers*—he took a rasping breath—*but I will try.*

No words came to her, and all thoughts were lost. She

could only move, fling her arms around his lowered neck, sob into the whiteness of his mane. He let her cling there and did not move until she breathed deep, stepped back. Only then did he turn toward the door.

*Take me to your father.*

TWENTY-FOUR

# THE KIDNAP

Any sounds from the street were distant, muffled in snow. Huge snowflakes were still falling past the window from a pal-ing sky. New York was out there, about to wake up.

Moonspill moved toward the door. "Wait!" she said, reach-ing beneath her tunic, searching. "I was wondering if the . . . the horn you gave me could be, you know, powered up? Maybe I could take that to him? It would be way easier—"

His thought interrupted her. *That is not possible.*

She couldn't find the chain. "What? Where . . . ?" She pulled the shirt out, waited for something to fall. Nothing did. The piece of unicorn's horn was gone. She turned to Moon-spill. "Oh my God. I've lost it."

He looked at her for a moment. *It does not matter. Its power lay only in the opening of doorways. It could not heal.* He had reached the door. *Shall we go to him?*

"Wait! I have to think!" Annoyed—*How could I have lost*

*the horn? When?*—she considered her options. The kitchen clock showed that it was already 6:15. It would be getting light soon. People would be around, snowstorm or not. How could she get a unicorn to . . . She didn't even know where the hospice was.

She ran into the kitchen, grabbed the phone book. The Yellow Pages listed "Hospices." There were a surprising number. She found "Compassion." Just four blocks away. She looked up. "You know," she said, "I think it would be better if he came to us."

*   *   *

A discreet brass plate on the front pillar said "Compassion." Other than that, and the wheelchair ramp to the front door, the brownstone looked exactly like any other on the street.

She'd called again. This time someone had answered. A nurse, surprised and delighted to hear from her. Yes, she could come now. No, her father wasn't . . . critical, not yet. They had him on high doses of morphine, which managed the pain but meant he mostly slept. She'd reduce the morning dose so Elayne would be able to talk with him, a little anyway. Give her half an hour to tidy him up, she'd said.

At 6:45 exactly, Elayne pushed the doorbell. She waited, looking up and down the street. There were few people out, fewer cars. The plows had been through, so she'd walked the whole way on the street, because the sidewalks were still thick with snow. But she wasn't that cold, not in her down ski jacket. After a hot shower and wearing her own clean clothes—she could take on anything!

The door opened. "Welcome," said the nurse, who was dressed not in a uniform but in a blouse and slacks. Only a small badge proclaiming her "Beatrice Whalley, RN" gave her away. She was black, middle-aged, with a large, open face. The hand she held out was big, the handshake firm. "Come! Come!" she said, keeping Elayne's hand, drawing her in, her accent the singsong of the Caribbean. She stood aside. "Stamp your feet there, honey. Get off all that snow. Brr! How I wish I was in Saint Kitts today, let me tell you."

Suddenly Elayne was really nervous. "I-I'm . . ." she stammered.

"So you are the lost child, eh? And why have you not come to see your father before, girl?" She scolded, but her voice was gentle, and she was shaking the hand she still held. "Well, never mind, never mind," she continued. "You're here now, that's the important thing. Come on, then."

Elayne stamped off the last of the snow, wiped her feet, then followed the nurse past a front room filled with books and magazines, and down a long hall to the back of the house. There was a little sitting room there, opening onto a glassed-in conservatory full of house plants. "The garden," Beatrice declared. "Bit chilly out the back now"—she gestured, to bushes shrouded in white—"but nice in here, is it not?" There were three doors onto the sitting room, all closed. She went to one of them. "And here . . . ," she said, "is your father." She knocked, then pushed open the

255

door. "Here we are, then, Alan. Here's that naughty girl of yours!"

Elayne took a deep breath and went in—to a room that was like any other cozy bedroom—except for the stand of plastic bags and IVs, the monitor on the bedside table, the wheelchair folded beside it. And the patient, of course.

He lay there, not looking noticeably different than he had ten days before—still sick as hell. But his eyes lit up when he saw her. "Elayne!" he cried weakly.

"Dad!" She rushed over, slid between tubes and machinery to hug him. *So skinny*, she thought.

"I'll leave you to it," said the nurse, turning to go.

The first sight had taken Elayne's breath. She just wanted to fall on the bed and weep. But four blocks away, a unicorn waited. "Wait! Could we—" She hesitated, then looked again at the wheelchair. "Is he well enough to sit in that . . . out there"—she pointed back—"so we can look at the garden?"

"Well . . ." The nurse checked her watch. "The day staff are coming in ten minutes, and I am meant to—"

"Please?"

The nurse looked at her for a moment, then smiled. "OK, child. Now help me here, Alan." In a series of simple moves, Beatrice had him up and into the chair, a blanket tucked around him. "He's all yours, girl."

Elayne pushed her father into the sitting room. As they arrived, a door opened upstairs and a woman's voice called out. "Beatrice! I need your help."

The nurse frowned, then smiled at Elayne. "You two have a nice visit," she said. "I'll be back soon."

256

She headed up the stairs. The door closed, cutting off voices. Elayne and her father looked at each other again.

"Where have you been, daughter of mine?"

"Long, *long* story." She took a deep breath. "Come on, Dad. I'm taking you home."

## TWENTY-FIVE

# CONNING

The first minute was tough—clearing the wheelchair ramp of snow with her boots, terrified that the day staff was going to show up any second. But once they were on the street, things went smoothly. She only had to push the wheelchair to the side twice to let cars pass. Driven by the terror that he might die from the shock of the cold, despite her ski jacket tucked around him, Elayne sprinted the four blocks home in four minutes.

There was a freight elevator at one end of the building. She took it, ran down the corridor to the front door they rarely used, unlocked it, pushed it open.

"Honey, I'm home," she called excitedly. She'd pulled it off! She'd brought a unicorn to Manhattan. She'd sprung her dad. Now all she had to do was introduce them. "Moonspill?"

No reply came. Apart from the faint humming of the

furnace, there was no sound. Wheeling her dad in a few feet, she stopped, let the door swing shut behind her. Where was he? The loft was large but open-plan. So unless he'd gone to take a nap in a bedroom . . . "Hello?"

Then she saw him—and realized at the same moment that the humming she'd heard wasn't the heating. It was him—Moonspill, lying between the sofas, his horn resting on the coffee table. "What the—" she said, stepping forward, shocked. She'd never seen him off his feet. His sides were moving, his breath making the sound she'd heard. Not a hum, now that she listened to it closer.

Moonspill was wheezing.

"What is it?" Elayne ran over to him.

*Air.*

"You want me to open the window?" She turned—but his thought stopped her.

*No. It is the air of this place. This world. What has man done to the air?*

"I . . ." What could she tell him? He'd left the world five hundred years before. A lot of crap had been thrown into the atmosphere since then. "Um, will you be OK? What can I do?"

*I will recover. I just needed to rest. I—*

Moonspill's thoughts, his voice in her head, were interrupted by another voice. "Tell me something, Alice-Elayne. Wherever did you find a unicorn?"

Her father was leaning forward in the wheelchair, his sunken eyes wide in astonishment. Elayne ran to him. "Dad, this is Moonspill."

259

"Moonspill? From Goloth? From our family story?" His eyes were bright. "Now *this* is what I call a hallucination!" He wheezed a laugh.

"Moonspill's not a hallucination, Dad. He's . . ." Elayne stopped again, no adequate words coming. Then her father suddenly strained farther forward, his eyes fluttering. After a moment, he said, "Yes. Yes, I will." And fell back.

His forehead was cold, clammy to the touch. She grabbed a pillow from the sofa, put it behind his head. Moonspill still lay there. "What did you say to him?" she asked, tucking her ski jacket up around her dad's neck.

*Only to rest. That all will be well.*

"And will it?" Suddenly she wasn't sure. Her father was slumped before her, his breath coming in little pants. Behind her lay Moonspill, his flanks heaving up and down. She was caught between a cancerous man and an asthmatic unicorn. If she hadn't been so terrified, she'd have laughed.

*Your father is very sick. And I am not . . . well.*

"But you *can* cure him, right?" Elayne was trying to keep the panic from her voice. After all that had happened! "You cured my ancestor."

*Beneath the poison, the weaver was strong. Your father is weak.*

"Are you saying"—she swallowed—"that the cure might kill him?"

*Perhaps.*

She hadn't thought of that. She looked beyond him, to the tall windows and the snow that had started to fall again.

Somewhere, a siren sounded, an ambulance rushing to someone else's aid. It trailed off into the distance, and in the sound she remembered all the ambulances that had taken her dad, the doctors who had worked so hard, the treatments that had given hope, the failures that had taken hope away. She looked at him, his wasted body, his tortured breath . . . and could only think of one thing to say, one word.

"Please."

Moonspill stood, lifting his horn from the table as if it were a great weight. Shaking himself, he joined her before the wheelchair.

*Do you love him very much?*

*Of course. He is my father.*

*It does not always follow.*

Tears came in a rush. "I love him beyond everything," she sobbed aloud. "It's always been just the two of us."

*Now there will be three.*

Moonspill knelt, as he would to bid her ride. Elayne threw off the ski jacket, and he laid his horn first on the shoulder, then slowly slid it till the tip was resting against her father's heart. For a moment, she was scared that Moonspill would slip, that ivory would plunge in and end her father's torment another way. But his horn was like a delicate nibbed pen, reaching out to fine paper.

Her dad's chest was reddened, as if fires raged there. His eyes shot open now, staring wildly at someplace beyond them all. He leaned forward, pressing flesh to bone. "Yes," he murmured. "Yes."

Moonspill's eyes were closed, as if he slept. Then, slowly they opened, those great lashes untwining like silken mesh. Elayne had gotten used to the depth of his eyes, the blue in them that was almost black, universes unfolding into distant time. But she'd never seen red before. It blazed there now, comet trails burning across the heavens.

Her father cried out, slumped forward, folding onto the horn as if it *had* driven into his chest. For a moment, none of them breathed, there was such stillness that Elayne thought she could hear the snow fall. Then, where the horn touched it, the skin began to lighten. It spread slowly, red flesh fading. She watched that patch move over her father's chest, expanding now with breath.

Light took her father's whole body—from his bald scalp to the toes uncurling on the metal boards of the wheelchair. And then that light changed, flooded with color. Not the heat of illness returning. The color of skin when it is . . . well.

One cry came from three throats. Moonspill fell back onto his haunches, while her father's eyes shot open, the light in them so different from before. There was no filter now between him and what he looked at. The illness, the drugs, the fatigue— all gone. She knew he truly saw—his daughter, the loft. A unicorn. The smile that came was for them. Only for them. And then he spoke.

"Alice-Elayne, my beloved daughter," he said, his voice deep and steady, with none of the quaver that the illness had given it, "I would give my right arm for an onion bagel."

## TWENTY-SIX

# VISITORS

The snow was falling even more heavily as Elayne turned back onto her street, the tumble of fat flakes drifting out of a dark sky making it seem like night. She closed her eyes to it, felt the cold strikes on her face; stuck out her tongue and caught one, imagined its perfect geometric shape dissolving there.

*When have I ever been this happy?* she wondered.

Upstairs, two of her favorite . . . beings were having major philosophical conversations. Her father was cured! She supposed the doctors would have to confirm it, but . . . it was clear to her. He was still weak, his body had been through so much. What he needed, she knew, was to begin a regimen of serious eating—which was why she was on the street. She'd gone for supplies—lox and bagels, cream cheese, milk, eggs. It was time for a celebratory feast.

When she was halfway down her alley, a tin can rolled— and the biggest rat she'd ever seen ran past. Yelping, she leapt back, squinted up and down the alley. But she couldn't see it, took another step. . . .

Something growled behind her. Elayne whipped around, peering through the snow. "Hello?" she called.

No answer. Nothing there. Except then . . . it came again. Not one growl this time. It sounded like . . . three. She started to back away.

"We bring you a message from the Lion, lady."

A shadow unfolded from a doorway. Elayne cried out, darting to the other side of the alley. The shape turned; she could make out a black cloak that covered from head to foot. Within the hood, she could only see the mouth. Lips moved, shaping words.

"And the message is . . . death."

A glimmer appeared at his waist—steel clearing leather, a dagger emerging from its sheath. The man stepped toward her. She swiveled the other way—to other shapes rising from the shadows there. And a growl. No, three growls, the little light reflecting off three sets of teeth.

Cerberus, the three-headed hunting dog of Goloth, was straining at his leash.

Elayne got out a scream, a little one anyway, backed up fast. The assassin had gotten closer, close. "Farewell," he said softly, raising his knife.

And then a pile of boxes and old blankets exploded. "Damn dogs," Malachi yelled, bursting from his nest. He hurled a can at the beast. "Why won't you let me be?"

The can caught one of the heads on its snarling snout; the

cloaked man jumped, turning toward the new threat. Elayne was as startled as any of them—but recovered first, darting at her slatted door. She hadn't locked it, just needed to get it up. Then she heard one word, shouted.

"Kill!"

A chorus of snarls came. Elayne, clawing at the gate, looked back to see the hound hurtle toward her, all those jaws wide and drooling. It leapt— Then it squealed, stuck in midair, as if it had hit an invisible wall. Something was wrapped around its legs, made of rope and leather balls. The beast fell, yelping, snarling, snapping.

The first assassin recovered, ran at her . . . but another figure stepped from the shadows and intercepted him. There was a swirl of cloak, something swung through the air, connecting. The man folded over it, fell to the ground, crying out in pain. Cerberus's handler ran forward, knife in hand . . . and got as far as Malachi, who lifted a trash can lid and smashed it on the man's head.

Elayne saw her chance. She yanked up the door, dove under, turned. She could see the men outside struggling to their feet in a sudden flood of light because the back door of the Lebanese restaurant had been flung open. She saw the chef standing in the doorway, cleaver in hand, yelling. She grabbed the rope, heaved the door, it hurtled to the ground . . . but just before it landed, sealing off sight and sound, a figure rolled under it.

Elayne fumbled for the light switch. *Please!* she thought. The light came on—and glowed in two pairs of eyes, quite close together. One set was small, dark, above a darting pink tongue. The others were pale blue.

They belonged to Marc.

Elayne stared at him—at him and his weasel—her breath coming in gulps. Outside, there was shouting, Malachi's stream of nonsense, the cook yelling loudly in Arabic. Then came the sounds of running.

"How . . . When . . . You . . . ," she managed to blurt.

"Is there somewhere warmer to converse, maid? My attire is not fit for winter, and I have followed the hellhound and his masters a long way."

"Oh. Yeah. Sure." Dazed, she led him up the stairs. But before the door, her legs gave out. She leaned against it, turned to him. "What the hell are you doing here? How did you get here?"

Marc seemed equally weak-legged. He leaned too. "When you and the unicorn disappeared into the tree, Leo was furious. On the instant, he dispatched his trackers and Cerberus—for we found that the doorway between worlds swung slowly closed. In a blind rage, he ordered them to kill you! I managed to follow." He swallowed. "It was hard, maid. Even Cerberus, who can scent a hare at a thousand paces, found pursuit difficult in this strange world. But he found you—or the unicorn, I think. They waited and watched for you. I watched them, and then"—he gestured outside—"then you saw."

"Well . . . thanks!" Elayne shook her head. It did nothing to clear it. "Um, I suppose you'd better come in."

She tried three times to get her key in the lock. But before she could, the door opened. Her father stood there, Moonspill

266

close behind him. "Well," her dad said, "more visitors. I hope you got enough bagels."

Elayne looked down, stunned to see that she was still clutching her bag of groceries.

* * *

While the weasel munched a can of tuna, Marc told his tale again over hot chocolate, bagels, and lox—and Pop-Tarts, one of the few other foodstuffs in the place, but one that seemed to make him happy. He ate seven.

When his mouth was particularly full, Elayne leapt in with a question. "So is Leo waiting on the other side for his assassins to return? Not to mention you?"

Marc swallowed. "He did not notice me slip through, I fancy. As for his assassins"—he shrugged—"they will either succeed or fail. He will not wait."

"Because he has to get back for the Games, and his coronation, right? If he hurries, he'll still only just make them. Good." Elayne snapped her fingers. "So he won't be there to stop us when we go back."

Moonspill, who had been standing at an open window breathing deeply, turned with his thought. *We?*

It was strange how decisions were made. She hadn't even thought about it before. She'd been too excited, too thrilled. But when she did think about it . . . it required no thought at all.

"What?" Elayne's father sat slowly forward on the sofa. He was wearing old clothes—cords, a chunky blue sweater way too big for him now, his pale face sticking out from the over-large neck. "What are you talking about? You are not going back."

"Dad—"

"Absolutely not." He raised a hand to silence her. "Moon-spill told me a little of what has been going on. What is still to come."

"You seem to be taking a unicorn in your loft remarkably calmly, Dad," Elayne interrupted, trying to distract him. She knew this tone of voice. In the year of his illness, he'd hardly said no to her once. But he'd had plenty of practice in the years before.

Distraction didn't work. "You forget—I have always believed in them." He reached to tap the emerald-colored book that sat on the table. But the slight smile that came, went. "And Moonspill has confirmed what's in here—that Goloth is still a cruel place ruled by a bloody tyrant. One who sent men to kill you. Who are probably still out there, right? Waiting for a second chance." He shook his head. "No. I won't let you go."

"Dad. Listen to me." Elayne reached forward and took his hands. "Look at what Moonspill has done for us. He's . . . returned the person I love to me. How can I do less for him?"

"It was in his power to help. But what can you do?" He turned to the window. "I appeal to you, Moonspill. You told me that you are a father too. Would you allow a child of yours to risk such peril?"

All of them looked at the unicorn. His words came, in her head—in everyone else's too, she supposed. *Allow? Each child has their own destiny, as do we all. It is up to them to decide how they reach it.*

"Destiny?" Her father picked up the book. "Are you talking about the promise our ancestor made five hundred years ago? You cannot expect my daughter to be bound by that."

*I do not expect—*

"Please," Elayne said loudly, interrupting them both. "Dad, it's not Alice-Elayne's promise I'd be keeping. It's my own. The one I make now."

Her father wasn't going to give up. "But . . . to do what? How would you even get into the city?"

"Sir, I can aid in that." Marc had finally cleared his mouth. His eyes were bright. "The weavers have long had a secret water gate by which they bring in things forbidden by the tyrant. It is just big enough to allow a unicorn to enter. It is close to the arena where the Games are held. Right below the castle."

"That's great!" Elayne leapt up, raising a hand for a high five. When he looked at it in puzzlement, she lowered it, turned to her dad. "You see, we've got a way in."

"Which Marc here knows. He can show Moonspill."

"But I am 'the unicorn tamer,' Dad. If the people are to rise up, as Marc hopes, they need to see me *and* Moonspill."

"My daughter the revolutionary!" he sighed, shaking his head. Then he turned again to Moonspill. "I ask again: would you force her to keep this promise?"

There came a pause, of breath, of mind. Until Moonspill answered. *No more than you can keep her by force, can I force her to go. It is, and always was, her choice.*

269

They all turned now to stare at her—three sets of eyes. Four if the weasel was counted, because he had ceased his munching to sit on Marc's lap. Elayne looked at each of them, beasts and men. Stared for the longest time into Moonspill's wondrous eyes. No pleas came. Finally, she looked into her father's, seeing them clear, illness-free. Seeing *him* really, for the first time in a long while, not his disease. "Dad," she said softly, "I have to go."

For a long moment, he studied her. Then she saw the concern fade—not disappear; it was still there, but something else joined it. "Daughter of mine," he said, "you are just like your mother—obstinate as hell!" He shook his head. "I knew the day would come when I would have to let you go. But I thought it would be out to terrible clubs, to listen to unspeakable music with unsuitable boyfriends." His great smile came. "I did not think it would be to the Land of the Fabulous Beast with a unicorn."

She dove across to him, hugged his boniness. "When do you go?" he murmured in her ear.

Thoughts intruded. *As soon as we are able. The Games will have begun. On the third, a unicorn will be sacrificed. And I cannot stay here longer.* Moonspill took a rattling breath. *I grow weaker by the hour and I will need strength for what lies ahead.*

Elayne tried to slip from her father's arms. "Tonight, then."

Her dad didn't let her go. "But how?"

Marc leaned forward. "By the way we came, maid?"

"Through the tapestry."

TWENTY-SEVEN

# THE CHASE

The plan was to wait till the middle of the night. Heavy snow was still falling, and that had helped cover them before, and kept a lot of traffic off the roads. They could only hope it would cover them going back.

Elayne didn't think she could possibly sleep—but did, dreamlessly, in her own lovely bed, for ten hours straight. Then she was up, showered, fed, dressed, and ready to go by ten. But the snowfall began to ease up at eleven and was done within the hour. It was Saturday night in New York. Midnight. Not everyone would be tucked up in their beds.

She chewed a nail. "What do we do? Wait some more?"

*No.* Moonspill's thought sounded as ragged as his breathing. *If I am to do what is agreed, we must go. Now.*

What had been agreed was that he would carry them both back to the Cloisters. Marc had said that when he followed the hunters through, some men there had yelled at them, but they had fled fast, Cerberus nosing the scent. Elayne could only hope that there wouldn't be any extra guards put on after such an incident. But watching Moonspill's flanks heaving with Manhattan's foul air, security guards were the least of her worries. She wasn't sure they'd make it as far as the river, let alone the Cloisters. "Are you sure you can do this?" she asked.

*I have no choice.*

She sighed, looked to Marc, perched near the window, studying the alley. "Any sign of them?"

He shrugged. "Nay. But they are two of Leo's best hunters. They will know how to lie in wait for prey."

"Oh, great! We might not even get past the front door!"

"Well, I think I may be able to help there." Her dad came from the kitchen. He had a phone in his hand and waved it. "When I called the hospice this morning, they were . . . a little concerned at my sudden departure, to say the least." He smiled. "I told them that I'd chosen to die at home. But I've just called them again and said that I've changed my mind. That I desperately need help. So they are sending"—he tipped his ear to the outside world—"that!"

They all heard it, the ambulance's siren, getting louder. Marc made the antiwitch gesture. Most things in their world he considered the work of evil spirits—though he'd been fascinated by the TV. Once his terror passed, it had been hard to pry the remote from his hand. Annoyingly, he mainly wanted to watch the Home Shopping Network. He slid down now from the windowsill. "Do we depart?"

All three were looking at her. She took a deep breath. "Moonspill's right. We don't have a choice. Let's go!" Pulling on her down jacket, she marched to the rear door, which led to the downstairs bay.

They'd talked about a distraction. Her dad had just provided it. Other than that, it was pretty simple: dodge the assassins; ride like hell. The same route seemed sensible. At least half of it was parkland and most of it bike paths, which only lunatics would be on at midnight in December in the snow. Of course, Manhattan had more than its share of lunatics—which might work to their advantage. Teenagers riding a unicorn? The cops would laugh at whoever called that one in.

Moonspill clopped down the stairs first; the others followed. They assembled before the metal-slat door. Her dad leaned on two ski poles. Moonspill knelt. Marc tucked his weasel into the front of his doublet and climbed on. Just before she followed, her father grabbed her, hugged her. "Be careful," he murmured. "And if you're not back within a week, I'll find a way to follow you through."

She hugged back. His arms felt great, warm, safe, and she really, *really* didn't want to leave them for . . . all that lay ahead. But Moonspill's breathing came in choppy bursts, and the ambulance siren was getting closer, closer, real close. It had to be turning into the alley, sounding as if it was coming from Gansevoort Street. So, with a last squeeze, she tore herself away, pulled herself up in front of Marc. Moonspill stood—and her father reversed one of the ski poles. "Every warrior needs a weapon," he said, handing it up to her. He turned to Moonspill. "Go well, my friend. And send her safely back to me."

*Another promise that will be kept.*

Her father nodded, then quietly slipped the key into the lock, turned it. Bending, he placed his fingers under the bottom slat. "All ready?"

She felt Moonspill's trembling. Marc's too as he wrapped his arms around her. She grabbed a fistful of mane, raised the ski pole, nodded. "As we'll ever be," she said.

The siren had gotten very loud, now coming from right outside the door. Giving a last wail, it died . . . followed by the sounds of vehicle doors opening, of voices calling. "And . . . ," yelled her dad, flinging up the door, "go!"

Cold air rushed in. Voices were instantly louder, together with another sound—a distinctive triple snarl. Moonspill needed no urging. The ambulance was right before the bay, but there was just enough room to slide by—once the EMT in the green uniform had thrown himself back, yelping, into the side of his rig.

He may have been too stunned to do more than cry out. But Cerberus wasn't, rounding the garbage cans where it had been hiding, three heads reaching before Moonspill had got into stride. One set of slavering jaws let out a howl of fury, one sank teeth into a white shoulder—and one closed over Marc's boot.

"Help me," he cried, slipping sideways, yanking Elayne with him.

She fought for balance, mane in one hand as Moonspill jerked. The dog was pulling Marc hard, Marc was pulling Elayne, they nearly fell.

"En garde!" came a yell. Her dad had been a fencer at

school, and there he was, doing his best lunge, stabbing his ski pole straight into one of the beast's noses. It squealed, released Marc's boot. The other head let go too, leaving a smear of blood on the unicorn's shoulder. The third head howled in agony. Hurt one, hurt all, it seemed. Moonspill, his hooves slipping on snow-slick pavement, finally got purchase and took off. Managing to glance back, Elayne saw two cloaked figures running from the shadows. Saw the ambulance crew scrambling back into their cab. Finally saw a scarecrow rising from a mound of cardboard. "Ride 'em, cowgirl!" yelled Malachi. "Yee-hah!"

They burst onto Gansevoort Street, Moonspill's hooves slipping again, sliding them into the road. There were shrieks— of brakes slammed on, of wheels failing to grip, of a woman in terror; then the crunch of metal into metal. But nothing collided with them. Moonspill found his balance and was off fast, heading for the Hudson.

Fast . . . but not as fast as they had come. Elayne could actually see the faces of people as they went past, mouths dropped in astonishment. She could read the street signs. And she could hear more than just rushing wind. Hear, for example, an unusual sound. She was no cowgirl despite what Malachi had shouted, but she knew hoofbeats when she heard them.

Though she really didn't like to move much, she had to look again, past Marc, whose eyes were screwed shut, his arms wrapped so tight around her she was finding it hard to breathe. And she saw horses. Two of them. Two of New York's Finest mounted police officers were chasing them! But something seemed wrong about them, and she looked harder. They were

275

about fifty yards back, and her vision was blurry with motion—yet she could see that something flowed behind them.

*Cloaks?*

She leaned forward, shouted. "The hunters! They're right behind us. Faster!"

How had the hunters gotten horses? Then she remembered the police stables on the Hudson she and Moonspill had passed. Following their trail down the greenway, the trackers would have passed—and smelled—them too. And helped themselves.

Moonspill grunted, didn't even think a reply. He did accelerate across Twelfth Avenue, turning onto the bike path . . . but only a little. The weight, the air quality? He was at his limit. When she glanced back again, she saw that the hunters hadn't gained—but they hadn't dropped behind either. Loping at their side was a dark figure. As she looked, its three heads lifted and it gave out that terrible triple howl.

There were other sounds—the hooting of horns, the whine of brakes, the shriek of tires trying to bite as drivers saw what they couldn't believe. And then the sirens began. Plural. Flashing red lights were coming toward them. The cruisers were a ways away, and then they were there, as engine and hoof gobbled up the gap. One of them mounted the curb, came onto the path, headed straight for them. But Moonspill did not deviate despite Elayne's scream, and, at the last moment, the driver swung hard in front of them and crashed into a chain-link fence. Moonspill swerved around it, and Elayne looked back. Saw the one car stuck, the other turning. Moving past it came the hunters.

More sirens—from in front, from side streets. Elayne caught an approaching sign: Fifty-sixth Street. So the cars pulling sideways across the path and road three blocks up were at Fifty-ninth.

Fifty-ninth? Central Park!

"Right," she yelled, and Moonspill turned, swinging onto Fifty-sixth. But there was another flashing light ahead, the cruiser pulling across to block the side street.

Not quite. There was a gap between cop and parked car. Wide enough for a unicorn.

"Yee-hah!" she yelled, like Malachi, as they squeaked through. Then they had the lights, all the way through to Eighth Avenue. *Left*, she thought when they hit it, and again Moonspill responded.

Two blocks, as horns blared and cars swerved . . . into Columbus Circle. They moved through the idling cars, onto the crosswalk, scattering late-night partiers. "Don't Walk" was flashing red, but it said nothing about galloping, and soon they were over . . .

. . . into Central Park.

There was a path, then a roadway to cross. She knew they didn't want to stay on that. Police cars would go faster on that. And from behind them, Elayne heard a deep howl. They weren't clear yet. "There!" she shouted, pointing at a gap in a fence. Moonspill took it. His great chest was going like a bellows.

*Are you OK?* she thought.

His reply came on a groan. *How far?*

"Uh, we're about halfway?" She said it aloud in the hope

that her voice would cover the lie better than her thought. But they could make up a lot of ground in the park. No cars. Few roads. Not many people.

Moonspill had slowed a little. And Marc spoke. "They still pursue us."

Those words, and the grass his hooves dug into through the snow, seemed to give him a little zip. Plus, Manhattan air was better in Central Park. Elayne guided them, with shouts, with thoughts, past playgrounds, over meadows, through trees. Cars may not have been able to follow them—but helicopters buzzed overhead, their searchlights crisscrossing the ground. Somehow they avoided their beams. Somehow they opened a gap between themselves and the hunters. They were riding horses after all. Moonspill was a unicorn.

A fading unicorn, Elayne realized—plus, the park had to end, and did. *How far?* he asked again. *Not far,* she replied, and he knew the lie. His head drooped, and he slowed, turning sluggishly through the gates onto 110th Street. They were moving at no more than a canter now.

"We're more than halfway," she called. "Way more."

*I do not think—I . . . cannot . . . breathe. . . .*

Howls came from behind. Closer.

"You have to. You . . ." She paused, thought. Thought hard. *Remember your mate. She will die in Leo's arena unless you save her.*

She felt the stirring beneath her. *Heartsease.*

*Yes. Heartsease. Ride to her. Ride fast.*

He sped up again. Now they were going almost as quickly as they had when they'd first come to Manhattan. Morningside Park passed in a blur, and then they were onto the pathways of Riverside Park, the Hudson glimmering beyond. They passed beneath the George Washington Bridge. "Ten blocks," Elayne shouted, then realized that would mean nothing to weasel, boy, or unicorn. "About a hundred breaths," she added, guessing wildly.

She probably wasn't far off. Perhaps they would have made it in about a hundred. If some cop hadn't figured out the impossible and guessed where they were headed.

"Freeze. Don't move."

A police car was skewed sideways, blocking the road to the Cloisters. There were no flashing lights, but lamps snapped on to blind them, simultaneous with the voice coming through the megaphone.

And they did freeze—at least as much as Moonspill's sudden halting allowed. Elayne shot forward onto his neck, Marc slamming against her. There was a squeal from the weasel squashed between them.

That distorted voice came again. "Step down from the horse. Do it now. Do it!"

They were blinded, terrified. Elayne sobbed. No! They were so close. No!

And then howls came, as if a pack of hounds were charging toward them. It wasn't a pack, of course. It was one dog. One three-headed dog.

The searchlight on the cruiser's roof snapped over suddenly to Cerberus. The beast froze, just as they had done. Then all three heads snarled . . . and the helldog charged straight into the light. Straight at the cop car.

"Shit!" came the yell. Followed by a shot—then another, another. Elayne couldn't tell if any hit, but if they did, they didn't slow the hound. There was a cry of terror. "Shoot it! Shoot it!" came a man's agonized scream. More pained yelps, more growls, two more shots. The searchlight shattered in an explosion of glass.

"Go!" she cried.

*Heartsease!*

Moonspill's thought came like a shout as he jumped. They flew over the cruiser. Elayne looked down, saw writhing, struggling forms, a muddle of legs and jaws. Then they were past, landing, and it was all she could do to stay mounted.

The circular driveway led to the wooden doors of the Cloisters.

"They come!" Marc cried, leaping from Moonspill's back. Elayne turned, in time to see the two hunters galloping up the drive, their horses so covered in the foam of exhaustion they looked as if they were swimming through it. One had had enough, fell as he arrived, his rider stepping off his back as the horse went down. The other man kicked his mount hard in the sides, the poor animal's eyes rolling white as he drove it forward. This hunter had a sword drawn and was whirling it above his head. His eyes were filled with the triumph of the chase, with the anticipated kill, shouting as he charged at them. The blade whirled close, she leaned away, raised a hand—and felt the slice of a blade across her palm.

He'd missed. Enough, anyway. But Elayne watched the sword rising again, death in it.

She did see death then . . . another's. Saw it in his eyes,

he was that close, eyes changing from triumph to terror as he stared down at the horn that had driven into his chest. Driven through it, Elayne realized, as his horse moved to the side, ran off whinnying, and he was left, legs kicking above the ground. Moonspill jerked his head, trying to fling the body off.

There was one other assassin, and he came now, flinging Marc aside, swinging a great club through the air. Moonspill was stuck, his head borne down by the weight on his horn. The club rose—and Elayne remembered what she somehow still held. Stabbing, she drove the ski pole into the assassin's shoulder.

It was no horn. But it was sharp enough, and his own momentum did most of the damage. He fell backward with a yell of agony—and Marc hit him with his club.

The man fell, lay still. They were all breathing hard now, clouds erupting from their mouths, from the huge white body, into the frigid air. For a long moment, breath was the only sound—until the whine of sirens came again, the whir of a copter blade, a radio voice frantically calling for backup.

*We go*, thought Moonspill. They rode up the stone arcade, paused before the doors at the end. Raising his mighty hooves, he smashed them in.

Yelps of pain blended with the instant wail of the alarm. Two guards were sprawling in the ruins of the doors they must have been standing behind. Daintily, Moonspill stepped over them. Marc leapt, clung, and Elayne helped him up.

"That way!" she cried. Moonspill lowered head and horn to step through three doorways, and into the last room. Finally, before the tapestries, he halted.

Elayne swayed. She thought she was going to faint any second, or vomit, or collapse into hysterical laughter. Goloth was a step away, through the slits an ancestor had left in warp and weft.

The tapestry turned in her gaze. Elayne slumped back against Marc, who held her, steadied her. A wet nose thrust into her ear. She giggled, wondering if it was his!

Shouts came from behind them.

*Now!* On his thought, Moonspill charged, leaping, driving horn-first at the cloth. Through the cloth.

Elayne tensed. But there was no impact, just a swallowing darkness. They fell into it. None of her senses worked for a while . . . until she smelled leaves. Until she felt bark against her cheek.

And then there was light, so much light it hurt. Flames moved everywhere, every way her half-open eyes could turn. Forcing the lids up, she saw herself—here, there, above, below.

"Mirrors! Don't look," she cried in warning. . . .

Too late.

## TWENTY-EIGHT

# BETRAYAL

It was a world of mirrors.

A thousand Elaynes raised blood-gashed hands into infinity. A thousand froth-daubed Moonspills, a thousand Marcs, stared. A thousand weasels, running at their reflections, pink nose thrust at all these rivals. Lit by a thousand torches, refracting off every pane of glass, filling the world with flame.

Elayne was looking up at all those unicorns. She'd fallen off, with no memory of doing so. Squinting, hand held up against the light, she tried to get her bearings. It was almost impossible. Everywhere she looked, *she* looked back, each of her at a slightly different angle. It was hard to move her gaze away. But she did, looked down to the ground—to grass, twigs, mud churned by boot prints. Leaves. It steadied her.

"Moonspill!" she cried.

It was no good. He was lost to reflection. But she wasn't.

They must have taken whoever had set the trap by surprise because no one was rushing forward to grab them. She rose, reached for his mane. She'd hurl herself onto him, cover his eyes, kick their way out of there!

A hand grabbed her hair, pulled hard, bending her head back; her fingers were torn from the mane, and she cried out . . . but not so loud that she could not hear the voice that spoke in her ear.

"No, maid. There is no escape now. There is only . . . obedience."

Her head was twisted around. She reached up to the hand that held her, grabbed it . . . but she lost all the strength she'd need to throw it off when she saw who the hand belonged to.

Marc.

He let go of her hair, grabbed both her wrists, pulled her face close to his. And it was as if she were seeing him for the first time. Seeing the real him. Not the vain actor, not the cocky thief, not the weaver-rebel. There was a set to his mouth, a certainty in his eyes, no hint of a smile in either.

"Obedience to who?" she said softly.

"The Lion, of course."

She shook her head. It didn't clear it. "So you're a . . . a traitor?"

"Nay, maid, I am the opposite. I am loyal to my king."

"But . . . why?" was all she could find to say.

"Why?" Marc smiled now, though it looked more like a sneer. He turned away from her, toward one wall of mirrors, a thousand hims turning to face himself, and called, "Are you there, Sister?"

For a moment there was silence, only Moonspill's now-gentle breathing, and the hiss of burning. Elayne noticed that the thousand flames were really one, a torch planted in the ground.

A gap opened in the mirrors. "I am here . . . Brother," Amaryllis replied.

It was like something broke inside Elayne, the cry she gave the sound of it breaking, as she sank onto the ground.

Amaryllis rubbed her eyes. "What took you so long?" she asked, pouting. "I was asleep when we heard you come. In a . . . tent!" she shuddered. "You know I hate to sleep away from my bed."

"Well, you are awake now," Marc replied briskly. "So do what needs to be done."

"I will." She came forward, looked down. "Would you like a sweetmeat, Ee-layne? No? Maybe later?" She laughed as she moved on, kept laughing, only stopping when she reached Moonspill. "Beast," she said to him. "I have waited so long for you."

Elayne knew her Moonspill was lost to his own image in the mirrors. That he could not hear the girl, could not feel her hand upon his neck. But Elayne could—like a slap. "No," she yelled. "Leave him alone. He's mine."

She lunged forward, but Marc seized her arm, jerked her back. "No, maid. He is Leo's."

"Yes," Amaryllis whispered, stroking the long white neck.

"Oh yes." Then she raised her voice and called, slightly louder, "Bring them."

The gap in the mirrors opened again, wider this time to admit two soldiers. One carried the bridle-muzzle with its cruel metal bit to hold his mouth, its mirrors to hold his eyes. Reins were already fitted to the canvas.

The second man carried something even worse. He carried a saddle.

A moan escaped Elayne, a single word. "Why?"

"Why what, maid?" Marc's voice was triumphant. "Why am I loyal to my king? Why do I help my sister to thrive? Why have I striven against those who would pull my soon-to-be brother-in-law down?" He bent closer, as the men brought the muzzle to Amaryllis. "Or are you asking why all this?" He gestured around, at all the Marcs gesturing back. "'Tis easy to answer. I told you the truth when I said that the king-elect was filled with wrath when you vanished. After all the care that had gone into your 'rescue,' your 'escape' from the dungeon?" His smile widened. "You cheated him of the unicorn of his dreams. In that moment of rage, and finding the doorway you'd vanished through not yet closed, he sent his best trackers and the hound Cerberus to take his vengeance. The door swung shut behind them. But I persuaded him to let me follow, to bring you back to"—he tipped his head—"this. And to the fulfillment of his great desire."

While he talked, Amaryllis had been slipping the muzzle over Moonspill's head, threading and tightening the straps. She nodded, and the men moved swiftly to the unicorn's side and threw the saddle over his back.

Elayne looked away, had to. Yet some of his words pierced the fog that was taking over her mind. "But if the door swung shut—how were you able to follow?"

She did not think he could look any more pleased with himself. But he managed it. "Because a door will always open—if you have the right key."

He stepped back, reached beneath his shirt, and pulled out the horn necklace.

As she saw it, two memories came together to form a picture. Her boast upon the deck of the fishing vessel, which she'd regretted, then forgotten. And the hug Marc had given her when Moonspill came for her in the fog, to bear her away. She'd thought it strange then. But it wasn't strange at all. Because she'd always known he was a thief. And, in that moment, he'd stolen the most precious thing she had.

The saddle had been cinched. Moonspill stood, with head bent, broken. And only then did Elayne begin to cry. More than the muzzle, more than the droop of his head, more than the blood of dog bite in the foam of exhaustion on his flank. They were going to ride him. Her Moonspill! She opened her mind to him, tried to reach him. There was nothing to reach.

Beside her, Marc had his hands on his hips, relishing what he saw, chuckling at it.

Tears could be for anger too, she discovered. She launched herself up from her knees. Her right hand was down at her hip, and she drove it up as she rose, drove it hard, straight as a horn, into his sneer.

It hurt her, a lot. But it hurt him more. He staggered back, raised a hand, pulled it away to gaze at the blood there. He bunched his fist, and for a moment it looked like he was going to punch her back. But then he turned away, shouting, "Throw her into the wagon!"

More guards came. They seized her, began to drag her through the mirrors, which were being collapsed, shuffled together like cards. The thousand Elaynes folded down to a hundred, a dozen, to one, a single standing frame. Within it, she saw Moonspill, head bent, horn tip on the ground, already smeared with soil. She watched as Marc mounted him, thrusting feet into stirrups, rising up in them, crying, "To the Games!"

## TWENTY-NINE

# PROPOSAL

They arrived in the middle of the night, having done the journey, from mountains to city, in two days and half a night. They'd barely paused to sleep for an hour at a stretch; barely stopped to pee, eat, drink, change horses. Marc was very much the leader now and drove them on. Through the slats of the wagon they threw her into, Elayne had heard the speech he made, urging everyone to hurry. Being the actor, it was very theatrical, very passionate. The Games had begun that morning and would continue for three days. Marc was determined to be there before the last, the most important day—to present the king-elect with this prize and no doubt receive a large reward.

When they'd rattled over cobbles rather than dirt, when they'd finally halted and her door had been unlocked, Elayne had stumbled out of the wagon into the courtyard of the Castle of Skulls. It was aflame with torches, and by their light she'd watched Moonspill, still blinkered, being led down that tunnel into the castle's depths. To her surprise, she'd not been taken there, back to a dungeon, but the other way, into the building, then up so many floors her legs went wobbly; finally, to a room. She managed to shed her clothes and kick off her sneakers, and was asleep as soon as she was between the sheets.

She was woken by a shrill blaring that had her groping for an alarm clock. But it was a trumpet, calling from outside. She looked for her clothes. They were gone. But across a big armchair was a linen shift. She put it on, stumbled over to the window. Judging by the sun, she must have slept till midafternoon.

She had a bird's-eye view—literally, as swallows flitted into the eaves just above her head. She knew the castle was at the top of a steep hill, but she had only ever come in the front way. Now she was looking out at the back—and she rubbed her eyes, not quite believing.

She was gazing down onto a stadium. The slope below her was one side of it. Farther down, bleachers began, descending in rows to an oval of sand. The stands were filling with people. There for the last day of the Games.

She shivered, and turned away. It was a gorgeous bedroom, larger and more lavish than the one they'd kept her in before, with a giant canopied bed wrapped in fine linens, a huge fireplace, lush tapestries on the walls. There was a table, stacked with every kind of food—candied fruits, creamy cheeses, smoked meats and fish, crusty bread. In its center stood a huge box of chocolates.

Yet a test of the door confirmed she was still a prisoner. If it wasn't the grim cell that Marc had "rescued" her from, it was still a jail. She spent a little time exploring it. There was a second door on the wall by the bed, almost a secret one, as it was flush to the wall like a hidden panel. Locked too. A door did open into a small room beside that served as the toilet. But that was it. The main windows opened, but she was so high up—no escape there.

She went back to the table, studied the food. She was starving after the scant meals of the journey. She made a huge sandwich, crammed with cheese, slices of meat. Heading back to the window, she was just about to bite into it when the screaming began.

The words were not in any language that a person could understand. Unless that person had received the gift of tongues from a two-headed snake. "Oh no," she said, laying down her sandwich on the windowsill.

Marc had explained the Games to her while they waited for the griffin stealing to begin. He'd said that each class in society, on the last day, got to hunt a fabulous beast. She couldn't remember who hunted what. But the scream told her *what* was being hunted.

"Help me!" wailed the manticore.

Slumping down with her back to the window, she realized that this gift was also a curse. Suddenly she wished she *was* in the deepest, darkest dungeon cell. She wouldn't be able to see. More importantly, she wouldn't be able to hear. Because her hands over her ears did nothing to block out the sounds, the roars and cheers of the crowd, the beast's shrill, still strangely beautiful cry, distorted by agony. It ended on a high-pitched, wordless shriek, swiftly drowned in the huge shout of triumph, in the stamping of feet on the bleachers' floorboards.

The noise reduced to the sound of something being dragged away. The crowd hummed, shouts and chatter rising up. That lasted for a while so, finally, wearily, Elayne hauled herself up. *Eat*, she thought. *I must eat.* The meat in her sandwich was rare, bloody, and she took it out. As she was doing so, the hum turned to buzz, building to a crescendo. "Oh no," she said. "No!"

Her fear was confirmed when she heard the cockatrice hiss.

It was quieter than the manticore. It did not cry out in words. But the "hunt" lasted way longer. She didn't hear its death cry—but the moment of its death had her kneeling clutching her stomach as if she were the one stabbed. That surge came, shouts, howls of delight, as another beast was slain.

There was a longer gap then, at least an hour, she thought, by the way the sun was settling in the sky. She even managed to eat half the sandwich. Just half—before the griffin chick began to wail.

Throwing the bread aside, she dived onto the bed and sobbed. Between that noise and the feathers in the pillow she shoved over her head, she managed not to hear too much. But she did hear men scream in agony as well; the killers did not have it all their own way. Then there was near quiet again.

Elayne swung her feet off the bed. Her legs were wobbly at first, but they got steadier with her pacing. She couldn't just lie there! Not when she knew there was one fabulous beast left to kill.

She checked the two doors again, jerked them to see if either would give. With the knife from the food tray, she managed to pry the window in the bathroom open. But there was nothing but sheer wall below that as well, falling all the way to the stadium. Frustrated, Elayne stepped back inside . . . and heard it. A scratching, coming from the baseboards of the wall. She looked. . . . *Eww!* There was a small gap between wall and floor. She saw a pink nose thrust out.

"Rats!" she yelped, instinctively backing away. She'd always hated rats! She was just about to run back into the bedroom . . . when the thought hit her. She did go into the bedroom—crossed it slowly to the food, crossed slowly back. Cheese seemed like such a cliché, but she'd grabbed some anyway, and a big hunk of bread and some meat.

She tried to remember what the amphisbaena had said after she'd been given the gift of tongues and she'd asked about talking to nonfabulous beasts. Something about them not having much conversation, as they were obsessed by their desires—and limited by their mouth and throat. But they'd said that some understood pretty well, depending on the creature.

The nose was still sticking out, sniffing the air. Taking a deep breath, Elayne bent. "Here" she said, laying the bread down gently. "This is for you."

The nose withdrew . . . then appeared again. A head thrust out. Eyes circled around the room, then fixed on her. There didn't seem much point in talking out loud. But she looked hard at the rat and thought to him—or her. *Take it. All yours.*

She stepped back, and it came slowly forward, eyes never

leaving her. Then it bent, nosed the bread, bit off a chunk, retreated a few steps to gnaw at it.

*There's more. Much more. Much as you like.* She paused. She didn't want to chat. So she thought her next words carefully. *Do you know the amphisbaena?*

The rat stopped eating. Stared up at her. Words didn't come. But a thought did. It knew the two-headed snake, for sure.

*Find . . . them. Tell them . . . Tell them I am here.* She put down the meat and cheese. *And afterward bring your family for a feast.*

Again, the sense came, an unspoken *Yes.* Darting forward, snatching the hunk of cheese, the rat then dashed for the hole and vanished.

Elayne stared after him—then shook her head. *Talking to a rat,* she thought. *Can it get any crazier?*

*Yes,* she realized. *Expecting the rat to do what I asked. Such a small hope . . .*

The thought made her stand. It was what Moonspill had always called her—his small hope. *And look how far his small hope has come. Why not a little farther? Why not?* So lost was she in that thought, the knock on the door made her jump. "Yes?" she called.

The lock turned. The door opened . . . and Leo was there. He studied her for a long moment. "Maid," he said at last, bowing from his waist in the doorway. He was dressed entirely in black; his long blond hair hung loose over his shoulders. In his arms he carried a red dress. He crossed to the armchair, laid the dress carefully over it. "This is for you," he said.

"Why?"

"Because I would have you even more beautiful than you are by nature's gift, when you are beside me upon the podium."

Anger steadied her. "Of course. You want to show off the unicorn tamer."

"No, lady." His voice stayed soft as he took a step toward her. "What I wish is to show off my queen."

The guy didn't take "no" for an answer! But instead of snapping, she took a deep breath. *Use it*, she thought. "I see. Quite the honor. Well, I would have to talk with the unicorn first, of course. . . ."

He flushed. She could see him fighting to keep his temper. "You will see him soon enough—in the arena. And when a king commands, he is obeyed. Instantly."

Elayne snorted. "That's not how it works in my world."

"We are not in your world"—he stepped up to the bed, put his hand on one of the posts, studied it as if he were look-ing for some flaw before he spoke, more gently now—"though perhaps you can be again."

She took a step toward him. *Careful.* "You'd let me go home?"

He caressed the wood. "I may. Upon certain . . . condi-tions."

"What conditions?"

He still wasn't looking at her. "That I accompany you." Elayne gasped, but before she could speak, he went on. "The player has told me of the wonders of your world. Someday I would see them for myself."

Elayne wanted to snap, "Like that's going to happen!" But

even if it was sometime in the future, he *was* talking about a way out. So she put a smile on her face. "But wouldn't you be scared that I wouldn't come back?"

Now he looked straight at her. "No," he replied, returning her smile, "for what mother would not return to her children?"

What little calm she had vanished. "Excuse me?"

"You are excused. I can see the idea surprises you." He started to slowly cross the room. "But think! We would make beautiful children, Alice-Elayne. And there would be no hurry. From the little I have heard of your world, 'tis certain that I would be too . . . inexperienced for it, as I am now. I would first learn of its ways, so I could deal with your leaders there as an equal." He nodded. "You would be my teacher."

He was right in front of her. He reached, his fingers brushed hers—and it was as if he'd sent an electric charge through her. But somehow she couldn't move it away. "You . . . you can't be serious!" she breathed.

His voice stayed soft. "Could not our worlds gain, each from the other? We have things to trade. Is it true that you have no fabulous beasts?" She nodded, stunned. "Come, then, maid. It was the beasts that chose to seal the door between worlds. Man did not choose. Is it not time to open it again?"

His hand closed over hers. He lifted it, began to draw her to him. And she knew she should let him kiss her, keep stringing him along . . . but, really, those lips! Those thin lips, puckering, getting closer, as his eyes started to close—

She slipped away, moved to the window, turned. "You don't need me. Why not just ask your spy, Marc? He's got the key to the door, after all."

Leo, who'd taken a step after her, stopped. "He has a key?"

She could see the shock on his face: Leo didn't know how Marc had gotten through to her world. The player was obviously keeping it—probably literally—up his sleeve. She'd given him away. *Serves the rat right,* she thought. *And that insults my buddy the rat!*

"Well," Leo muttered, "I will deal with the ambitious player later. But you, maid, you will hear me and—"

She'd had enough. "No, you hear me. Do you know what would happen if you 'opened the door'?" She half laughed. "Trust me—within twenty years, your gold would be stripped out of the mountains, your fabulous beasts would all be in zoos. Goloth would have turned into one great big theme park—and God help you if you have oil! You think your streams are polluted now?"

"That will be for the king to decide—"

"No. It won't. Believe me, it won't."

He'd taken a step toward her. She thrust out a palm. "And believe this too—you need to find yourself another queen."

He went red. Elayne thought he was going to start shouting. But then a trumpet sounded outside. He looked to it, breathed deeply. "You are . . . not like any woman of Goloth, Alice-Elayne. And I have always said: as the new king, I will be willing to listen as well as to command. We will have time for more . . . *discussion* later." He forced a smile onto his face. "But now the arena calls. It is the moment of destiny. My people will see what a king I shall make when I fight and slay the mightiest of unicorns."

She remembered the death cries of the other fabulous

beasts. "Fight?" she said, putting all the derision she could into one syllable.

"Aye, maid, fight. What sport would there be if I but slew it? What victory? Think ill of me if you will, but remember the griffin who would have taken you and judge then if I am a coward." He crossed to the door. "Ho, there!" he called. It opened on the instant. "You will bathe, dress," he said to her, beckoning in four men who carried a tub of steaming water between them into the small room that passed for a bathroom. "There are jewels for your hair, for your person. . . ." He gestured at the packages two maids carried. "Obey," he added. "For if you do not, these"—he waved his hand—"will persuade you. Whatever is to pass between us in the future"—he smiled—"you *will* be beside me on the podium come sunset. You will take my hand and acknowledge the people of Goloth. And you will cheer with them as you watch me slay the fabulous beast."

Elayne wanted to tell him where to stick his jewels and just let them try and dress her. But what good would she do Moonspill locked in this room? Out there, perhaps their small hope still lived.

The servants bowed, left the room. She did not hear the lock turn, but she knew they weren't going anywhere. Leo went to the other door, the one sunk into the wall beside the bed. He turned and looked back as if he would speak again. Then he just bowed stiffly and left. She heard a lock, Leo sealing her in. Now that he was gone, so was her defiance. She leaned against the wall by the window, listened to the hum of the crowd below.

She pushed herself off the wall, crossed to the smaller room.

The bath was there, fragrant steam rising from it. Putting her hand in, she found the water was deliciously hot but not scalding. There was nothing she wanted more than to lower herself into it, to drift into a sweet-scented dream, to wake up somewhere else, anywhere else. Because whatever Leo said about a fight, she knew it wouldn't be fair. All that was left for her was to obey . . . and watch Moonspill die. With a choked sob, she grasped linen at her hips, started to pull—

Froze!

There was a noise. Not from outside—from within the room. She looked at the baseboard, thinking—hoping, even—that the rat was back. Then she realized that the noise was coming from what passed for a toilet in a castle—a hole cut into a stone bench. A person squatted—and let the pipe and gravity take care of the rest. She approached on tiptoe, ready to run.

Something slithered up the hole. Yelping, Elayne backed up against the bath and got stuck there for a second—the second it took to recognize that it was a snake that appeared. And spoke.

"Verily! 'Tis the maid!" it said.

"Awesome!" said a second head, sliding into view. "And, check it out! Bathtub! Coo-ool! 'Cause I am, like, totally covered in shit!"

## THIRTY

# DOWN

Amphis looked at Baena—or vice versa—and then they lunged as one out of the toilet and dropped onto the floor. Elayne stepped back, too stunned to do more than babble. "What the . . . How did you . . . ? When did you . . . ?"

"We were waiting there," spoke one head, "until the tyrant departed."

"Boy, did he ever take his time!" said the other, eyes rolling. "He was, like, 'You will obey, maid!' and you were, like, 'Yeah, right. Take a hike!'"

Elayne had to smile—the impression was so good it was like Leo was back in the room. Though she knew *she'd* never talked like that!

The other head shook. "I apologize, maid, for Baena's lamentable attempt at—what would you name it?—'teenspeak.' He was ever frivolous." Amphis slithered closer, forcing Baena to turn away to follow. "As to the 'how'—we'd heard that you had returned and Moonspill was taken. We were lurking nearby when news came of where you were."

"My rat?" Elayne exclaimed, pleased.

"A rat, certainly. They communicate by thought and spread news swiftly by this means. One came to us"—he turned to glare at the other head—"and once I had prevented Baena from consuming him . . ."

"What can I say? Guy's gotta eat."

". . . he told us where you were held. So we thought to rescue you. We have always known ways in and out of the tyrant's dwelling. This one is . . ." He sniffed. "I apologize again, and this time for our scent."

He looked down at the brown stains that, it had to be said, were mainly concentrated at his other end. There, Baena spoke. "Brother, when I stink, we both stink." He craned around to look at Elayne. "Can we use your bath?"

Elayne figured that their need was greater than hers. "After you," she replied. "Or . . . maybe not."

"Sweet," hissed Baena.

They slipped into the water, splashed a lot, twisting and looping as each end helped the other cleanse. The water darkened, and the herbal scent was replaced by something that made Elayne move away. Finally, they slid out, headed straight to the fire that glowed in the grate. They curled up there, the two heads close together resting on a coil, eyes halfclosed in pleasure.

She stared at them for a moment. "Um . . . guys?"

Four eyes shot wide open. "We forget ourselves, lady. 'Tis rare that we bathe in such delight."

Elayne had been thinking while they washed, thinking hard. "You say you know ways in and out of the castle. Bigger than that, right?" She gestured at the toilet.

"Aye. Some."

"Big enough, say, for a unicorn? Two unicorns?"

Both heads rose. After a long moment, one spoke. "Maid, 'twill be hard enough to rescue your good self—"

The other interrupted. "Nay, dude, listen to what the girl has to say."

"Just this." She crouched, so her eyes were level with theirs. "I can't leave without Moonspill. And Heartsease. I just can't."

Amphis considered, turning to look at his twin. "And 'tis true also—the world suffers now, with two unicorns in it. What will it be like when there are none?"

"Right on!" Baena turned too. "So are you, like, thinking what I am thinking?"

Both heads nodded. Both spoke. "Jailbreak!" He—they—slid back over to the toilet hole. "This leads to the sewers. They run beside the dungeons of the arena. Let's go!"

"I am not going down there! I wouldn't fit and—eww! It's so gross."

"Nay, 'tis a foolish idea from one with half a brain." The two heads glared at each other, and then Amphis continued. "I have another. Yet first you must clothe yourself."

She was still wearing only the linen shift. And they'd taken her New York stuff. "In what?"

"In all your finery! The tyrant's gifts—jewels and all."

"Why?"

"Mayhap the trappings of a lady shall confuse any we meet."

"Besides," added Baena, "if you're going to the prom, you need a kick-ass dress."

Elayne couldn't help it—she laughed. It was hard to button herself in—but she swiftly discovered how versatile snakes' mouths were. There was little she could do with her hair, so she gathered it all up and pinned it with an enormous diamond-studded clasp. Then, to her joy, she discovered they'd overlooked her sneakers. She'd kicked them off the night before, and they'd gone half under a curtain. She slipped them on. Now she'd be ready to run.

"OK," she said, tying the last double knot. "What now?"

Amphis and Baena slithered over to the door. "Check this out," whispered Baena, and then began to speak . . . in his dead-on impersonation of Leo.

"Ho, there!" The door opened a tad, but Amphis lunged into it, slamming it shut. "Nay, do not enter. Disperse to your several tasks. I will bring the lady down. Away, or feel my wrath!"

Elayne felt he kind of overplayed it. But the eaves of the castle were studded with the skulls of those who'd failed to heed their king. The servants outside didn't hesitate. They went fast, and as silently as the ancient floorboards in the corridor allowed.

"Cool, or what?" Baena chuckled.

"Shh!" commanded Amphis, listening. When all was silent outside, he opened the door a crack, peered out. "Gone," he whispered. "Come!"

"Where?"

"Down," he replied.

They were on the top floor, so they made for the stairs. She wasn't sure who was leading. At each landing, they paused, peered around the corner. But every corridor was deserted. Nearly everyone was at the Games, she supposed, required to be there to bear witness to Leo's triumph. They went down five flights and met no one.

Until they got to the main floor, to the great stone courtyard she'd always entered by. The outer doors to their left were shut, barred. To the right . . .

Three heads peered around the wall. Then they all jerked back. "Guards. Two of them, with spears," Elayne whispered. "They are at the entrance to the tunnel, the one they took Moonspill down."

"Shall we brazen it out?" asked Amphis. "Mayhap you could tell them we are another beast for the Games."

"No way," replied Baena. "Too risky." He grinned. "Besides, I got a better idea."

"What, prithee— Erk!" Amphsis was cut off as Baena grabbed his head in his mouth and hurled them out into the courtyard. It amazed Elayne how much speed they built up immediately. A whirling blur shot across the open space and disappeared between two pillars opposite.

One of the guards cried out. She peeked, figuring they'd be looking where the action was. They were. Both had their spears lowered, both were coming forward . . . until one shooed the other back to his post at the tunnel and came slowly on alone.

Flattening herself against the pillar, she looked again. The guard was still peering into the shadows on the other side. Weapon thrust before him, he took one cautious step in, another—

*Whoosh!* He was gone, feet leaving the ground as he went. There was a muffled yelp, the clatter of metal falling. Then— nothing.

"Where are you? Answer me!" a man called.

Elayne watched. The second guard was moving slowly, almost in the middle of the hall, away from the pillars, spear thrust out before him. "Are you there?" he called again. And then something came bouncing out of the darkness. Both Elayne and the guard jumped as the object rolled to a stop at his feet.

It was a helmet. The guard bent to pick it up. It was a mistake.

A whirl of snake, spinning out of the darkness, smashed into him. He seemed to explode, spear going one way, helmet the other, legs up, head down. He landed and didn't move while the whirl circled him once then slowly settled, like a rolling Frisbee, wobbling onto the ground.

"Swiftly," Amphis hissed at her.

"Coming," she said, snatching up the spear. They hooped again and rolled. Elayne ran. There was no time to hesitate, at the darkness, at the steep incline before them. The tunnel spiraled down in tight circles around a central stone column.

There was a torch in a bracket at every bend, which began to pass increasingly swiftly as their pace built.

Elayne was just starting to get scared, bracing herself for the tumble that must surely come, when the floor leveled and she slowed. Not by much. Not when the torches multiplied and by their light they saw, about twenty paces ahead, a metal grille that blocked the tunnel. There was a tall, square door in it. It was open, and there was a man standing in it.

"Gods," he cried, frozen by the sight.

But they were still all speed. "Yahh," she screamed. Leveling the spear, she charged. He took off, yelling, and Elayne plunged through the door and on down the tunnel, which changed from earthen walls and floors into paved, stone-lined corridors. They heard his feet ahead, slapping on flagstones. Then, over his shrieks, they all heard another sound: the steady beat of a drum, the hum of a crowd, building, building.

At some kind of junction, they halted. Corridors spoked off in all directions. Straight ahead, at the end of the long tunnel the man had taken, was light—daylight, not torchlight, more men there. The running man joined them, gesticulating wildly, screaming. All turned their way.

"Swiftly," called Amphis, pulling back into the center of the hall, out of sight, "to Moonspill."

"But which way?" She looked at all the tunnels. There was nothing to distinguish them.

"Your call, girlfriend," said Baena. "We'll lead these dudes down other ways."

She chewed her lip. "But how do I choose?"

The two snake heads looked at her. One spoke. "If you

have tamed the unicorn, you are joined to him forever. Listen to your heart."

"But I haven't . . ." Her gaze jerked wildly over the entrances—there had to be at least seven of them. How was she meant to . . . ?

Then a certainty came over her—and she just knew. "There," she said, pointing down the tunnel. "He's there."

"Then go to him," cried Amphis, shouting over the footsteps that echoed nearer, over the cries of many men. He rose up, Baena's head slipping into his mouth. They spun away, down the opposite corridor from the one she wanted, uncoiled for a moment. "Here!" they cried in the voices of two guardsmen. "She is here!" Hooping up, they shot away.

She stepped into the shadows, watched as the men ran past her and up the tunnel in pursuit of the shouting snakes. Then, taking a deep breath, she ran to find her unicorn.

## THIRTY-ONE

# REUNIONS

Perhaps if her heart hadn't told her, her nose would have. The farther she got, the stronger the scent. A musk made up of terror, suffering, cruelty.

There were caves every twenty yards or so, on either side of the tunnel, with thick iron bars joining floor to ceiling at their front. These had doors in them, and many of them were open. On the floor of one glittered the colored scales that a cockatrice had shed. In the next, at the base of a wall, Elayne saw five quills that the manticore must have flung in despair. The third cell she passed had feathers among the straw, fallen from the griffin chick. Goaded out of their cells, driven from darkness into the light of the arena above, to die at man's hand, for man's pleasure.

Then she came to a cage that was locked. "Heartsease!" she cried, leaning the spear against the wall, stepping up to grip the bars.

The unicorn stood in the center of the cell, staring back with huge blue eyes. She was smaller than Moonspill, more delicately built.

"I am Elayne," she said. She didn't know if Heartsease would know of her, but the unicorn hobbled a step forward, her forelegs joined by some sort of manacles. She didn't "hear" a reply, though. No thoughts came to sound in her mind. "Looks like I am a one-unicorn kinda girl," she murmured, adding more loudly, "Where is he?"

Heartsease turned her head to the right, her horn running across the bars, sounding notes on them. *There*, she was saying, as clearly as if she'd said it out loud.

"I'll be back," Elayne said.

Footsteps pounded nearby, echoing down the stone tunnels, and she froze. Then shouting came. "No! She went this way. *This* way, I say!" and the footsteps retreated. Elayne crept on.

They hadn't even bothered to lock his cage. Why should they when the blinkers were still on him, that cruel, blinding mask, its straps biting deep into the white flesh? He was slumped on his side, flanks heaving as if he were still breathing the tainted air of New York. "Moonspill," she cried, running in, throwing herself down upon him. He jerked at that, head coming up. Then he collapsed again.

It was hard to get the mask off—harder because of the tears. But she managed, yanking the hideous device off him, throwing it down onto the filthy straw that covered the cell floor.

He was as dirty as the straw. Elayne didn't care. She threw her arms around that stained white neck.

His voice came into her head sluggishly, as if he were

309

struggling up from some great depth. *Alice-Elayne*, he thought. *You have come.*

*Of course I have. Did you think I would abandon you?* She hugged him again, then began to tug at his neck. Come on. Up.

He made an effort to rise . . . then fell back. *I cannot.*

"Yes!" she hissed fiercely. "Of course you can. The mask is off. There are no mirrors here. Get up!"

Again, his words took a long time to come. *They have poisoned me with a drug. It weakens me. It will wear off a little by the time they take me up to the arena—only enough to let me give a good show, no more. I will still slip into the red rage but without even the strength that it usually brings.*

Elayne remembered Leo standing there, telling her it would be a fair fight. Lying again. The son of a— Wait! She sat up. *Did you say that you were poisoned?*

*Yes.*

*But . . . a unicorn's horn cures poisons.*

It took an age, but he answered. *Not his own.*

"No, but . . ." She jumped to her feet. "Wait here," she cried, unnecessarily.

She ran back down the corridor, more shouts echoing along it. Amphis and Baena were still leading guards astray. But they couldn't do it forever.

Heartsease's cage door *was* locked—but the key that fitted the huge mechanism was hung on the wall beside the bars. It took all Elayne's strength to turn the key in its hole. Then, kneeling, she yanked open the clasps on the leather hobbles.

"Come," she said, throwing the door wide. "Moonspill needs you."

Elayne ran back, Heartsease following. When they reached the other cage, the unicorn moved into it. Moonspill tried to rise, failed again. But Heartsease knelt and brought her muzzle down to touch his.

Elayne turned away. Their joy at the reunion was overwhelming, their thoughts entirely their own. She had to admit it—there was a small part of her that was just a little jealous.

She heard a grunt, turned back. Heartsease was caressing Moonspill with her horn, slowly, from his tail all the way up, crossing his horn with hers like sword blades before moving to his other side. Her white horn gleamed, reflecting even the paltry light of the cell, passing that light into his gray flesh, transforming it. She came up his neck again, over his muzzle, finally laying the tip of her horn against the tip of his, gazing into his eyes—a twinned-blue stare. It held for a long, long moment, during which Elayne became aware again of the distant drumbeat, of the rhythmic stamping of feet, building, still building. Down a corridor, men shouted . . . and then Heartsease ran the length of her horn down the length of his, halting at his brow. Elayne watched the dullness leave his eyes, saw the light return. Then he was up, tail filling as if with air, whipping from side to side. Elayne stepped forward, laid her hand beneath that spiraling horn.

*Better?*

*Yes.*

*What now?*

*Now?* His great eyes widened. *Now mount, and we will ride from the city. There's not a gate raised or a spear forged that could stop two unicorns.*

"But where do we go?" she said aloud.

*Home. I made a promise to your father, to return you safely to him.*

*Dad!* she thought. But something held her back. *And after that? What will you do?*

She felt the sigh shudder through him. *It is finally time for the last unicorns to leave Goloth.*

"Oh." After all that had passed, she felt strangely deflated. "So that's it? We all just . . . leave?"

*I have my Heartsease.* He turned to briefly nuzzle at his mate's neck. *You have made my tiny flame of hope blaze bright. Your father is healed. What else is there?*

What else? There was something else, she knew. She heard it in that distant beating drum, in the stamping feet. Up above, a tyrant stood, waiting for his triumph, the blood of fabulous beasts staining the arena before him. If they fled now, Leo might be thwarted for a time—but she had no doubt he would find some way to cling to power. There were spikes to spare on the walls of the Castle of Skulls.

*Wait.* She laid her hand on Moonspill's brow. *You remained in Goloth when all the other unicorns left. Because you felt . . . responsible. You saw what each Leo did, saw the cruelty, the spoiling of the land. You tried to counter it. But maybe*—her breath came fast, shallow—*maybe this is your chance to actually end it.*

He stared at her for several heartbeats. *What mean you, maid?*

*I know my weaver ancestor only meant to leave some hope to a people who would have little. But these people believe it to be a real prophecy. A maid. A unicorn. The death of tyranny.* She took a deep breath. *Maybe today is the day that prophecy should come true.*

She was looking deep within his eyes. Saw the pupil contract as his thought came. *It would be a redemption I had not dreamed of. And yet*—he shivered—*to do what must be done, to end the tyranny as I would end it, I would still need to think in the arena and not run mad. But their spears would send me into the red rage. Unless . . .*

*Unless?*

They were so joined, his thought blended into hers, almost the same words in each of their minds. *Unless I was tamed.*

They were frozen. It was Heartsease who moved, backing fast away from them, her head rising and falling in alarm. Moonspill's stare, his mind, left, went to his mate. Gradually, she calmed, stared back, and Moonspill turned again, his thought returning to Elayne. *She speaks my fear, what I have always feared. What will it mean if I surrender to you? What will I become?*

Elayne gazed at the two unicorns, their huge eyes fixed upon her. The power that was in them! It made her want to sit down. She was gazing into the wisdom of centuries. She, who had lived all of fifteen years!

"Listen," she said, aloud, so her thoughts would reach Heartsease too. "From the moment we met, we've been trying to figure out what taming means. We know your ancestors—

your own mother and father—must have been 'tamed' to allow those heroes to ride them, yeah? But you don't believe that they gave up their pride, their true natures, do you?"

*No.*

"Then why would *you* have to . . . 'surrender'? Maybe"—she bit her lower lip—"maybe you don't need to give up anything. You only need to find someone *worthy* enough and let them in."

*Worthy?* Moonspill stepped toward her.

"Yes!" she said, her face flushed. "We could do this!" Forget destiny and prophecy! I want this for my weaver ancestor, murdered by a Leo. For his daughter, who made a vow she . . . she somehow asked me to keep. For Goloth, which deserves better than to be ruled by a tyrant. I want this for you—and not just because you saved my father. But because I think you need this too. I want to help"—she reached up and laid her hand on his neck—"but I only can if you consider me worthy. And let me in."

For a half dozen heartbeats, the silence held. She was lost once more in the universe of his eyes.

*Worthy. Yes, my Alice-Elayne. Yes. You are.*

And, bending, he laid his head against her chest. They had tried this when they hadn't known each other very well. This was different. Before, he'd intruded into her mind, taken over, made her sleep on command and awaken at his bidding. He did not command now. Neither did she. His thoughts still filled her head. But this time, for the first time, hers filled his too.

*Well!*

The thought, the memory of that word in their joined minds, made them both laugh.

Another thought came, from beyond them. *Well, indeed.* It did not surprise Elayne that Heartsease's voice was near as deep as her mate's. *After all the torment, to have found this, now.*

For a moment they stayed like that, the three of them. And then, from above, sounds intruded. A cacophony of drums, trumpets, shouts, stamped feet.

The Games of Goloth were approaching their climax.

*Can you do this?* she thought.

*Yes, maid. For you will be there with me now.*

*You bet I will.*

Moonspill stepped away, bent to Heartsease, the two of them joined by spiraled ivory, eyes shut tight, and thoughts Elayne did not hear, did not desire to. Then Moonspill took a step toward the entrance. "Wait!" Elayne called aloud, and he halted. "He's got so many men, so many weapons. Why not"—she bent, picked up the awful mask—"let him continue to think you are coming to him 'poisoned'?"

Rarely had she heard him laugh—and now, for the second time in a minute, she did, heard that deep-throated hum. Turning to Heartsease, he leaned against her. She bent to him for a moment, turned, and left the cell.

*She will await my call in her cage.* He reached his horn down, nudged the muzzle in her hands. *Put this on me again, Alice-Elayne. They are sure to remove it for the fight. So let me live with my reflections a little longer.*

*You won't have to.* Elayne bent, scooped dirt from the cell floor, rubbed it into the small mirrors inside the eyecups. He lowered his head, and she fastened on the mask, cinched the last strap. Then she laid her hand on his neck. *Ready?*

He pawed the earth. *Yes. After five hundred years, I am ready.*

He threw his head high and ran the tip of his horn against the stone ceiling. Sparks exploded.

*Tyranny will die!*

## THIRTY-TWO

# THE HUNT OF THE UNICORN

She had just closed the door on Heartsease's now unlocked cell and hung the key back on its hook when they came. Four of them, running down the corridor, skidding to a stop when they saw her. Then they charged, grabbed. There were too many to resist, and Elayne didn't need to anyway. She knew that they would take her where she wanted to go.

Back to the junction they went, then up a slope toward the light. As she got closer to the square entrance, the drum-beat, the rhythmic stamping that had been underneath her every breath like a pulse, grew louder. This close, she could hear the chanting too.

"Hunter! Hunter! Hunter!"

Inside the entrance, a man halted them. It was the king's high steward. He made that "Witch, avaunt!" gesture at her, then pulled one of the guards to him and whispered questions. He must have got the right answers, because he was suppressing a smile as he turned back to her. "You have caused us much trouble, maid," he said. "Now, come!" He beckoned, then reversed his hand. "Halt!"

Elayne stood still as he walked around her, tsking. Her dress was splattered, her hair askew. She could feel drying mud—she hoped it was mud!—on her face. So she was not sorry when the steward dispatched a guard, who soon returned with maids and buckets. Two proceeded to dab, wipe, and brush her down, while another tried to tame her hair.

Soon enough the steward snapped, "It will suffice," and gestured everyone away. Then he reached into a pocket and pulled out a red silk scarf. He tied it around her neck in a loose knot. "Come, maid," he said, stepping back, offering an arm. She accepted his offer, feeling the wobble in her legs. They halted again, in the shadows beneath the arch of the entrance. Not many in the crowd would notice her yet. But she could see them.

Her dad used to take her to see the Yankees sometimes. She always loved that moment, especially at night games, when she stepped out of the concrete halls of food vendors and beer sellers and into the stadium itself. The wave of feeling she'd get from that mass of eager people crammed together. And though there were no great towers of floodlights here, the setting sun had been caught in huge mirrors—*they love their mirrors, these people!*—so that the whole stadium dazzled.

*How many are weavers?* she wondered, looking at the hordes. The man on the boat who'd helped her escape had said that there would be a lot, or people sympathetic anyway. Waiting for a sign. Hoping.

The steward signaled to a pair of buglers beside the entrance. They blew a fanfare. "Come," he growled, and marched her in.

After the darkness of the tunnels, she found it dazzling in the light and raised a hand to shade her eyes. But the crowd must have thought she was waving because the chant of "Hunter!" was swiftly replaced by another single word, delivered at twice the volume.

"Maid! Maid! Maid!"

"Forward," growled the steward. They climbed two flights of stairs. Halting, he ordered her to wait while he entered a separate area, like a box in the theater. Leo was there, surrounded by courtiers and soldiers. She saw Marc, dressed well, no longer as a poor player, his cover now quite blown. Next to him sat Amaryllis, in something vast and pink.

Elayne focused on Leo. The steward was whispering to him. He went white, glanced at her, then his color slowly returned as the steward talked more. Leo nodded, stood, stretched out an arm, beckoning her. The shouts redoubled, alternating both their names now. "Leo! Maid! Leo! Maid!" When he took her hand, they rose to a roar. They stood there, the focus of all those stares, that raucous acclaim. Elayne didn't like it, but she would play along—for the moment.

They sat. The drum began again, and others joined it. The cheering stopped, replaced by an excited buzz of voices. Leo leaned into her, his breath in her ear. "So you escaped, maid. Tried to free the unicorn. And failed." When Elayne shrugged and said nothing, Leo continued. "'Tis well that you did . . . fail. For you would have disappointed many people." He gestured to the crowd, then lowered his voice to a husky whisper. "Myself more than any other."

*Unbelievable!* The man was relentless. Yet Elayne had been thinking hard while they'd fussed with her clothes. She'd done everything she could for Moonspill—except, perhaps, lull Leo. So she leaned a little closer to him now. "Sire, I would like a little time to consider your . . . your generous offer to me," she said, her own voice as low as his.

She saw different things on his face—suspicion, mostly. But he was playing a role, half for the crowd, half for her. And he stuck to it, tried a smile. "Then may I hope?" he murmured.

Two could play that game. "My lord," she replied, leaning closer, giving a little smile in return, "surely all men may hope?"

She thought he might kiss her then. And she was prepared to grin and bear it. But it was he who now became aware of all those silent stares. He rose suddenly, stepped to the front of the box, raised an arm, commanding silence. "People of Goloth," he declaimed loudly, "the sun sets. On the morrow, it will rise on a new reign, a new Leo to rule over you. Once he has proved his right to sit on the throne of hunters and kings. Once he has slain . . . the unicorn!"

He ended on a shout, a shout echoed from twenty thousand voices. "Unicorn! Unicorn!" they cried. Leo turned, snatched up Elayne's hand, and kissed it. Still holding it, he stretched to arm's length. "Will you favor me, lady?" he said loudly, and pointed to the scarf the steward had tied on her.

*Ah, so that's what this is for,* she thought. Reaching up, she gently slid the silk from around her neck, held it out. He took it, raised it high. "My lady's favor," he cried, tying it around his own neck. Then, to a roar from twenty thousand voices, he left the box, disappearing down the tunnel she'd come up.

Everyone sat. The roar subsided to general chatter. Vendors moved around the stadium selling food, drink. She almost expected someone to start yelling, "Hot dogs! Get your hot dogs here!" No one did, but a servant brought her a goblet. She gulped, realized it was wine . . . then gulped some more. She was thirsty after all that chasing around, and wine did fine. Better than fine.

Glancing around the box, her eyes met Marc's. He was sitting three rows away and was forcing a smile onto lips that, she noticed, were still delightfully fat from when she'd socked him. He started to rise, obviously planning to join her—to try to ingratiate himself, no doubt, with the possible future queen. But a hand shot out, and Amaryllis jerked him back down, sending a look of pure venom Elayne's way.

Elayne smiled sweetly at her, then turned back to the arena. Men were scrambling all over the arena floor, transforming it. . . .

"Wow!" she said, sitting forward when she realized what was happening. There was no doubt about it—The Unicorn Tapestries were being re-created before her. Not from silk and spun wool but with real flowers and trees, planted in real earth.

A small army of men worked on different areas, shaping scenes unbelievable swiftly. A miniforest sprang up, near the entrance to a tunnel that had to lead to the animals' cages below. Beyond that . . . Elayne blinked, not quite believing. Sluice gates had opened, and water was now pouring along wooden channels, cunningly concealed by vegetation. A fountain was erected, and near it five men were unloading a small oak from a horse-drawn wagon, planting it into a mound of earth.

The scene shifted to a more open piece of ground, a grassy area strewn with flowers, the trees small and set back so they didn't block anyone's view. *"The Unicorn at Bay,"* she murmured. Finally, almost reluctantly, she looked to the arena's end.

Sheets of painted wood were being raised, hammered into place—the Castle of Skulls, in miniature. A small earthen hill was thrown up, swiftly covered in grass sod, studded with flowers. It looked beautiful, peaceful. Elayne knew it wouldn't be for long. Knew what was to happen on that gentle slope.

It was a near perfect re-creation of the tapestry *The Unicorn Is Killed*.

Elayne shivered. Suddenly she was uncertain—of anything. The arena's transformation? It was like a dream unfolding. . . . No, a nightmare! And it was getting worse. The last touches were applied, the last flowers planted, the last trees driven in. The army of workers withdrew, leading away their horses, taking all their tools. A few better-dressed men walked among the areas, checking, adjusting. Then they too quit the field, and the drums that had pulsed as the work was done, ceased. A silence came, shocking in its suddenness, as if everyone had decided not to breathe for a moment. Elayne knew she didn't. Only her eyes moved, seeking, seeking . . . she didn't know what.

The silence ended—shattered by the howl of a single dog. It came from the tunnel and then was lost in an avalanche of barking. A pack of huge hounds burst from the darkness there, straining at leashes, their handlers fighting to hold them back. The crowd roared at the sight of them, stamping their feet, the wooden stands reverberating, vibrations shuddering through her. One man raised a bugle, blew two notes, low and high, commanding silence again. In that silence, other gates opened on all sides of the arena, and silently men marched out of them.

They were dressed just like the men she remembered in the tapestries—rich doublets of every color; bright satin leggings; short, fur-lined cloaks; feathered caps. There had to be one hundred of them, each man armed with both spear and sword, marching in to take up their positions on the field, filling all the different areas. But they did not turn to face the tunnel. They turned to face the hill.

Another shrill call from a different bugle. Everyone looked to where it sounded . . . and watched Leo march in, alone, and take his place at the top of the hill. He was dressed in a flowing, pleated crimson coat that fell to his knees, his head covered in a hat of whitest fur. He also had a sword at his belt and, in his right hand, a spear. Its vast, leaf-shaped blade caught the last light of the dying sun as he turned to face the length of the arena. Beneath the tip, wafting in a slight breeze, was the scarlet scarf—his "lady's favor."

Near silence came again. Only the snapping of pennants, the whimper of hounds, the hiss of held breaths. Then Leo raised his spear, there was a great crash of drums . . . and Moonspill ran out of the tunnel.

Elayne clamped her hands over her ears—though it barely blocked out the shouting of one word from thousands of mouths.

"Unicorn!" yelled the crowd. "Unicorn!" Over and over it came, rolling from the arena floor back up to the sky. Everyone there was screaming it.

He stopped, his white flanks heaving. Someone had tidied him up a bit; the filth and straw that had clung to his ribs were gone. But to Elayne he still looked sick. And she felt sick too. What had she been thinking? What was going to happen? Even if he was no longer poisoned, how could Moonspill— weakened, starved, tortured—how could he charge through that whole arena, through men with spears and dogs with teeth, and, on that green hill, kill a king? How could—?

*Maid.*

She heard the word clearly, far clearer than any of the shouting around her. Because the word sounded only in her head. *Moonspill?* she thought back.

*Be with me, Alice-Elayne. Help keep me from the red rage.*

She took a deep breath, exhaled slowly. *I am with you,* she thought.

Within the screams of the crowd came yelping. The dogs' leashes were slipped, and they ran forward. "A force of hounds" the Cloisters guide had called it, for they were trained to hassle but not attack, driving panicked prey through the forests to the point of a hunter's spear. They ran at him now, snarling, snapping, taking little nips at his legs.

Moonspill jerked forward, running to where the stream wound before a fountain and men with spears stood around and jeered. But if they were playacting the tapestry story, Moonspill wasn't. One dog ventured too close and was caught by a hoof, sent sprawling sideways. Another snarled closer, and Moonspill drove his horn into the beast's side—a horror greeted by cheers from all around.

Elayne swallowed—but she did not look away. *I am with you*, she thought.

The unicorn splashed through the stream. There was no pausing to "con" it; he wasn't going to play any role for them. He ran through—and was brought "to bay"—surrounded by a hedge of bright-pointed spears. He kicked out, shattering some weapons, parrying others. But there were just too many, and some found their mark, opening up wounds, leaving slashes of blood. Elayne clutched herself where every blade bit, joined to him in a way she had never been before. She sensed his agony, scented his terror . . . and then something else. It was as if a wave of blood slid over her mind. Redness filled her eyes. She yearned to strike out at the huntsmen, to kill—

"No!" She screamed the word aloud, shook her head hard, ignored the people who stared, leaned forward to grip the balcony before her . . . and look straight at Moonspill. *I am still here*, she thought, louder in her mind than any shout. *Don't leave me.*

The red wave receded. But no thought returned.

The hunters drew back. They were not trying to kill him, she remembered. The blades sank in a little to draw blood, to sap his strength. Dogs rushed him again, driving him on as the spears parted, their bloody work done. When Moonspill staggered clear of them, at the base of the small hill, his head drooped, his horn thudding onto the turf before him.

*Moonspill?* she cried silently.

Still no reply. Trumpets sounded. The handlers went in, roughly seizing the hounds, slapping muzzles on them, beating them into silence. The crowd had fallen silent too. They all leaned forward, staring, and Elayne leaned too. He looked so broken, his horn in the dirt.

*Moonspill,* she shouted again in her mind. Again, nothing came back. She bit her lip till the blood ran.

Leo stood unmoving at the top of the hill, gazing down. Then he began a slow descent of the slope, lowering his spear as he came. Halting before the unicorn, whose eyes were closed, bloodied flanks heaving from exhaustion, the man lifted the weapon above his head and looked around the entire circumference of the arena before he spoke.

"I am Leo, sixteenth of that name. And I claim the crown of the hunter-king."

"Leo!" came the roared response, shouted again and again. Silently, he took the acclaim. Then he lowered his spear into two hands, stepped forward on one leg, braced. And when the silence was complete again, he thrust.

It was such a little sound. A kind of *clack*, nothing more. But Elayne could see, because she was staring so very hard, the spear tip held a handbreadth from the crimsoned white chest. Moonspill holding it there with his horn.

Elayne gripped the balcony. No noise came now. But words did, words that no one else would be able to hear . . . because they sounded inside her head. Perhaps in Leo's too.

*You shall not.*

Leo shouted, pulled back the spear, and stabbed. Again the horn moved, faster than sight, knocking the shaft aside, the man slipping in order to keep his grip on it. Crying out, Leo slashed the blade back—and the block that met it was so hard it knocked Leo, who still did not let go of his spear, three paces to the side.

He was crouched, staring up. *He* was the one panting now—now it was Moonspill's turn to attack.

The silence in the arena was near complete, the only sound wood on horn, as each thrust was blocked by the spear shaft, the desperate man retreating each time, the unicorn advancing. At the top of the hill, with only a fall behind him, Leo screamed his rage, drove with all his might. But Moonspill parried again—and flicked, plucking the weapon from the hunter's hands, knocking it away to clatter against the arena walls.

Something scarlet floated in the air between them. And just before it sank, Moonspill shook his head, twining the scarf around his horn.

Leo fell to his knees, arms stretched wide. He did not cry out for help. Perhaps he knew he would not be answered. It was up to the king-elect to kill his unicorn and prove his right to the throne. The people of Goloth, his guards, were all as bound by tradition as man and unicorn.

Leo's eyes were open, staring into the eyes before him. Elayne knew the universes he'd be seeing there. Knew that pity would be found in none of them.

She had done this. It was she who had asked the unicorn to stay and fulfill the prophecy. To achieve his destiny. She had every reason to hate Leo, and did. But to see him killed because of her? *Moonspill*, she thought, on a sigh, not as a question, not as anything, expecting nothing.

And she was surprised.

*Maid.*

She stared at them, the man and the unicorn. And she realized that it was beyond her now. It was between them.

*Do what must be done*, she thought.

*I will.*

She could not turn away, though she wanted to. Had to watch as Moonspill rose up on his hind hooves. His front ones flailed over the prostrate man. It would be the matter of a moment to bring his hooves crashing down. Another to plunge the horn through the frail body.

But Moonspill did neither.

Instead, he gave out a great roar, shattering the silence. No one but Elayne would have heard anything other than terrible fury. Heard the call within the roar.

*Heartsease!*

It took only a moment for the call to be answered. Another unicorn's cry sounded like an echo in the tunnel, and she was there, galloping through the lowering spears of dumbstruck men, riding to her mate's side. Then, as one, they flew down the hill. The arena gates lasted only a couple of twin hoof strikes before they fell outward.

Words came. Only for her. *Black Tusk*, Moonspill thought.

Then they were gone, leaving the arena to its silence. Silence of a very different kind. A world, holding its breath. Elayne looked at Leo, sprawling on the ground. Alive, which was a bitter relief.

*But if the tyrant isn't dead, what about tyranny?* she wondered.

She glanced around the arena again, at the silent masses. Then found that she was rising to her feet. Lifting a fist. Yelling a word that had been buzzing in her head all afternoon.

"Weavers!"

## THIRTY-THREE

# THE RIDE

*Another first,* Elayne thought. *I've started a riot.* Though, looking around, she wondered if it wasn't more of a revolution. Perhaps they began the same way. Benches flying. People attacking each other. Particularly around her. It was the "royal box" after all. A lot of objects were being thrown at it.

Dodging debris, she couldn't decide which way to run. Then, luckily, she didn't have to. "Gotta fly!" a head said, as the amphisbaena slithered up beside her.

It had all been too much. She was a little slow. "Can you fly?" she asked, as a goblet just missed her head.

"Duh! No. But we can— Erp!"

One took the other in its mouth. They formed a hoop. "Prithee, if you squat and brace your arms before you, you may fit," said Amphis.

"Really?" It looked like a tight squeeze, but she managed

330

it, her neck bent down under the coils, head turned to the side. Which is why she saw . . . "Wait one second," she cried, rolling out.

"Maid," they called, but she was already halfway across the box, heading for the mound of pink material she saw under a chair. "Hey there!" she said.

Amaryllis looked up, hatred briefly displacing terror on her face. "Witch!" she hissed.

But Elayne wasn't interested in trading insults. She was interested in only one thing. "Marc," she called to the figure huddled beside Amaryllis.

"Maid," he said, wincing as a helmet flew over their heads.

"It's been a helluva party, but I really have to be going. But I wouldn't want to leave without"—she reached into the top of his doublet, found what she was after—"this!"

It seemed a pity to break the silver chain. But the piece of Moonspill's horn, given to her namesake and ancestor, was the truly valuable thing. She pulled hard, let it dangle between them for a moment, then clutched it in her fist. "Later," she said, and, ignoring the twin squawks of rage, ran back to the amphisbaena.

"How's this work again?" she asked, somehow squeezing in. She no sooner had than the snake took off, spinning between fallen benches and chairs. Elayne caught a glimpse of the few soldiers forming into ranks at the front of the box and of a much larger group of men and women massing before them, screaming.

"I feel sick," she yelled.

"Close your eyes," one called back. And then they were powering down some stairs, with the sounds of riot and revolution fading behind them.

She opened her eyes, saw an archway. It gave onto a square that they bowled across. "Oooh," she retched, just keeping the wine down. Every once in a while she'd open her eyes to see revolving houses, carts, running men. She always wished she hadn't. So when she glimpsed houses on the bridge revolving past, she yelled, "Guys! Stop! Stop!"

They rolled a few more turns to the bridge's end, pulling to the side as horses clattered toward them, ridden by shouting men. Her vehicle unfolded quite suddenly, ejecting her onto her legs, which buckled straightaway. Collapsing, she tried to stop the spinning world, nearly puked—then everything steadied. The stadium was on the far side of the city . . . but smoke was already rising from over there in three spiraling columns. A trumpet sounded a rally and was suddenly cut off. Screams carried clearly, along with the sound of smashing.

Elayne bit her lip. "Oh my God," she mumbled. "What have I started?"

A snake's head rose beside her, staring where she stared. "'Twas a long time coming," Amphis said. "You were but the spark to a fire already laid."

The other head rose. "Burn, baby, burn," added Baena with glee, before turning. "But now we gotta blow!"

Elayne looked at him. "Listen, you! I never *ever* talked like that."

Scaly lips widened to a smile. "I've added my own stylings! So sue me!"

Amphis took Baena's head in his mouth, forming the circle. "My brother speaks truly, if poorly," he mumbled through a mouthful of snake. "Blow we must. Mount!"

Elayne eyed the contraption distastefully. "Whither?"

"Anywhere away," came the reply.

"Not just anywhere," she said. "Moonspill said to meet him at Black Tusk."

"Then we shall take you thither. Mount!"

"No way." She stepped back. "Sorry, guys, but I'm not riding to the mountains like that. There has to be a better way."

She looked around. At the bridge's end were the same stables at which she and Marc had outfitted for the previous journey. She went over to the door of the main barn. "Hello?" she called. There was no reply. She looked in, saw several horses in stalls. But riding? She'd never ridden alone, was always led.

She chewed her ragged lip. Perhaps she'd have to try.... Then she looked out the back door, into the yard. There was a small wagon there, a horse in its traces. Maybe its owner had run off to join the fun in town. The wagon itself was filled with water jars, dried food, hay. She stepped up to the open door of the house. There was an alcove on the left, clothes dangling from hooks. "Anyone home?" she called.

No reply. "Give me a minute, guys," she said, and began to peel off her dress.

\* \* \*

The horse was docile, slow—which suited Elayne just fine. When gallopers came from either direction, they pulled over, hid. Some were soldiers, some citizens. It looked like the forces of Goloth were mustering on both sides. Others had simply fled: they passed many deserted villages, where they could help themselves to what they needed. And it wasn't as hard to get a horse into and out of traces as she'd supposed it would be.

On the fifth morning, she was woken before dawn, a snake's head whispering at each ear.

"Rise and shine!"

"Come, maid. We must away."

"So early?" She yawned. "OK, I'll get the wagon hitched."

"Uh-uh. Just untie the horse. He'll find his own way home. You can walk from here. Unless you want a ride?"

She walked, they rolled. Within an hour, in the presunrise light, she got her first glimpse of Black Tusk. Elayne stopped when she saw it, while the amphisbaena unhooped. Twin heads rose up beside her.

"'Tis time, maid. We needs must part company here."

"Here?" She frowned. "I thought you were taking me all the way."

"No can do. You'll be fine, trust us. And we got places to go, people to see."

"People?"

"Well"—Baena grinned—"rats. The road makes us hungry."

"Gross!"

"Don't diss it till you try it."

"And they helped us, remember?"

"True. Maybe I'll switch to moles." Yellow eyes narrowed as he considered. "Nah! Come on, Bro. Let's roll!"

"But . . ." She coughed.

"A moment, Brother." Amphis leaned away from the other's mouth. "Lady, you have graced our land with your beauty. Whilst your deeds? Ah, sagas will be told of them, of your coming, of your courage when all was lost. I myself have begun to compose a modest epic in iambic pentameter to celebrate the— Erk!"

Baena seized Amphis's neck, clamping down. "Enough with the poetry already!" he mumbled. "Later, girlfriend!"

"Leave be, rogue—" Amphis spluttered.

"Wait!" she called. But they were gone. She watched them rolling down the track until she lost them in the predawn gloom. She looked nervously around. How could they have left her? What if there were fabulous beasts about?

Then she realized why they had left. . . . Because there were. Was. One.

*Alice-Elayne.*

She jumped, turned . . . and there he was. "Moonspill," she cried in delight.

*Maid.* He tossed his head, then knelt. *Shall we ride?*

*   *   *

They rode east at a gentle pace, toward the growing light. Away from Black Tusk, the oak door beneath it. She had been thinking of her dad, dreaming of home, all the way to the rendezvous. Now she was so close, though, and knew that she'd be leaving soon enough, she was content to just be with Moonspill for a while. She knew, as well as he, that this was goodbye.

*Where is Heartsease?* she wondered.

*She rides farther east, seeking shelter from the troubles of man.*

"Troubles," she said aloud. "What have you heard?"

*Rumors only, borne on the wing. Birds see the world differently. The ravens are happy, for there is much death—in the streets, and in the fields, of Goloth.* He gave what could have been a sigh. *This land has had enough of tyranny.*

*You knew this would happen, didn't you? That's why you didn't kill him.*

Moonspill snorted. *I did not kill him because I do not kill unless I must. Or unless the red rage takes me. It is why I needed you with me. No one deserves to die for doing what they cannot help, be he man or manticore.*

*Even Leo?*

*Even he.*

Elayne wondered about some of the people she knew. Was Leo still alive, fighting for the throne? Which side was Marc on? Would Amaryllis find it difficult to get chocolates during a revolution?

The unicorn began to pick up the pace. Elayne, who was already clutching his mane quite hard, clutched harder. *Um, Moonspill,* she thought, *what are we doing?*

*Remember when you first rode me? How I told you I would not let you fall?*

*Yes.*

*It is as true now as it was then. All you have to do is believe it.*

Dew sparkled on the grass and the bushes, though Moonspill was going so fast it became like flashing diamonds, glistening as they passed. Soon they were galloping up a steep slope, the ground increasingly gouged and torn, potholes and trenches everywhere. But he didn't slow down. He did the reverse.

Elayne took a deep breath—then released one hand. After a moment, still centered, she released the other—and gave herself to it, to the speed, to the power. Flinging her arms behind her, she leaned into the wind their speed created, and laughed. She knew he had her.

They reached the summit in a flash—and Moonspill pulled up so suddenly she was flung onto his neck, had to grab his mane again. A pit lay before them, a deep gouge in the earth that ran, she could see, for fifty paces either side.

Behind, the endless grasslands. Ahead, this chasm as wide as the one he would not risk jumping with her on his back the day after she'd come to Goloth.

His thought was clear. *We should go around it or turn about.*

*No.* Elayne's thought was clear too—and different. *We've done the impossible so many times—why not once more?*

He hesitated for a moment, only a moment. And then his laugh came, that rare, great rumble in his throat. *As my lady commands.*

He moved back fifty paces, turned. She leaned forward, needing to say it, to whisper, into his great velvet ear. "Fly!"

Sucking in breath, Moonspill began to run. Hooves swallowed ground in great, four-legged leaps. In both their eyes, earth blurred. There was only speed and air. His legs landed together on the crest's very edge. Bending deeper than he ever had before, he sprang up, powering them out over the void.

They slowed, or so it seemed to Elayne, the land below only just passing, as if frozen. They began to fall—and Moonspill stretched his forelegs almost straight before him, his rear legs back, horn thrusting, a white arrow seeking a mark. Finding it. Hooves touched earth, the cliff edge crumbling as they hit it . . . but they were already past, into long, soft, wet grass that began almost at the far edge, skidding, spinning slowly to a stop.

"Yes!" Elayne shouted, flinging her head back, her arms wide.

They were looking down into another valley, a river cutting through it, stands of willow on its banks. There were forests, large and small, making a random checkerboard of the vast grassland. In the distance to the northeast were the mountains of the griffin, snowcapped, backlit. They watched that glow turn fiery . . . and then the sun burst up like a flaming ball, flung by some giant, unseen hand. Sunbeams flooded the plain.

And Moonspill turned, ran past the rent in the earth, heading back the way they'd come. He'd broken straight into a gallop and rode now as if racing the sun across the land. He'd always moved fast—but this was different. He wasn't fleeing or desperately running to a rendezvous. He was running for the pure delight of it, sure-footed whatever the terrain, grass or stone or riverbed, soaring over large rocks as if he were winged.

It was over, too soon. As he slowed, the landscape came into focus for her. They were once again beneath Black Tusk. The valley narrowed to a forest track, which had once been lit by flame, lined in mirrors. They passed the lightning-charred tree, crested the slight rise, entered the small bowl of land. Twenty paces before them was the oak.

"My stop," she said. She didn't know any way to do this, except fast. So she slipped off his back and walked quickly toward the tree, horn held out ahead of her. She wasn't even sure how this worked. But if that rat Marc had figured it out—

*Alice-Elayne.*

She stopped but did not turn, focusing ahead on bark, leaf, branch.

*Look at me.*

"Can't, just now."

*Look.*

She turned, squinted. Sun rays poured over the slope behind him, lighting his every curve. The light was the reason her eyes teared. She'd have held back otherwise.

*Look there*, he thought, gesturing with his horn toward a bush.

She looked. And realized that what she'd thought were blossoms was something else. "The scarf," she cried.

Moonspill delicately lifted the scarf with his horn and brought it to her. *My lady's favor*, he thought, and draped it round her shoulders.

She held it to her face. It was soft, the most wondrous of silks. And the scent! There was a musk to it, sweet and deep—the scent of unicorn.

There was no pretending about the tears now. But she wasn't going to spoil the silk. So, tying it around her neck, she wiped her face on her sleeve and smiled. "Thank you," she said.

He turned, without a thought, and trotted back to the rocks that formed the bowl's narrow entrance. She went to the oak tree, pausing there to look back over her shoulder. She raised an arm, not trusting her voice.

Still, no thought came. But he rose onto his rear hooves, his front ones pounding the air before him. The power of him! She staggered back, leaned against the oak, and heard him at last.

*If your need is great, call to me. For I will come.*

"So will I!" she cried, reaching forward. But she tried to push herself off the trunk with the hand that held the horn— and suddenly everything was moving back. She was falling, feeling nothing but space opening behind her, seeing nothing but the darkness sweeping over her, and a last flash of a unicorn dissolving into sunlight. Then she was tumbling, over and over, free-falling through a void.

Her ancestor, the genius weaver, had put little slits into the warp and weft of his tapestries to create curve, light, shade, expression. Tiny, like a unicorn's hope—yet large enough to fall through.

"Ow!" she cried, thumping onto a polished wooden floor.

She lay there on her side for a while. Above her a unicorn moved. Young, small, he leapt out of a stream.

"Hey!"

At the entrance to the room stood a man, a badge around his neck. "I thought everyone had gone," he said, annoyed. "The museum's closing, miss. You can't just sit there gawking!"

He came over, offered an arm. She pulled herself up. His eyes widened as he took in her clothes. Then he shook his head. "What is it with you girls and unicorns anyway?" he sighed.

Elayne took her time. First she checked that the scarf was still around her neck. Then, tucking the horn into her pocket, she looked around the whole room, taking in every tapestry, before she replied.

"Well . . ."

# Author's Note

When Nancy Siscoe, my editor at Knopf, asked me what I was going to write for them next, after completing my Runestone Saga, I was stumped. I hadn't felt the usual spark that starts the fire of a new story. Nothing came for a while. Then I looked at my left pinkie.

I wear a signet ring on it, a bloodstone, which I inherited from my father. Engraved upon it is the crest of our family. A unicorn.

I'd worn it so long, I no longer paid it much attention. But that morning I studied it and wondered what power, if any, this symbol had had over my life. What did the unicorn mean? How had people regarded it over the centuries? Did it have any relevance to the modern world?

And so, a spark. Research fanned it into a flame.

One of the first things I found was the Unicorn Tapestries in the Cloisters, the medieval department of the Metropolitan Museum in New York City. Even in reproductions, these Renaissance masterpieces dazzled. But in person, they overwhelmed. They are made, essentially, from straight lines of colored wool, going down, going across. Yet the distinct men and women, flora and fauna, they depict, the vibrant action that takes place . . . staggering! And there was the tantalizing mystery of their origin.

The Tapestries were the way into a new story for me . . . and literally became a doorway to another world—to Goloth, Land of the Fabulous Beast. (Why stop at the unicorn? I thought. Let's have them all!)

There are turning points in the process of writing every novel. They can be flashes of imagination at six in the morning, when a character does something you didn't expect. Or they can be an encounter with someone who points you in a different direction. Which happened, quite literally to me, on my second visit to the Cloisters.

I wanted to reenact an incident in the book, when the unicorn rides through Manhattan. No unicorns being available, I rented a bicycle. I am a great believer in the idea "Good luck? Bad luck? Who knows?"—how you curse something that goes wrong, only to discover that if it hadn't, some other really great thing wouldn't have been able to go right. As it happened, I cycled to the Cloisters—without a bike lock. I was convinced I could sweet-talk Security into looking after my bike for twenty minutes while I spent a little more time with the Tapestries. *Wrong!* Between protocol this and regulation that, and despite the charm of my English accent, they were having none of it. Frustrated, I grumbled my mantra, "Good luck? Bad luck? Who knows?" and set out on the unicorn's ride that I'd written in my basement in Vancouver. Elayne and Moonspill needed to travel from the museum somewhere north of 190th Street down to my heroine's loft at 14th Street. From maps, I figured they'd ride down the greenway—the bike and pedestrian path that runs along the west side of Manhattan. But here in person, I couldn't find a way onto it! I cycled ten blocks south, looking for a sign, got annoyed, doubled back . . . and met Cordelia.

She's one of the park gardeners—the Cloisters sits in Fort Tryon Park. When I explained my story, the unicorn needing to get swiftly down to the greenway, she said, "Wait a minute," and found a map in her jeep. "Thought so," she said, pointing. "You don't have to ride ten blocks south. If you go just a little north of the park, the greenway begins there."

I could have kissed her. Then kissed her again when, just as I was mounting up, she called me back to the jeep. "We are always finding things in the undergrowth," she said. "Look what I found this morning!"

It was a sword—a fencer's foil, no less. I am an old fencer, so I took it as a sign of extreme good fortune. As I did her parting words. "I grew up around here," she said, "and I love the Tapestries. I've always wanted to ride a unicorn through New York."

You and me both! I thought, setting out on what turned out to be another great adventure.

Of course, Cordelia was just one of the people who helped me in the writing of this novel. My wife, Aletha, was her usual insightful, calming self; while my son, Reith, came up with a wonderful idea one day as I drove him to kindergarten. I was puzzling over how a unicorn might think. When I consulted him, he contemplated for a moment, then said, "Through his horn." He was a little startled by my yelp of joy!

There are, as always, several authors to thank. Adolfo Salvatore Cavallo wrote the terrific essay in the Metropolitan Museum's book *The Unicorn Tapestries*. Joe Nigg wrote a fantastic book called *Wonder Beasts*, which opened up the world of mythical creatures to me. Then there was the elegant *The Lore of the Unicorn* by Odell Shepard, in which he mounted a passionate defense of the unicorn as a creature that deserves to live, not solely in myth, but in our hearts too. There were also many websites and even YouTube videos where I was able to study weaving techniques.

A novel's creation has so many elements. For an author to be free to write well, he needs great professional support. My agents at United Agents Ltd. are first-rate at this, both Simon Trewin, my main adviser there, and Jane Willis, who deals with young adult fiction throughout the world. Both give terrific feedback too.

I have praised Nancy Siscoe, my editor, before and will not embarrass her again . . . much! But she has worked her magic one more time, as ever challenging and provoking me to do my very best. I went to New York to see her after I delivered the first draft. We brunched in Brooklyn and walked and talked for hours. The subsequent drafts are a result of this collaboration, which I value so highly. We often fight like not-so-fabulous beasts, but it is all about the end result, never the ego. And every fight resolved made the book so much better.

Now it is time to let my unicorn run free, to make his own way in the world. Moonspill, that is. Another unicorn sits on my little finger, rearing up in a bloodstone. I am not sure I have answered the question that became the spark, then the fire, for this novel: What does that unicorn mean?

But I have had a huge amount of fun trying!

C.C. Humphreys
Vancouver, Canada
March 2011